ABBY, VIRTUALLY

ABBY, VIRTUALLY

A NOVEL

RONEN DIVON

NEW YORK

LONDON • NASHVILLE • MELBOURNE • VANCOUVER

ABBY, VIRTUALLY

© 2019 Ronen Divon

All rights reserved. No portion of this book may be reproduced, stored in a retrieval system, or transmitted in any form or by any means—electronic, mechanical, photocopy, recording, scanning, or other—except for brief quotations in critical reviews or articles, without the prior written permission of the publisher.

Published in New York, New York, by Morgan James Publishing. Morgan James is a trademark of Morgan James, LLC. www.MorganJamesPublishing.com

The Morgan James Speakers Group can bring authors to your live event. For more information or to book an event visit The Morgan James Speakers Group at www.TheMorganJamesSpeakersGroup.com.

ISBN 9781683509073 paperback
ISBN 9781683509080 eBook
Library of Congress Control Number: 2017918935

Cover Design by:
Megan Dillon
megan@creativeninjadesigns.com

Interior Design by:
Christopher Kirk
GFSstudio.com

Publisher's Note: This novel is a work of fiction. Names, characters, places, and incidents are either products of the author's imagination or used fictitiously. All characters are fictional, and any similarity to people living or dead is purely coincidental.

In an effort to support local communities, raise awareness and funds, Morgan James Publishing donates a percentage of all book sales for the life of each book to Habitat for Humanity Peninsula and Greater Williamsburg.

Get involved today! Visit
www.MorganJamesBuilds.com

This novel is dedicated to women everywhere.

All beings are beautiful souls;
having no gender, skin color, or ethnicity.

CHAPTER 1

NEW DELHI

"Dear Abhaya,"

Abhaya's eyes skimmed the rest of the email.

"Thank you for submitting a bid. Unfortunately, we have…"

Unfortunately. That was the word she dreaded. Staring at those ill-fated letters for a prolonged moment, Abhaya felt spasms of anger bubbling inside. The anger morphed into thunderous rage. She raised her arms and slammed her fists onto the heavy oak table, rattling her keyboard and mouse. With her mouth contorted in fury and large almond-shaped eyes opened wide, Abhaya's face echoed the fearless Goddess Kali bent on destruction.

"Abhaya dear, are you okay?" Her mother's melodious voice rang out from a neighboring room.

Abhaya collected herself, plucked a lock of stray hair off her forehead and placed it behind her ear. "Yes, Mom," she called back, struggling to keep her voice from wavering. "Just a difficult math problem," she added.

She disliked deceiving her mom, but Abhaya had lied to her nonetheless. No equation was too challenging for her since she was at the top of her class. But she knew her reply would appease her mother. And more importantly, it would keep her from entering her fourteen-year-old daughter's room.

Making sure to log off her computer desktop, Abhaya grabbed her red Nike backpack and a matching iPhone. "I'm headed over to Janaki's," she called as she rushed out of the apartment.

"Don't be late for dinner!" came her mother's hurried reply. "Not again. Your father will punish you this time!"

Abhaya, her long black hair rippling behind her like a speedboat's wake, barely heard her as she shut the door.

"This is the eleventh refusal!"

Janaki was listening, sipping a hot cup of Masala chai.

"E-l-e-v-e-n-t-h!" Abhaya slumped in her seat. "I just can't take it anymore."

They were seated in the shade of an old banyan tree in Janaki's large backyard. Janaki's backyard was a luxury Abhaya's family had never known. Janaki's father was one of the wealthiest New Delhi fabric merchants, and Janaki's family not only had a sizable suburban house but also a private courtyard. Abhaya had never had a yard or even a room of her own. Instead, she had shared her room with her older sister since the day she was born. More than anything, she wanted a room of her own. A yard was a close second. Abhaya loved it back here, but today even its beauty could not soothe her.

"You know what they say," said Janaki, trying to sound as encouraging as possible, "the twelfth time's the charm!"

"Yeah, right," replied Abhaya. "That's what you said the eleventh time."

"But you're such a brilliant programmer!" declared Janaki. "Even Mr. Pandit always says so."

Abhaya knew Janaki was trying to cheer her up. Mr. Pandit was her favorite teacher. But Abhaya couldn't help being gloomy. She tugged at her hair.

"Why do you think your proposals aren't being accepted?" said Janaki.

Abhaya sulked. She knew with Janaki that she could just be herself. The two had been friends for as long as they could remember, practically inseparable. Abhaya did not seem to envy Janaki's good fortune of being born into wealth, and Janaki was always supportive of her friend's intellectual achievements.

"Beats me," Abhaya said. "It has been three months since I listed with this online freelancing website, posting to every possible bid that I thought I had a chance of winning, and nothing. No explanation. Just an automated rejection." Abhaya paused. "'Unfortunately,'" she muttered. "I hate that word. I tried pricing myself low, then high, then somewhere in between. I tried various qualification descriptions, but nothing. Nil. Zero. The clients posting on that website always pick someone else." Abhaya's face came to life, wearing the mask of a fierce warrior, making her attractive features all the more stunning. "God," she sighed, "I hate those automated replies!"

They sipped their hot chai, keeping silent for a while. Beyond the tall stone wall in the backyard, muffled sounds of honking horns on the busy streets provided Abhaya with some familiar comfort, serving as a reminder that she was not alone in her pain. Everywhere in the world, there was daily struggle.

Yet in the middle of the struggle, the earth never stopped showing its loveliness. The setting sun colored the skies with a divine palette from dark red and fiery orange, to purple and incandescent blues. The air felt a little less humid as a twilight breeze brushed through the oval leaves of the banyan tree.

The ancient banyan, thought Abhaya, the "Kalpa Vriksha", the tree that fulfills all your wishes. Why won't you fill any of mine?

Her attention drifted back to the dramatic sunset. It was Abhaya's favorite time of day. It gave her hope no matter what the day had been like. Not a single window in her home faced west. If she wanted to watch a sunset, she had to go up to her apartment building's rooftop.

"When I have my own place," Abhaya muttered, not realizing she was speaking her mind aloud, "my bedroom will have a window to the west."

"What was that?" asked Janaki, raising her eyes from a social media site on her phone. "What place?"

"Oh, nothing." Abhaya's face now reflecting some of the skies' pinkish shades. This was her secret desire, and one she did not even share with Janaki.

"Abhaya, sweetie, are you staying for dinner?" Janaki's mom called out.

"Oh no!" cried Abhaya aloud, pulling her phone out of her bag to check the time, "I'm late!"

By the time Abhaya made it back home, her family was already seated at the dinner table. Old, large and a real antique, the heavy table took up about two thirds of the open space of the small apartment's dining area. For her mother, this table was much more than a piece of inherited furniture. It was a connection to her aristocratic past.

Abhaya's father welcomed her with a visible frown. "Again?" He did not need to raise his voice. His tone sufficed: quiet anger wrapped in a coat of disappointment, his dark eyes narrowed beneath knotted eyebrows. Hung on the wall behind him sat the Goddess Durga, framed in golden colors. Riding her tiger while her eight arms held various holy artifacts, her warrior expression was forgiving compared to his.

Abhaya knew her father's tone all too well. It was a trap. Her dad was looking to draw her into a fight, one she was bound to lose. Her friend Janaki likened Abhaya's father to a naja naja, a cobra lying in wait, preparing for the right moment to strike. "I'm sorry, Father. I have no excuse," she said in the most apologetic voice that she could conjure. Given her spicy character, that was quite a tall order.

"Sorry my arse!" hissed Jeevana, Abhaya's older sister.

"Jeevana!" Dad snapped. His unexpectedly sharp voice caused Abhaya to flinch. "What is this?" he demanded. "I do not tolerate such language in my house!"

"Sorry, Father," said Jeevana. A moment later, she added, "But please remember to call me... Jane."

Abhaya sneaked a peek at her with a mixture of curiosity and terror. She questioned her sister's timing. After all, Jeevana was anything but stupid. *Doesn't she realize that's the wrong thing to say, especially when he's already angry?*

"I absolutely will not!" yelled her dad. "We gave you a beautiful Indian name, and I will call you by no other!"

"Devidas-ji," reasoned his wife Kamalakshi, "we have been through this already. We want to be supportive of Jeevana's career. Jeevana was instructed to have everyone call her by her new work name so that it will come naturally to her."

"Jane, Mom. Jane, not Jeevana!" said Jeevana.

"Sorry, Dear," replied her mom, "Of course, I meant Jane."

"A career?" said Abhaya, jumping at the opportunity to poke her sister. "You call working at a lousy call center for an American company a career?"

"Quiet, Abhaya!" lashed her mom.

"Jane," her dad uttered distastefully, "I will not stand for this!" He stood up, his chair screeching against the old stone floor. "I have lost my appetite." He turned, left the room, and then the apartment.

"But Ji!" Mother said, "you haven't touched your dinner. Please...." She left the apartment, rushing after him, her voice fading into the building's staircase like an echo within an echo.

"Thanks, Sis!" Abhaya said to her sister, cheerily.

"What for, you brat?!"

"Being that I was late for dinner yet again, and you just bailed me out, Jane." Abhaya chewed the name with a mocking American accent.

"Laugh all you want. During training, we learned that research clearly shows Westerners respond much better to a name like 'Jane' than 'Jeevana.'"

"Who cares what Westerners think?" replied Abhaya. Imitating her father's voice, she said, "'We gave you a beautiful Indian name,' one that should make anyone fall in love with...." Abhaya stopped mid-sentence, her mouth agape.

Jeevana looked at Abhaya like she'd lost her mind.

"But of course!" Abhaya called aloud. Her mind was racing. *How could I have missed it?* "You're a genius, Jee!" she said to her astonished sister. "I mean, Jane!" she corrected herself, this time without mockery.

Before Jeevana could collect herself, Abhaya was gone.

With her parents out, and her sister eating by herself, Abhaya knew her time alone in the bedroom was limited. No one knew of her work online. If her super-conservative father ever found out, the old desktop computer she gained after much begging would be gone in a blink, and with it, many of her hopes and dreams. Her father simply could not know. As for her sister, she reasoned that while Jeevana may be more modern and working for a company providing services for the West, she could not be trusted. Abhaya had few all-but-faded fond memories of sibling tenderness, but that was when they were both much younger. As they grew up, they grew apart, each in her own little universe. Only necessity, stemming from poverty, made them share a room. Otherwise the pair would have stayed apart. On good days, the two would keep up a polite façade, but on bad days, their hostilities could shame any political rivals hot on a campaign trail.

Abhaya's calculating mind worked out that Jeevana, a slow eater, would be done in about fifteen, twenty minutes at best. Her sister would then enter their room on her way to take a shower and change from her official working clothes into a mundu, the simple traditional sari her father expected her to wear at home. Her parents, she knew from past experience, would be awhile. Whenever her father lost his temper and performed a

"Bollywood-style exit," as her friend Janaki nick-named it, he took at least an hour to cool down. That meant that Abhaya had a quarter of an hour to safely work online, then wait for her sister to pass through, and then another fifteen minutes for her sister to finish showering and dressing. Half an hour in total was just enough time for what she needed to do.

She opened a website connecting freelancers with prospective clients and started typing. She kept one eye on the screen and the other on the door. When a lock of stray hair fell over her forehead, Abhaya ignored it. No time to waste.

CHAPTER 2

NEW YORK CITY

John Reynolds could remember better evenings. Sitting at his computer, the twenty-two-year-old college dropout petted his black angora cat Tess that laid across his legs. The sounds of rush hour traffic from two floors below rattled his nerves.

This week was over before it started, he thought. One of those weird time-space mysteries where you inhale on a Monday and discover it's Friday by the time you exhale. Taking his hand off Tess, he rubbed his pale blue eyes, sinking his knuckles in a little too forcefully. He was not just tired. He felt frustrated, beaten down. No matter how he turned the numbers around, the totals he needed to see in the spreadsheet were not there. Tess, realizing her human was no longer at her disposal, rose to her paws and rounded her back, her nails piercing John's pants in the process.

"Ouch!" he yelped, staring at Tess. "You've got to stop doing that! Just because I'm not showering you with affection doesn't mean I don't love you."

Tess, indifferent, leaped from his lap and headed to sip water from the kitchen tap, one John always kept dripping for her sake. Just in case something happens to me one day, and I don't make it back home, he told himself. Gazing at Tess, John stretched his long skinny legs, spread his arms above his head, and yawned, his face resembling Edvard Munch's The Scream, if only for a moment.

His studio's doorbell buzzed at its usual deafening volume. He jumped off his chair. Grumbling, he glared at the door. Why do I need such a loud doorbell for such a tiny apartment, he thought, and not for the first time. Tomorrow morning I'll go to that hardware store down on Third Ave and get a new buzzer. Something more relaxing, maybe with birds chirping or soft wind chimes...anything other than that firefighting brigade!

The doorbell buzzed again. He clapped his hands over his ears. Oh, if only whoever is there would go away.

The doorbell screeched on relentlessly, demanding attention like one of his impatient patrons at the East-West Cafe. Unable to ignore it any further, John shuffled toward the door, looked through the peephole.

It was Rachel.

He had not expected to see her today. Even at the end of a long workday, she looked radiant, her stance tall and self-assured. Or maybe it was just his perception. John noticed his pulse increasing a touch, his heart beating a little faster. He took a long, deep and happy breath and opened the door.

"What's up?" Rachel snapped, fists firmly planted on her hips. "Did it really take you a w-h-o-l-e five minutes to cross your e-n-o-r-m-o-u-s apartment? Or you just enjoy keeping a damsel waiting?" She brushed past him, letting herself in.

Gathering his wits, John searched for a comeback line, but his mind was working in slow motion. Too much number crunching over the past few hours made his brain feel like mush.

"Well," he said, finding a retort, "in fact I do like to keep them waiting. But only the real ugly ones."

Rachel was already putting the kettle on in the tiny space Manhattan dared call a kitchen. "Is that the best you can do?" she said, an amused smile curling around her fire red lips.

Realizing his defeat, John did not bother answering. Instead, he went back to his desk, pointed at his screen and said, "I just can't make it work, Rache. Our budget's too tight."

"Tea or coffee?" she asked, setting up two mugs.

"Uh, I think I'll switch to tea this time," replied John. "One more cup of coffee and I'll be bouncing off the walls."

"I thought your tolerance for coffee knew no limits," mocked Rachel.

"I thought so, too," muttered John. "I must be getting old."

The kettle's cheerful whistle began, making him smile.

"You know," said Rachel, "we could always use one of those freelancing websites, the ones where web developers put themselves out for hire. My office uses them occasionally." She poured the boiling water into a mug decorated with the words, "I'm a BIG boy."

John watched her shoulder-length bob follow the tilt of the kettle. He loved the way her red hair curtained parts of her face. It added to her mystery.

Turning to look at him, she caught his stare. "What's up?" she asked.

John snapped out of it. "Nothing," he replied. Realizing she had spoken to him, but unable to recall what it was that she had just said, he prompted her in a different direction. "Remember when you gave me this mug?"

"Of course," she replied gingerly. "It was when you graduated high school, a big step for you. One step above infancy."

He smiled. Her quirky sense of humor was yet another quality he admired.

"How's your sleep these days?" she asked.

"Not great," he admitted. "Still having all sorts of weird dreams." Smiling, he added, "Research indicates that people with strange dreams tend to be the creative types."

"That, or they're just imbeciles. And in your case, it's likely the latter." Rachel laughed.

"But of course." John gestured dramatically. "That's why I have friends like you."

"Uh-huh, but let's not get further off-topic," she said.

"Which was?" said John, his tired mind struggling to remember.

"How about it?" Rachel asked. "How about using a programmer from a freelancing website?"

John took a deep breath. They had been through this before. "What's good for your large ad agency and its deep pockets is not necessarily what we can afford."

"On the contrary," Rachel countered. "It's much better for a small startup such as ours."

John felt his heart soften. She had referred to the venture as "ours". He was not always sure if her heart was in it. Every reference she made to it as theirs made him happy.

"This is the best solution for a small budget since you can dictate the amount and see who bites," she continued.

Where did the "us" go? wondered John, noting she switched to "you."

"We can't afford screw-ups."

She handed him his tea and sipped from hers, a large mug with the NASA logo that she had bought him as a gift from her Florida trip. It had been "her mug" at his place. "Besides," he added when she had said nothing, "the programmers on those sites are mostly from Pakistan or India, or God knows where. They don't speak English very well, and they're here today, gone tomorrow."

Rachel examined him over her steaming tea. "How do you know so much? You told me you never go on those sites."

"I don't," he admitted. "But I read about it online. Lots of horror stories."

"So now you believe everything you read online, huh? You're the one always lecturing me to take 'news' on the web as nothing more than gossip."

John ignored her sarcasm. "Ours is a very sensitive project. We cannot afford patenting the idea–way too expensive to file a patent–so whoever our developer will be, he must be someone highly reliable, someone who can keep matters confidential, someone who won't steal our idea and do it on his own. You know how the Chinese have this reputation for reverse-engineering everything and ignoring international laws. I'm not–" then, realizing his slip, "we are not going to give my–our–idea to some guy from the Far East, or India, or some other god-forsaken place."

"Oh, please," said Rachel. "Go ahead and stereotype. I thought that we don't classify people by ethnicity."

"Come on!" he said. She was getting on his nerves. "You of all people know I'm not a racist!"

"Right," responded Rachel, concealing a smile. "You just demonstrated your racism, again."

"How?" protested John.

"By using the word 'racism.'"

Noticing John's ears turning red, Rachel burst out laughing.

John cracked an embarrassed smile, once he realized that she was just teasing. Seems like she won this round as well, he thought.

They both sipped their teas.

"Still, let's face it," she said. "The budget is tiny, a mere ten grand. I'm handling the graphic design, so there is no out-of-pocket cost for that. We said up to seven grand would go toward programming. The mobile app and website interface take a certain expertise that neither you nor I have. The rest will be for other expenses, such as hosting and things.

But it's unlikely you'll find a US-based programmer to do the job for so little money."

"I know," said John. He paused for several long moments, his forehead wrinkled. "But," he continued, "I'm just not yet ready to accept it. Give me more time."

Sighing in exasperation, Rachel took one last sip from her cup, got up, placed it in the kitchen sink and picked up her coat and bag. "Take all the time you want," she said, heading toward the door. "I have a job that pays."

Thinking, she paused for a moment. "By the way, did I tell you about the job offer I got from the West Coast?"

He shook his head.

"Of course I didn't. It just happened this morning." Ignoring or otherwise oblivious to his panicked face, she continued, "John, you're the one who'll be running out of dough soon." With her back turned to him as she opened the door, she added, "When that crap finally hits the fan, don't count on crashing at my place. I may be already gone."

She never saw his face falling.

CHAPTER 3

NEW DELHI

It was late evening. The Delhi horizon turned a deep blue, decorated with remnants of purple. Kamalakshi, Abhaya's mother, walked with her husband along the sacred Yamuna River. The air felt fresh after the veil of humidity lifted off the city.

Kamalakshi watched Devidas' face. He seemed calmer than he was half-an-hour ago at the dinner table. Now he seemed reflective.

He swept his arm in front of him, including the entire river in his gesture. "This river, a tribute to the goddess Yamuna, is such a close representation of worldly affairs. Here you see our sadhus, the holiest men, in prayer to the divine, and but a hundred feet away, others are washing their dirty laundry. Yet the great Yamuna takes it all in. She never complains."

Kamalakshi lowered her head, concealing a smile. Yes, she heard Devidas speak of this many a time, almost lecturing, as if before a group of eager students. Speaking this way seemed to relax him somehow.

They walked in silence for a spell.

Kamalakshi, experienced with his walks, said nothing. She gave her husband time and space to work things out in his mind, getting the venom out of his system. Only then would he be ready to return home. As with previous family fracases, she joined him, first following from afar and then closing the distance, walking by his side.

"Why are you doing this?" he once asked her after calming down. "Why do you follow me?"

"Because I love you," she replied. Her response had been instantaneous, but she would often ponder the same question herself. Was it love that drove her to stick by him, or was it fear of being left alone? She was always afraid that one of these days, he would take off and leave her and their children to join an ashram, disappearing from their lives forever.

On the other hand, perhaps it wasn't just fear. She did enjoy his company. As conservative and hard-headed as he was, she felt, more than heard, his wisdom, and she found it to be soothing. In a world that was rapidly changing around her, he was her anchor, and her first true love.

She also knew that with people such as her husband, wisdom came at a price of much inner turmoil. Being brought up in a very traditional Indian family, Kamalakshi recognized her place by her husband's side, her position in the family's hierarchy. She was not without a voice, but she was an expert in practicing self-restraint and was skilled in commanding her own wishes and desires. She knew all there was to know about making sacrifices of her dreams, as often as it may be required, in order to serve her husband and family. This had been ingrained in her since childhood, as if into her very DNA.

Devidas continued. "The blessed Goddess keeps the water clean and pure, that is until it enters Delhi." His voice became grave. "We then contaminate this divine offering so much that the polluted water is deemed deadly. As my guru says, it demonstrates all that is wrong with this world." Devidas paused.

Kamalakshi did not much care for this guru. Devidas had often told her that his guru was his spiritual guide, a person Devidas revered as second only to God. While respecting the notion of gurus, she had grown up in a traditional environment. Spiritual guides were as common as dead fish floating in the river. Her own personal experience had been that most were charlatans. But she could never tell her husband that.

Devidas picked up where he left off. "God and his demigods gave us all these wonderful gifts—clean, fresh water, all sorts of material manifestations of His divine nature. But losing respect for our traditions, we humans, we took all that we could. We abused, we wasted, and we didn't care one bit for anything beyond our immediate enjoyment."

They passed near a group of teenagers sitting by the waterfront, all engaged with their phones.

Devidas looked at them and frowned, as if this was all the proof needed to make his point.

Kamalakshi noticed her husband's darkening mood. Trying to shift his disposition, she asked, "Please, Ji, please tell me another one of your Yamuna tales."

Devidas took the bait. His voice brightened. He retold the tale of Yamuna's birth, and how Yamuna's scheming mother, the Goddess Sanjana, convinced her father, the Sun God Surya, to ignore his older son when the time came to bestow the grown-up children with responsibilities. She had Surya assign duties only to the two that had come from her own womb, Yama and Yamuna. Yama was given charge of Dharma, the laws governing the righteous way of life. "And Yamuna," continued Devidas, "was given the status of a holy river. Bathing in her waters, one cleanses himself from the sufferings of death."

Kamalakshi knew there was more to the story—the part about Shani, the elder son, and his trials with his mother and father—but she did not press Devidas to continue. If he chooses to end the story here, she thought, that is just fine with me. She could feel his mood sink again like a large parcel placed upon her husband's slim shoulders.

"I say this with a heavy heart, a very heavy heart." Devidas paused for a long spell, considering his words. "But I see no other way than to discuss this difficult matter with you. I have been carrying this load with me for a while now, hoping the situation, by the grace of Lord Ganesha, would resolve itself, and he would open up a path, some way out. But unfortunately, my impurities may be too many and a resolution did not come." He slowed to a standstill, brought his palms together in front of his chest and seemed to be praying.

Kamalakshi waited by his side, her head down, her thoughts concealed. Bile rose in her throat.

Devidas continued. "Our financial situation is grave. They just let go a dozen people. They let me stay on in bookkeeping, but I can already sense another pay cut coming." He began walking again, taking a turn that led them away from the river and toward home. They passed a college's beautiful park. "I am already so ashamed at having to allow Jeevana to drop out of college." He stopped and surveyed the academic buildings from afar before continuing. "For God's sake, she was accepted on full scholarship! So bright, such a future! But what was I to do? It was this or...." He let his words fade away.

"Or me going to work," Kamalakshi whispered.

Devidas pretended not to hear her.

"It is not right. But at least she is not yet a married woman, and this is just temporary." His words, Kamalakshi knew, were his indirect answer. He would never allow his wife to get a job.

"I am sure my bosses know what they are doing," he said, but it sounded to Kamalakshi like he was trying to convince himself. "Soon enough we will thrive again. I am sure, yes, I am quite sure." He repeated this in a whisper, as if doing so would make it come true.

"I am sure, too," said Kamalakshi. She tried to sound cheerful, but her voice cracked.

Out of the blue Devidas asked, as if the thought had just occurred to him for the first time, "Why didn't she insist a little more that they not change her name? 'Jeevana' — such a pretty name, and powerful too. Giver of life. I picked it myself–do you remember?–when I saw how feisty she was, such a feisty little baby...." He drifted off into silence, into memories of happier times, with Kamalakshi walking by his side.

CHAPTER 4

NEW DELHI

During an extended break between classes, Janaki waited for Abhaya on a bench under a pipal tree, their favorite spot. The ancient pipal was their school's mascot. Its leaves were heart shaped and its branches produced a large number of figs that the students enjoyed around mid-April. The Pipal School for Boys and Girls was a public school, and although Janaki could have enrolled in a more prestigious private one, she insisted on going to the public one, knowing that Abhaya had no other option.

So busy was Janaki checking her Facebook page on her phone that she did not notice a boy her age approaching her. Tall, his hair was disheveled, and yet his shirt and pants, though quite obviously secondhand, were clean and neat. His large brown eyes had a brightness to them, and combined with a high forehead, they gave him an intelligent and friendly look. Those eyes were open even wider now, matching his anxiousness.

"Uh...excuse me," he said after standing unnoticed by her side for several minutes, his voice cracking.

Janaki lifted her head, startled.

"I'm so sorry," he now whispered, surprised himself by her response. "I didn't mean to...."

"What do you want?" asked Janaki, her tone harsher than she had intended.

The boy looked panicked.

"Well?" demanded Janaki, now impatient.

He looked around. "It's a private matter," he said, his voice trembling.

He's a good-looking guy, thought Janaki, examining him more closely. Her hard expression softened. She thought his name was Chetan, but she wasn't sure. Janaki's mind wandered, her gaze turning dreamy. Big eyes, hmm...I like that. He reminds me a bit of that actor I saw once in a movie. Now, what was that movie?

"You see," he added, "it is a matter of the heart, and I'm not very good with these sorts of things."

Unaware of her actions, Janaki arranged her disobedient hair. She hadn't really heard what Chetan had just said. Maybe, she thought, my prince just arrived! She smiled warmly at him, hope gleaming in her eyes. "Yes? I'm all ears."

"It's... It's about your friend? Abhaya?" He went on. "I... I... wanted..." Janaki's face fell.

He might have noticed Janaki's disappointment had he not been so enmeshed in his own confusion and embarrassment. Janaki cursed herself for believing that this handsome boy could possibly be interested in her.

Janaki was beginning to find it more and more difficult to ignore Abhaya's attractiveness. While looks presented no obstacle when the two were young children, Janaki struggled to turn a blind eye to the way boys were now staring at her beautiful friend. Janaki was ignored. That was not easy for her, especially since Abhaya seemed oblivious to how their bodies were changing.

Over the past year, Janaki found herself feeling a little envious of Abhaya. It was a new emotion for her. That is, as far as her best friend was concerned. Still, she could not ignore how this sentiment was slowly invading their relationship, spreading like wild weeds or cancer.

Janaki did not like it one bit. Not that she herself was ugly. There was just nothing that special about her. She was plain, her dark hair dull and messy despite endless visits to the best hairstylists that money could buy. Her mane seemed to have a rebellious mind of its own. Even Janaki's long eyelashes, usually a desirable feature, seemed a little grotesque on her somewhat puffy face. Janaki thought they looked like decorations someone forgot to remove after the holidays.

Before she had a chance to respond, "Hey, Janaki!" Abhaya's voice rang out nearby. "Enough with charming guys. I have some exciting news!"

The boy blushed, mumbling, "I'm sorry" one more time before taking off.

Janaki tried to push her hurt feelings aside, but the lump in her throat wouldn't go away so quickly. Not giving Abhaya the chance to question her about the exchange with Chetan, she turned to her and snipped, "So, what's up?"

Abhaya seated herself on the bench next to Janaki, playing it cool though struggling to contain her excitement. Her face flushed.

"Well?" asked Janaki.

As thrilled as Abhaya was, she was enjoying the suspense. Abhaya looked around to make sure no one was within earshot. "I won!" she whispered.

"Won what?" asked Janaki, confused.

"A bid for a project, you dummy!" answered Abhaya, elbowing her friend.

"Oh, I see. Well, congratulations."

"'Well, congratulations,'" Abhaya quipped, imitating her friend's cold wishes. "Is that the best you can do?"

Janaki realized she wasn't being a good friend and snapped herself out of it. "I'm sorry," she said a little more cheerfully. "I was distracted. Really, I'm very happy for you. I know how much it means to you."

"Distracted?" Abhaya said, not missing a beat. "Does that boy and you... and I don't even know his name!"

Janaki blushed.

Abhaya saw. "Come on, Janaki, did he ask you out?"

"Stop it," pleaded Janaki, her self-restraint fading.

Abhaya looked at her strangely.

Janaki regained her composure. "It was nothing," she added. "Really, nothing to report. You know, if something ever happens in that department, you will be the first to know."

Abhaya let the subject drop.

The bell rang. For some students, it signaled the last class period, while for others it was the end of the school day. Abhaya and Janaki headed back in to their class. Out of the corner of her eye, Janaki saw Chetan pick up his Taekwondo logo embroidered bag and head out. She found herself wondering if he was standing there watching them from afar the entire time. Chetan joined another large fellow that was waiting for him by the school's gate, and they were soon both gone out of view.

CHAPTER 5

NEW DELHI

At the Support Center, Jeevana was back in her chair after a brief ten-minute break. With shifts that lasted ten and twelve hours, every small break was as essential as a passing rainshower to someone lost in the desert. Jeevana's next call was from an American customer. By the time that her screen displayed the caller's basic geographical information such as country, state or province, time zone and one of the many companies that her call center served, she had already recognized the accent. A small handwritten note taped to her monitor reminded her to "Smile. Your voice will sound friendlier when you do." She forced a smile on her tired face and recited the script: "Good evening and thank you for calling Tough Toys for Bad Boys. My name is Jane. May I ask for your name?" Jeevana's English was flawless although her Indian accent was discernable.

"Yeah, hi. This is Jim." Jeevana noted the customer sounded anxious and irritated.

"Good evening Jim. How may I assist you?" she said with all the pleasantness she could muster.

"Yeah, well, I placed an order through your website three weeks ago, and it never arrived though you guys charged my credit card."

"I'm so sorry to hear this, Jim. Can I please have your order number?"

"Yeah, I have it right here. It's 6570426," said Jim, his thick New England accent making it difficult for her to understand.

"I'm so sorry, Jim, I didn't get that. Can you please repeat?"

"6-5-7-0-4-2-6. Did you get it this time?" He muttered under his breath, "Freakin' foreigners."

Jeevana flushed with embarassment. As her training dictated, she chose to ignore the comment. She keyed in the order number. Her computer was working superbly slow, as sometimes was the case.

"Yeah," barked Jim, "So what's up with that?"

"I'm so sorry, sir, the system is a little slow. I'm still waiting for the order screen to come up."

"Stop being so sorry all the time," burst Jim, "and just do your freakin' job!"

"I'm so..." started Jeevana again but stopped herself. Instead she just said, "It is almost here."

She was beginning to lose her cool. Her day had already been long and tedious, and now this, but she had a job to do, and she would do it well.

"All right, now, you just listen to me, Jane, or whatever the heck your real name is," he growled. "Either you tell me where my order is right now or credit my money back to my card. I don't have time for this crap!"

"Sir, I would gladly assist you," said Jeevana, but in her struggle to keep pleasant, her accent became even more pronounced. "If you don't mind, please hold on for a little longer, as the system is a little slow today."

"Yeah, I bet you it's slow every day! That's the problem with you freakin' people. Never mind, I'm gonna cancel this order and get it somewhere else."

The phone line went dead. Jeevana felt as if she had been slapped. Try as she might, she couldn't stop her eyes from tearing. Just then, the customer's order came up on her monitor. The purchase was for an adult blow-up doll. Her eyes still blurry, Jeevana squinted at the screen. She couldn't believe her eyes. "This is what all that was about?" she thought. In an instance, the irony seized her. Here was a grown man acting like a child, throwing the mother of all temper tantrums until he got his way, only to discover that the candy he coveted was utterly sour. She burst out laughing, stifling her giggles with her hand over her mouth.

"What is this?" The man's voice was loud. He was directly behind her.

Glancing over her shoulder, Jeevana jumped to find Eshaan's face just inches from her ear. Looking no more than eighteen years old, Eshaan was the nephew of one of the call center's owners. That fact explained his quick rise to supervisor. Peering at the monitor, a crass smile stole across his face.

Jeevana blushed. "It was an order," she stuttered, "for an American client."

Eshaan nodded and winked at her, his grin still plastered across his face as he stepped away.

Far from being funny, his antics made her feel dirty. At first, Jeevana thought he had left to check in with another worker. In fact, he had backed away a few feet, measuring her figure. She could feel his gaze stripping her bare. Once again, her vision blurred as hot tears streaked down her cheeks, humiliated and shamed. This is not the life she had wished for herself.

CHAPTER 6

NEW YORK CITY

It was 8:00 p.m. An ensemble of street noises accompanied Rachel as she walked to John's apartment. Her heels clacked against the cement, adding to the continuous hum of the city. To Rachel it sounded like a large heart, pumping life through the veins of the city. The City that Never Sleeps.

She wouldn't be sleeping either. Her mind was on other matters. John's long shift at the East-West Café had just ended, and she had promised to bring by her latest mock-ups for their project.

She arrived at his building. Its faded walls and iron steps were now a familiar part of her life. She climbed the three flights to his door and walked inside.

"You don't knock anymore?" John glanced up with a wry smile.

"No," she said. "I've got the mockups."

John reached for them and spread them over his keyboard. "Wow! I love your design for this screen."

This was one of John's qualities that she secretly adored: his child-like peals of delight whenever he was impressed.

Despite her feelings, Rachel replied blandly, "I knew you would." The only child of an business attorney and a math teacher, Rachel was brought up to conceal her emotions.

Her father's voice echoed in her mind. "Showing emotion is a weakness," he told her time and again. "Emotions are like playing with a deck of cards. One must learn to control them if you ever hope to win the game." He must have known what he was saying; his law-firm made a fortune. Death found him at fifty-four, two months prior to Rachel's college graduation. His death left her wondering about the wisdom of this teaching, yet so ingrained were his words in her mind that having a poker-face in any situation was second nature to her.

"How about this screen?" Rachel pulled up another design on her laptop.

"Wow!" responded John.

Rachel suppressed a smirk before asking, "And how about you? Any luck with finding a programmer?"

"Yes! I can't believe I didn't tell you!" he said. "I found someone on one of those websites you suggested."

"What did I tell you? What did I tell you?" said a cheeky Rachel.

John either did not notice or was too excited to care. "Here, let me show you." He sat down on one of his two chairs and pulled up a page on his laptop. Sliding his chair closer to Rachel, their thighs almost touched beneath the small table.

She pretended not to notice.

A profile page of a programmer filled his screen. Most prominent was a photo of a good-looking blonde woman with pale skin and blue eyes. If Rachel had not known better, she could have sworn it was the face of a fashion model, but she kept her mouth shut. Maybe not all programmers were nerdy-looking. The attractive woman on the screen seemed to be in her early twenties. Her name, the webpage announced, was Abby Smith. A small UK flag decorated the country of origin spot.

"She's British," explained John, "but she currently resides, temporarily, in India. I appreciate the fact that she's European and not Indian-born."

"Interesting that someone with such a fair skin would be living under the unforgiving Indian sun," hissed Rachel.

He pointed to the screen. "See! She can program in PHP and java... exactly what we need! And, she has experience developing phone apps."

"A true wonder woman. All that's missing is the headband and the cape. By the way," Rachel said, "you forgot to mention how good-looking she is. Was that a consideration in your selection?"

John's face turned red. "Of course not," he protested.

"What is it John? Are your cheeks red? Red is Wonder Woman's cape color. She might like it...." she said with a smile. Point made, her voice became calmer, her composure regained.

On the cushioned corner chair, Tess rose to her feet, licked a paw, circled her tail a couple of times and then went back to sleep, her purr becoming a gentle snore.

CHAPTER 7

NEW DELHI

Her last class over, Janaki sat alone on a bench under the pipal tree. So many Instagram posts to review, so little time, she thought.

As silently as a grasshopper, Chetan appeared by her side. He stood perfectly still.

Janaki noticed him out of the corner of her eye but made him wait. After a few moments, she muttered, "Abhaya isn't coming." She had not bothered to lift her head.

"Oh, I'm sorry," Chetan murmured, "but it's you, Janaki, that I came to see."

Janaki raised her eyes this time, Instagram all but forgotten, and her face flushed.

"Are you done for today? Do you have another class?" he asked.

She nodded yes.

"May I walk you home, so we can speak in private?"

Janaki agreed. She led, making sure to take the longer way home. Walking slower than her usual rushed pace, she refused to let her hopes get the best of her. She waited to hear what Chetan had to say. The winding path took them through a neglected part of town. Janaki felt uncomfortable when they passed by several young men eyeing her every move.

Chetan must have noticed her discomfort, because he positioned himself between her and the onlookers.

Janaki's heart soared. She summoned the courage to grasp the arm of her protector.

Chetan braced a bit but said nothing. As they turned a corner and entered a quiet park, he finally spoke, "Janaki, I'm not sure how to say this. I'm not very good with expressing my thoughts."

Janaki's heart was pounding. She dared to wish, did he change his mind about Abhaya? Will he ask me out?

Chetan took a long breath and then said, "about Abhaya...I think I love her."

Janaki's heart sank. It was as if it had torn itself from her body and flung itself out of an airplane. A wave of hatred washed over her, hatred at Chetan for daring to raise her hopes but also hatred for Abhaya. Vileness flooded her so intensely that she felt most of her strength draining out.

"She's so smart and pretty...." Chetan went on, unaware of the effect his words had on his companion. "I've had these feelings for a long while but was too shy to do anything about them. I still can't."

Janaki felt dizzy. Losing her footing, she gripped Chetan's arm.

"Are you okay?" asked Chetan, turning to support her. "You seem so pale, and your eyes...."

"Yes, it's... it's just that the heat is suddenly getting to me," Janaki replied.

The day was not particularly hot, but Chetan seemed to buy her story.

"Here," he suggested, pointing at a bench nearby. "Let's sit for a moment." No sooner did they sit down than he continued, "And then the thought occurred to me. You, Janaki, I look at your face, and I have a feeling you're a kind person, and Abhaya is your friend. Maybe you could help me?"

Janaki said nothing, her breath shallow and strained.

They sat without speaking. A light breeze blew through the tree branches, jolting Janaki back to life. "Sure," she said, her calculating mind trying to work things out. She realized that if she refused, Chetan would find a way to approach Abhaya, and she, Janaki, would be out of the picture. The only way for her to remain relevant was to agree. "I'll help you," she said.

CHAPTER 8

NEW DELHI

That afternoon Abhaya was in her room, coding. P!nk's "The Truth About Love" was blasting through her earphones. Abhaya knew better than to play the songs she liked aloud on the computer's speakers. Despite having only basic English, the mere chance that her mom — or even worse, her dad! — could walk in on her and catch some of the lyrics filled her with dread. It was not a gamble she was willing to take. She checked her newly set up ePayMadeEasy.com account and was delighted to see that a payment had already been deposited: $500! More than she ever imagined she could have. And that, she knew, was only the start.

Abhaya's mind returned to the moment she had decided to seek work online. It had followed a premonition, a vision of the future that had come to her in a dream. She had had only two or three visions in her life. Each had heralded significant changes in her life.

This particular premonition happened early on a Saturday morning. She awoke at dawn, atypical for her weekend sleep pattern of a late morning in bed. Trying to fall back into sleep, she dreamed that she was being physically attacked. The dream was so vivid, it seemed as if it were actually happening. A crowd of men, New Delhi locals she did not recognize, stood around her, their mad eyes undressing her before their greedy hands reached out to tear her clothes off. She awoke again, this time with a start. She did not dare to go back to sleep.

Abhaya dressed and went for a walk along the river. She stayed close to populated paths, fear still gripping her mind. What did it mean? These vivid dreams always meant something.

Yet she questioned herself. Maybe her dream was nothing but a byproduct of a story she'd seen in the news. A young college student had been sexually assaulted while riding a bus. A gang of men brutalized and raped her. She died a few days later. The local news covered the story for weeks, angling to blame the young woman for being promiscuous in her look and dress. Then the international media got involved, proclaiming that India was a place where the victims were blamed. Indeed, her own parents had told her to be careful of how she dressed and looked at men so that she did not give them the wrong idea. Her parents talked endlessly about what the young woman must have done to invite such an attack.

Abhaya knew without a doubt that it was not the woman's fault.

A chill ran down her spine. She shivered.

Abhaya knew then that her dream was a warning. If she stayed in New Delhi, she, too, would experience the same fate.

She was flooded with an overwhelming desire to move out of her parents' small apartment, out of this futureless city, and away from this backward country. She felt as if she would suffocate if she did not break free.

If I could only find a way, she thought.

The trail she followed had taken her to the newer part of town where large high-tech buildings were popping up everywhere. A large billboard caught her eye. "Looking for a better tomorrow?" it said in large royal-blue letters. "Aim High and find your future with High-Tech, the fastest growing company in India. Make lots of money. Variety of positions available. Call…"

Abhaya's mind screamed in delight. That's it! The answer was right in front of her eyes.

But she would not apply there. She was too young, too inexperienced, and besides, she had no desire to stay in New Delhi.

Her mind raced with new ideas. Her step quickened as she turned toward home. She had heard that one could find work online via freelancing websites. She knew she had the goods; she was a talented programmer, the best in her class, and heck, the best programmer her school ever had. Her teachers always praised her and a few even called her a prodigy.

As soon as Abhaya returned home, she searched the apartment to see if anyone was home. She was alone.

Perfect! she thought. She logged on and searched for such websites. Picking one, she set up her profile within an hour and started bidding on jobs.

Snapping herself back to the present moment, Abhaya refocused. She clicked on a favorite browser link, taking her to the freelancing website page that she had recently modified. Here was Abby Smith, her avatar. Abhaya thought that if she could have controlled her rebirth into this world, this fictional Abby was who she would want to be. Her recent online experience had taught her that Caucasians had it easy. That and having a Western name. At the same time, her lighter brown skin was a privilege in India that she took for granted; she had not been aware of the status it bestowed on her.

Funny, she thought, here I was mocking Jeevana for being called Jane, and I end up as Abby. She had selected Abby's photo almost randomly. First she picked the name. "Abby" was obvious since it was close enough to her real name. "Smith" was generic enough. Then she Googled the name and came upon a photo of a real Abby Smith, but one who was into fashion. She would therefore be unlikely to encounter this fake profile on a programming services website. Right that minute she wanted to be that Abby Smith. Life would have been so much easier for her. Maybe living in London, Paris, or New York, in her own small apartment, away from this miserable life. She and her John Reynolds....

Daydreaming, Abhaya did not initially notice the Instant Messenger prompt that popped up on her screen. When the blinking chat icon caught her eye, John had already sent her three messages. Her heart leaped. It was not often that John Reynolds communicated with her via messenger. Chatting with John was having a little piece of her fantasy come to life, her future away from the place fate had intended for her.

She would trick fate. She was Abhaya, the fearless one. Nothing could stop her once she put her mind to it.

John R.: Hi there, Abby! I'm happy with the code you sent yesterday and have deposited a payment to your account. Did you see it? All good?

Abby: Yes, very. Thank you!

John R.: How's the weather on your side of the globe?

Abby: Good. It's hot, but that's usually the case.

John R.: How do you handle it?

Abby: Don't forget that I'm used to it.

John R.: Used to it? Isn't England much cooler?

Abby: Right Well, I grew up in the southern part and we had no air-conditioning :-)

John R.: Smart aleck ;-)

Abby: Yes, that sounds just like me. Say, isn't it late night in New York?

John R.: Very late. But such is the glorious life of an entrepreneur.

Abhaya's phone buzzed. She quickly peeked at it:

Janaki wrote, "R we still on 4 2morrow?"

Abhaya texted a puzzled emoticon. "on?"

"We're off school the next few days. U 4forgot already? We're set 2 meet @ at Tagore Garden & walk 2 Rajouri Garden Mkt."

John buzzed through. "Abby, are you still there?"

Abby answered him. "Sure. Where else would I be?"

"When do you think you'll have the next part of the app ready?"

"I'll try to finish it over the next five days. Would that be okay?"

Janaki buzzed in. "Abhaya? Helloooooo? U there?"

Abhaya turned her attention to Janaki. "sorry, what?"

"So r we on 4 2morrow?"

John texted next. "That's perfect!"

Abby answered him. "You've got it."

Janaki was next. "Someone there with u?"

"No, of course not!"

John texted, "I think I'm in love!"

Abby was shocked. "What?"

Janaki texted, "yrutakingsolong2getback2me?"

John continued. "With my programmer! Bright, pretty, smart aleck and quick! Good night. :)"

Abby's face flushed. "Good night John! Xoxo"

Janaki sent an angry face emoticon.

Abby replied to Janaki. "Sorry, sorry. Just busy with work. Yes! We are on for tomorrow."

CHAPTER 9

NEW DELHI

Jeevana had just finished the morning shift and was getting ready to leave. Collecting her handbag, she was startled to find her supervisor, Eshaan, suddenly by her side.

Jeevana did not like him. She never had. From her first day at this job, even before he started bothering her, she found his sense of self-importance irritating. Full of himself and smug, Eshaan preferred to dress as a Western gangster. In her mind, that was absolutely ridiculous, even if his narrow face, thin mustache and sparkly eyes fit the bill.

"So, what's up, good-looking?" he said as if playing a role in a film. "Leaving already? Are you free to catch a movie tonight?"

Jeevana's long face must have disclosed her true feelings.

"What's the matter?" Eshaan snapped. "You don't find me to be good enough for a college dropout such as yourself?" The sharp edge in his voice reminded her of the small knife he often flipped open at work to clean his nails.

Undeterred, Jeevana threw her handbag across her shoulder. "Excuse me," she said, "but I need to go."

Instead, Eshaan followed her to the empty entrance hall before rushing ahead of her at the last moment. Blocking her way to the door, he whispered teasingly, "A kiss and I'll let you go."

Jeevana stared at him, utterly shocked. This behavior was far from proper, even in a company not known for rigorous workplace ethics. But who could she tell? Eshaan would easily deny it, and a complaint from her would probably lead to being fired.

"Eshaan! Where are you?" came a shout from the shift manager, Eshaan's superior.

Taking advantage of his brief distraction, Jeevana bolted forward, accidentally brushing shoulders with him as she slipped out of the building.

"No worries," she heard Eshaan calling behind her. "There is always tomorrow!"

Walking home, Jeevana kept on looking over her shoulder, half-expecting Eshaan to follow her. She knew he was back at work, but fear gripped her heart. Her workplace provided transportation, but that was mainly for the late shifts. She could have taken the bus, but since every rupee counted, she did not mind the walk when she had the time. It was good exercise, too, she reasoned, especially after sitting in front of a computer for hours on end.

With Eshaan's advances still on her mind, Jeevana passed by the University of Delhi campus, adding insult to injury. It was there that she once attended college before dropping out. She found herself stopping by the large open gates. Not that long ago she was part of that institution, looking forward to graduating with honors in chemistry. Now a wall made of material thicker and stronger than iron and cement separated her from her dream of becoming a renowned scientist. Her mind flashed back to a moment in her childhood.

It was a neighbor, Mr. Rajeeb, that sparked her love of chemistry, all by making a comment that hit the right chord at the right time. "You see, child," he told her in his deep yet gentle voice, "everything in this material world is made of elements: elements discovered and elements yet to be discovered. A person who understands these elements holds the key to the universe, much like a... hmm... a cook having all sorts of secret ingredients at his disposal."

Some years later, young Jeevana realized that Mr. Rajeeb, an atheist, stopped short of mentioning God and instead replaced him with "cook."

At home, her dad, a devout Hindu, seemed to believe the opposite: the material plane was nothing more than maya, an illusion. Jeevana learned early on to avoid bringing up Mr. Rajeeb's perspective in front of her father. Just mentioning his name would send him out on one of his "rage-walks." But when she was accepted on full scholarship to the University of Delhi, even Devidas was proud of his daughter, the brightest in her class. "The cream of the crop," the science teacher Mr. Pandit used to say. Just look at me now, she thought bitterly.

Back home feeling tired and beaten, Jeevana rushed to her room. "Jeevana, dear," called her mother after her, "I heated a plate of Baingan Bharta for you."

"Thank you, Mom," replied Jeevana, "but I'm not really hungry."

Entering the room that she shared with her sister Abhaya, Jeevana's mood remained foul.

Her sudden entrance provoked panic in Abhaya.

Abhaya, sitting at the desktop they both shared, abruptly logged out. "You're home early," she said, as if it were a complaint.

"No, not really," replied Jeevana. "I'm actually on time. What are you up to?"

"Nothing," answered Abhaya.

"Said the Cobra to the mouse," responded Jeevana, undressing to shower. "I know you well enough. You're surely up to no good."

"Wait a minute. Are you implying you're a mouse? I always suspected that," said Abhaya, trying to divert the conversation.

Jeevana wrapped a towel around her naked body and turned to face her sister.

"Listen to me," she said, "Cyberspace is no joke. There are a lot of perverts and nutcases out there. If I find out that you're meddling where you shouldn't be, I'll make sure you get no more access to this computer."

"You can't do that!" called Abhaya, panicked.

"Oh, yes I can," answered Jeevana venomously. "As you may recall, Father was anything but happy bringing this computer home, into our room...."

"Yes, but you had no objection," Abhaya interjected. "After all, you use it, too."

"And I agreed so that, unlike me going through high school without a computer, you could use it for homework."

"That's not fair," said Abhaya her voice devoid of its previous aggression.

"Well, little sister, you had better get used to it. Life isn't fair." Jeevana turned and left the room, heading to shower.

Abhaya set a timer for ten minutes and brought up her work-screen, but a small voice at the back of her mind continued to shout, that's not fair! It's simply unfair!

CHAPTER 10

NEW DELHI

On the first day of vacation Abhaya and Janaki walked along the busy pathways of Rajouri Garden Market. Abhaya loved the energy of the market. Along the narrow streets, there were tables displaying everything from fruits and vegetables to housewares and furniture to cheap electronics to clothing items. Tables lined both sides of the road, concealing the storefronts behind them.

Abhaya would lose herself in the sounds, sights, and smells that blended together in the crowded streets. Merchants yelled out their daily deals while a thick stream of shoppers strode by like a human river, moving to a disorganized logic, mirroring the rising and falling crests of the nearby Yamuna. The air was filled with the rich aroma of spices. Loud Indi-pop played from different stands, mixing rhythms of East and West into a cacophony of sounds that somehow resulted in an awkward harmony. The skies above the narrow hectic streets were covered with colorful saris hung out to dry in the searing sun, their shadows dancing playfully in the light breeze. Cars, scooters, bicycles and pull-carts made their way through the crowd, miraculously without colliding, honking upstream like lost goslings in search of their mothers.

As if by mutual agreement, Abhaya and Janaki avoided discussing school and the tests just taken. From experience, they both suspected that Abhaya had probably aced hers easily while Janaki had struggled for barely passing marks.

Janaki picked a safe topic. "How's it going with that project you won? We never really had much of a chance to talk about it. How did you win it? What was different this time around?"

"Well," said Abhaya, smiling, "Didn't you say that the twelfth time is the charm?" Mulling over her words for several moments, she added, "I owe it partially to my sister."

"To Jee?" asked Janaki. "What does that nosey piece of work have to do with it?"

"Long story short," replied Abhaya, "I owe her my new pseudonym!"

"You mean like a new name?" asked Janaki.

"She didn't realize it, but she gave me the idea," explained Abhaya. Quoting her sister, she added, "'Research shows that Westerners respond better to people with Western names,' so I figured they are less likely to hire a programmer named Abhaya." She paused, aiming for a more dramatic effect, expecting her friend to urge her to continue. Sure enough, her expectations were met.

"Go on!" pressed Janaki, biting a nail, a habit she had tried to break with modest success.

Abhaya continued, "After I realized there may be something to what my sister said, I went to my online profile on that freelancer's website, deleted it and started a new one." She paused again, a twinkle in her eyes.

Right on queue Janaki prompted, "And?"

"In comes Abby!" announced Abhaya, spreading her arms wide and curtseying like a stage actor, introducing herself to the world.

Janaki stared at her friend confusedly. "Comes who?" she asked.

"I reinvented myself," explained Abhaya. "I called myself 'Abby Smith,' added a fake photo of a nice looking Western woman, invented a whole new bio and described Abby as someone who was born in London but had to relocate with her family to India some years ago because of her father's military career, and," she broke off to take a breath.

"Wait, wait!" called Janaki. "When was your father in the military? You never mentioned that!"

"No!" exclaimed Abhaya, "it's just my fake bio." She gave Janaki another moment for it to sink in and added, "It worked! I answered three new bids and one of them, a John Reynolds from New York, hired me!"

"Wow!" called Janaki, her hazel eyes widening. "But wait," she added, her eyebrows arching even more, "is that allowed? I mean, let's face it: you're cheating."

"At this point, I don't really care anymore," said Abhaya. "I always believed in playing fair, but if people out there are judging me by my name and looks, then all bets are off." Biting her upper lip, she remembered what her sister told her. "And anyhow, there is nothing fair about this world."

"But won't they catch you?" persisted Janaki. "I mean, the clients or the people that run that website?"

Abhaya was struck by the fact that Janaki was not much concerned with her friend's renunciation of honesty but rather more interested in the risk involved.

"Maybe," replied Abhaya, "although I don't see how anyone can check on me as I plan to deliver good on the job." She let the sentence hang. "The way I see it, all that really matters is the quality of my work–not that I'm from India, or a teenager or," she added, "a woman."

"Look at you," smiled Janaki with a pang of cynicism, "a fighter for women's rights."

Janaki's tone did not go unnoticed by Abhaya. Conditioned for instant retaliation by her constant fights with her older sister, Abhaya's mind sharpened a sarcastic response. Instead, she took a deep breath and let it go. Janaki was her best friend. She can forgive her, their unspoken pact of 'no jealousy' unbroken.

"How is Naja Naja taking it?" asked Janaki.

"My father?" said Abhaya. It was not often that Janaki used the nickname she had given Abhaya's dad, a person she disliked. "My father, as you very well should know," replied Abhaya, "is not aware of any of this. And it goes without saying that it should remain that way."

The last thing she needed was for her father to learn of her secret life and confiscate the computer. She had no doubt that was exactly what he would do if he ever learned that his younger daughter worked, and especially for Westerners. He was already deeply distressed by the effects that contact with the Western world was having over her sister, even outside the workplace. Abhaya saw his severe looks and heard his comments when Jeevana would occasionally forego her traditional salwar kameez pantsuit in favor of jeans, casual tops, and other such fashions. But, for the most part, he did not forbid her sister from doing as she wished. Abhaya wondered how he tolerated it.

"Your sister didn't snitch?" inquired Janaki surprised.

"She doesn't know," replied Abhaya.

"You mean she hasn't a clue?" Janaki wondered. "How come? You share a room for heaven's sake. Is she blind?" She brought her hand to her mouth and was biting her nails again.

"No, she isn't," assured Abhaya, thinking how little Janaki knew. Janaki never had to share a room with anyone, not only because of her family's wealth but also because she was an only child. "But Jee isn't really home much. She works very long hours, and when she's not at work, she finds things to do that keep her away and then goes out with her friends."

"Can't really blame her," said Janaki letting go of her nail. "With the all-prevailing Naja Naja watching, I wouldn't want to be around much either." She paused before saying, "I'm just surprised that your father allows her, I mean, to go out that much."

Abhaya found herself somewhat irritated by Janaki's repeated snubbing of her dad. God knew she did not like her father much these days either, but she never made fun of Janaki's parents, let alone with such malice. Yet she said nothing and instead replied, "she's twenty-one, and she pays my father rent. It's true that he makes her life difficult, but we all have learned to live with the way he is, even if..." her voice turned sorrowful, "it's been more difficult these past few months. More than the usual."

"I don't get it," admitted Janaki. "How is it that a daughter pays rent to her father for staying at the family home?"

Janaki seemed oblivious to Abhaya's changing mood. Of course you don't get it, thought Abhaya. You never experienced the financial stress my dad has to endure.

While contemplating how to best answer her friend, Janaki yanked her aside, removing her from the path of a honking motorcycle. The abrupt scare made Abhaya lose her train of thought.

They walked in silence for a while, each busy with her own ideas. The sun moved lazily across hazy skies, and an occasional breeze provided relief from the increasing heat. Several streets later, Abhaya and Janaki passed by a sadhu, a holy man, seated on a small carpet whose original colors must have faded decades ago. Half-naked, the sadhu's groin was wrapped in a traditional orange cloth, symbolizing renunciation. The old man's leathery face was smeared with white ashes. Only his thick grey beard and his forehead weren't white. From there, his remaining hair was collected into a bun atop his head. A bright red stripe ran from his hairline to the bridge of his nose.

His posture meditative, the sadhu's shut eyes suddenly popped opened. He stared directly at Abhaya, but otherwise he was as still as a sphynx.

The unexpected change in the man's expression caused Janaki to jolt. She tugged hard on Abhaya's arm, but Abhaya did not budge. Abhaya returned the sadhu's gaze, defiance in her dark almond eyes. The two stared at each other for a long moment, locking eyes, transfixed.

As suddenly as it all had started, the sadhu closed his eyes, a trace of a smile on his lips. The rest of his face remained as expressionless as mask. Abhaya blinked several times.

Glancing at Janaki, Abhaya saw horror and confusion on her friend's face. As she could not herself fathom what just happened, let alone explain it to Janaki, Abhaya elected to pick up their conversation where it was left off. "I was telling you about the project I just won."

"Oh, yes," responded Janaki, as if snapping out of a dream, "Is it going well?"

"Oh, you know." Abhaya sounded scattered even to her own ears, as if still under enchantment. "Pretty good."

"Tell me more. What's it about?" Janaki urged.

Surprised by the unexpectedly sharp tone, Abhaya raised an eyebrow.

"Please?" added Janaki hastily.

"Well," complied Abhaya, "it's actually quite interesting. It is a phone app that allows the user to record whatever sound they want and then turn it into a ring tone."

"Cool!" responded Janaki. "Any sound?"

"There are a few guidelines," explained Abhaya. Her enthusiasm to discuss her work began to energize her, removing the languished feeling of walking the streets. Her pace quickened. "But that's the easy part. Then there is a whole e-commerce section where users can trade or sell their own ringtones. This is what I'm working on now."

"I see," said Janaki.

"I completed the first part of the project on time and on budget. Actually, I even delivered a little ahead of time. John, my first client that is–I have a few more clients now, but John would always be my first–was very happy. Shortly after, he sent me the next part of the project to do. He also wrote a very positive review for me on the freelancing website, rating me five stars!"

"Great," said Janaki, her voice devoid of emotion.

"Yes," agreed Abhaya. "Once I received that first rave review on the first segment, it all became so much easier. I guess other clients on this site consider the reviews more important than the cost. I was able to increase my hourly rate for new bids, and still get other jobs. I'm actually making some decent money!"

"But how do they pay you? After all, you don't have a bank account, or do you?" Janaki had underestimated so much about her friend that she wondered what else did she not know.

"I've managed to set up an ePayMadeEasy account," answered Abhaya.

"A what?" asked Janaki.

Abhaya explained how this online payment system works.

"So how much did you make?"

"To date?" asked Abhaya, and then, tilting her head up, narrowing her eyes, she whispered while calculating. "I'd say roughly about two, no, wait, I forgot the job I'm doing right now–altogether, probably closer to three thousand dollars, that is, American dollars," she replied casually.

"How much?!" asked Janaki again.

"About three thousand," grinned Abhaya. "I told you it's some serious money."

Janaki fell silent.

Abhaya was excited. Telling her best friend made it all more real. As if it were an omen, a brand new black Mercedes was passing by, its silvery emblem glittering in the sunlight. The driver did not seem to need to honk; the crowd reverentially parted ways for it, a vehicle that seemed to have an authority of its own.

"Have you spent any of it yet?" Janaki asked.

"No," replied Abhaya, "and I'm not planning to anytime soon."

"Why not?"

"Well," replied Abhaya, "first, I need to figure out how I can do that without drawing my family's attention. The last thing I need is for my father to find out. And second...." She stopped short.

Janaki looked at her with a puzzled expression. "Yes? Second?"

Abhaya drew in a deep breath. "This can never be repeated," she whispered.

"What?" asked Janaki.

"What I'm about to tell you," replied Abhaya, her expression severe.

Janaki halted, brought her hands to her hips, and turned to look at Abhaya. She had her most offended look on her face, the one she had used with Abhaya's sister since they were eight years old.

"Okay, okay," said Abhaya, trying to appease her friend, "I would have told you eventually. I just didn't plan on doing it so soon."

Janaki didn't move. She didn't even seem to breathe.

"Well, I have been planning this for a long while. The truth is that I'm saving this money so when I'm sixteen, I can get away."

"'Plan to get away?'" repeated Janaki, wetting her lips. "You mean run away...from home? Run away?! But why?"

"I need my own space," Abhaya whispered fiercely, "my own freedom." *You wouldn't understand*, she thought. *You never had to share a room with a sister, never had to worry about money.*

"But your family!" said Janaki, panic creeping into her voice. "Your mom would be heartbroken!" And a moment later, adding in a voice barely audible, "And me..."

Abhaya said, "I'd let them know I'm okay. I wouldn't be rejecting them. Ultimately, they'd understand, or at least I hope they would." She had told herself this to quiet her conscience so many times that by now she almost believed it. "I can't tell them yet," she added, "though I wish I could. At any rate, even when I can tell, I wish someone else would do that dirty work for me. No doubt my father will go ballistic."

"But what about us?" Janaki gasped. "You're my best friend!" She felt tears welling up and turned her head so Abhaya couldn't see.

Abhaya did notice but did not comment. She just said, "We'll figure out a way to stay in touch. Don't worry. And besides, it is not like it's happening tomorrow. There's plenty of time. Let's not think about it for now."

A long silence ensued. By now they were out of the noisy market area, entering a quiet, well-groomed street of posh stores, the kind that Abhaya could only dream of patronizing. Stopping by a storefront window of expensive handbags, Abhaya pointed to a stylish purse tagged with a price worth $100.00. She murmured, "This is the one I'd been eyeing. Once I find a way to release my money...."

Abhaya saw Janaki looking at her reflection in the glass. Janaki looked frustrated, angry, maybe even envious.

Was that possible?

Abhaya couldn't understand it. Why would Janaki feel that way?

"I'm not leaving soon or anything. And you'll always be my best friend."

Janaki gave Abhaya a tight smile and turned toward home.

Abhaya followed.

CHAPTER 11

NEW YORK CITY

"Yes," Rachel answered John's call impatiently. She was not in a good mood. An elaborate graphic design that she had submitted earlier that day, one that required many long hours of preparation, had been ruthlessly rejected. How she hated such clients, the know-it-all types who were anything but. These puffed-up creatures more often than not were covering their own insecurities by demonstrating what she came to nickname a "childish superiority complex."

The conversation was still burning in her mind.

This client sneered at the drawing. "What's up with this blue color? It looks meek."

"Meek?"

"Yeah, meek," he said.

Exactly what you can expect an imbecile attorney to say. How predictable! He didn't even know it wasn't just blue, it was cobalt blue. She had tried to explain that cobalt blue was a color used in the production of Chinese porcelain, that it is a noble and classic color, projecting style, tradition, importance. She knew more about colors than they could have ever imagined. But her words fell on deaf ears. Not a great day.

She could remember other times. Fresh out of college, everywhere she looked, design patterns emerged: lively designs, classic designs, good designs, bad designs, designs that she, Rachel, could definitely improve on. She was going to make the world a better place, one project at a time. And she did, at least for a while, until she learned that the world–or rather, some people–did not care for her sharp eye, keen creative mind, and light hand. Nor did they care for her fast tongue, something that her boss grew increasingly impatient with. He reminded her that their clients do not want to be proven wrong.

Imbecilic idiots, the whole bunch of them, she thought. Her love of her profession was dwindling. The joy of designing was being sucked out of her bones by such clients like life drained from a fly in a spider's web.

"It's not your profession that's the problem," Mr. Greenberg told her one Saturday morning. He was one of the elderly New Yorkers that she made a habit of visiting monthly, part of a volunteer visiting program for senior citizens.

As impatient as Rachel was, she had no such issues with the aged. They all loved having her over, welcoming her warmly with open arms. Rachel felt it was almost unfair. It was she who was supposed to be doing them a favor, and yet more than once, she was on the receiving end.

"No, not your profession, but rather your location. New York City is a wonderful place, but for every yang there is a yin. For every wonderful attribute, there is also a negative. I hate to say that, as I would not wish to see you gone, but for your own sake, you may want to consider relocating to another place with a different pace, at least for a while."

He may be right, thought Rachel bitterly. A true Manhattanite, she had a hard time imagining herself living anywhere else but New York City, yet....

"Listen up, Rache," exclaimed John on the other side of the line, "I've got some good news!"

Rachel sighed. She could use some good news right now, although what would count as good news, she couldn't tell. She knew all too well that John was easily excited by just about anything. "That programmer I hired...that we hired," he quickly corrected, "well, she finished the next phase of the development ahead of schedule!"

"Oh great," responded Rachel. Right then, she could not have cared less about their project.

"What?" asked John. "I thought you would be a little more ecstatic."

"Oh, but I am," replied Rachel. "You just can't see me doing my happy dance right now. Here, let me twirl one more time."

Trying to hide his dismay, John went on. "It means that we are only one step away from launching our beta! We'll be able to test this app with actual users much faster than we thought!"

When Rachel remained silent, John continued, "You know, it was a good thing you suggested I look for a programmer on that website."

Ignoring his compliment, Rachel's lips remained sealed, her mind still arguing with the arrogant client over the meaning of the color cobalt. He had said, "That color reminds me of the blue equivalent of puke green, you know, that wishy-washy color of old fashioned hospital wards and clinics. It reminds me of a place where sick people go to die ... a hospice, or something."

Of course, thought Rachel, what else would it represent to creeps like you?

"This Abby," said John, "she's really great, very very talented. I never met a programmer with so many capabilities and dedication. And soooo affordable."

Still, Rachel remained mute.

"Is that The Koln Concert with Keith Jarrett playing?"

Rachel still didn't answer. He knew it was Rachel's favored album for whenever she was feeling down. Surely that would make him realize that she would rather be left alone. With a wry smile, she also knew that he wouldn't hang up, because she would be even more offended.

When she was in these moods, he couldn't win. But he would put up with her, she knew. The thought made her feel a tiny bit better.

"Abby always responds when I message her." Unaware that he was upsetting Rachel even more, he added, "all hours of the day and night.... I don't know how she does it!"

"Well, good for you!" growled Rachel. Her limited patience with John's blathering about this Abby had reached an end. It's not enough that I was tortured at the office today by a complete amateur, she thought. Now I have to listen to this B.S. about this geeky, gorgeous, wonder woman! "So now, all of a sudden, you like foreigners?" Rachel barked. Enough was enough. She was upset, and someone had to pay the price. John was an easy target. "First you bash them all, those Chinese, Indians and Pakistanis, then you abuse them by paying a ridiculously low fee." By now, Rachel was spitting her words rapidly. "Hey, you know what? Maybe you can bring back slavery? You and all these freaking a-hole attorneys."

Rachel's words fell on deaf ears. John, used to ignoring Rachel's sarcasm and too drunk with his own excitement, hardly understood a word she was saying.

"Do you understand the meaning of this?" he asked, exhilarated though a tad confused.

"No," answered Rachel, "but I'm sure you're going to explain."

"It means," continued John, completely missing the cliff-dive the conversation was taking, "that we will be able to maybe see revenues much faster than the business plan called for–that it may work out better than I planned!"

Rachel pretended to be excited, "Yay! Now, first of all, John, what happened all of a sudden to the we as in 'we planned'? Second, John," pronouncing his name as if tasting Brussels Sprouts, "Abby this, Abby that–why don't you just buy a one-way ticket to India and marry this woman? I'm sure she would love that. And, you'll save a bundle of money since you won't need to pay her, being that she'd be your wife and all. Abuse your relationship with her like... like... like you're abusing me!"

With that, Rachel hung up. She so wished that her phone was an old-fashioned one. She could have gotten the satisfaction of slamming the receiver down, but that was a misfortune of modern technology.

Acid churned in her stomach. She felt a little dizzy, and her head started pounding. Heading to the bathroom, she washed her face with cold water and then sat on the toilet trying to calm down. She tried focusing on something else–anything, even her breathing—in order to clear her head. Minutes later, a wave of regret washed over her. He didn't deserve it, she thought. Poor silly John. He was just so excited to share the latest with me. How could he have known I was having a really lousy day? Tears gathered in her eyes. She liked John. In fact, she liked him a lot. Maybe even more than like?

No, she was not ready to admit that, not even to herself, at least not yet. But if it's not love, then why do I feel so envious, even enraged, hearing John praising another good-looking, talented woman?

She used the back of her hand to wipe the salty drops her eyes shared with her lips. There were too many emotions to handle right now.

But the thoughts of John wouldn't go away so easily. Deep down, she already knew that he nurtured romantic feelings about her. She kept this at bay, at least for now. She wanted John as a friend, a good close friend, a business partner. Any step beyond that was dangerous waters. If this old cherished relationship turned into a romance and went bad, poof! There goes the friendship.

Not now, her thoughts swirling. Not now. Too much on my mind to handle this right now. File it for later, for another calmer time.

At the same time, her conscience lectured her. "You need to call him and apologize for the way you hung up. He really didn't deserve it." But her pride would not let her do this. Pride goaded her. "You can do it tomorrow. Enough humiliation for one day."

Yes, I'll call him tomorrow, she decided. Tomorrow is another day. It was almost the weekend. She would suggest that they meet up for breakfast, a nice Saturday or Sunday brunch at his favorite diner. She would apologize when she called and maybe explain his poor timing when they would meet in person.

CHAPTER 12

NEW YORK

John gazed at the blank screen. Did she just hang up on me?

He couldn't believe that. Maybe the line dropped. That happens sometimes. Darn service providers. They charge a fortune and then the line drops in the middle of an important call.

Or, he wondered, did I miss a cue? After all, Rachel cannot be at fault. She was too perfect in his mind while he was the clumsy one. Did she actually say I abused our friendship? That I abuse her? I must have misheard. She was speaking so fast. But what did I say to make her so angry?

He knew he was a bit of an awkward bird, that he could not always read the writing on the wall.

But where did I go wrong this time? What was it that I said? Should I call her back?

He considered this course of action for a moment.

No. She was obviously not in the mood. That music in the background should have warned him; The Koln Concert with Keith Jarrett improvising at the piano. It was Rachel's favored album for whenever she was feeling down, a sure telltale sign for the leave-me-alone foul mood.

But he had been too excited by his news to hear it.

His earlier delight over the project's progress was now all but gone. John felt himself sinking into an icy bottomless ocean. And not just any ocean, but a cobalt blue one, Rachel's cherished color. His cat, Tess, was watching him from her favorite spot by the window.

John turned to her. "What?" he asked defensively. But wise old Tess knew better than to respond. She turned her eyes away from him, lifted a paw and licked it. John felt alone, lonely, abandoned, and maybe even betrayed. Betrayed, and no less by the person he cared most for in the entire world.

His cellphone buzzed. So startled was he that the device almost slipped out of his hand. A text message came in. Maybe it's Rachel?

Abby: What's up, Long John?

John was not sure when, but at some point earlier in their messaging, Abby decided to attach this nickname to him, maybe upon learning that he was six feet two. He was not sure if she realized that the nickname had other meanings as well. Still, he thought it was cute of her to call him that, so he let it be.

John: Not much, just wrapping things up and calling it a day. BTW, I'm very pleased with the progress you're making.

Abby: I'm pleased to be pleasing you ;-))

Well, thought John, at least someone still likes me.

John: Nothing like a programmer as smart as she is pretty! OK. Gotta go. It's late. 'Nite.

Eager to see this day gone, John pressed the power button off just as Abby's last message came in, one he did not see:

Abby: xoxox

CHAPTER 13

NEW DELHI

Abhaya face flashed the widest smile humanly possible. "Yes!" she shouted ecstatically, "he likes me a lot!" She reread his messages several times over, and another idea sprouted at the back of her mind. Many people have called me smart, but no one has ever called me pretty. And he's called me pretty twice! He must really mean it. Maybe–and this was the thought that scared her as much as it delighted her–maybe he's even in love with me!

Happy news is not that happy unless it can be shared with someone else, and so Abhaya decided to share this with her best friend. I must text Janaki! She thought. Heck, it's already 8:30 a.m. We are off from school, but lazy bones should get up. She knew Janaki was in the habit of keeping her phone on, even at night.

Abhaya texted her. "Janaki! Wake up!"

A few minutes passed until Abhaya's phone buzzed softly.

Janaki texted, "Abhaya, it's way 2 early."

Abhaya replied, "Never too early for some good news. Meet me at Starbucks? The new one they just opened? 10 a.m?"

"Ok, ok. But make it 10:30 a.m. This princess needs more time 2 get ready."

"See you soon."

CHAPTER 14

NEW DELHI

"This time," said Abhaya, as the two were waiting in line at the Starbucks on Netaji Subash Place, "I'm treating."

Janaki eyebrows rose. She said nothing.

"You see," Abhaya, who never offered to pay for anything in the past and seemed to always take it for granted that Janaki would take care of the bill, felt compelled to explain, "I found a way to cash some of the money I made from my online work. I can only cash a very limited amount, and even that at a great cost because there is a hefty fee involved, but at least now I finally have some money at my disposal!" She was glowing.

Janaki listened, her expression a stone sculpture, revealing nothing. Once their order arrived, the two friends found a vacant table. "So, what's up?" asked Janaki flatly. If she was irritated, Abhaya was too absorbed in her own excitement to take note.

"Well," said Abhaya, with radiant eyes, "I think I'm in love!" She said no more, obviously expecting her friend to jump on this juicy piece of news and question her relentlessly.

"Oh, you are?" said Janaki. She sipped her steaming drink, blowing on it on occasion.

Abhaya, a volcano about to erupt, tried to prolong the sweet moment. She was hoping her friend, whom she knew loved gossip, would be so much more curious and excited. Her reaction was disappointing. *If Janaki can pretend to be disinterested, I can play that game, too!*

"Well," she responded, "on second thought, perhaps I really shouldn't say anything else. It may be too early." She was hoping to see Janaki losing her cool and begging for information, but that did not happen.

Janaki remained silent. She was taking small sips from her cup, her eyes wandering around as if, so it seemed to Abhaya, other people in that coffee shop were much more interesting than her best friend about to spill her guts. Whatever thoughts were running in her friend's mind, Abhaya was unable to guess. She thought she knew Janaki so well. Silence lingered.

Abhaya was becoming irritated. This was not like her. Deciding to proceed anyway, she gushed, "He's tall and handsome and smart, too!" she added.

"Right," responded Janaki. "I expected nothing less of your future prince charming on a white horse." Janaki took a large gulp of her coffee. Her face turned in digust, as if the drink had soured suddenly. She plopped her half full cup on the table a little too firmly, causing some of the brownish liquid to erupt. "Are we done here?" she asked, sounding displeasure. "Unlike some of us, I do need more time to prepare for the up-and-coming tests." Without waiting for a reply, Janaki got up and took off, leaving Abhaya sitting there with her mouth wide open.

What is wrong with her? Abhaya just could not figure it out. It was a beautiful morning and she was in no rush. Taking her time with her coffee, Abhaya enjoyed herself. To heck with Janaki. I'm well on my way to achieving my goal, especially now that I can cash some of my earnings. Another year of hard work and I'll have more than enough to get me out of this miserable place for good! Abhaya imagined herself in the streets of New York. In her fantasy, she looked a lot like Abby, her avatar. A little older and dressed in the latest fashion, she strolled along Fifth Avenue, window shopping. The tall handsome guy by her side? Long John, her love.

"Excuse me miss, may I sit here?" a crusty voice shook her out of her daze. Her eyes took a moment to focus. The middle-aged man standing opposite her, patiently awaiting her reply, was a Westerner–pinkish skin, curly blond hair, green eyed–but his speech had no trace of an accent.

Abhaya blinked, her mind trying to bridge the contradiction between his voice and his appearance. He smiled, revealing a longtime smoker's yellow-brown teeth. She could smell his cigarette breath all the way across the table. It made her stomach turn. There was something wrong about all this, as if West meeting East produced a monster rather than romance. Abhaya half-smiled.

"It's okay," she said hurriedly. "I was just leaving." With that, she picked up her bag and left, not looking back.

CHAPTER 15

NEW DELHI

Abhaya was helping her mom with dinner. Ganesha, the half-elephant deity that imparts wisdom and removes obstacles, stared down at Abhaya from his concave nook embedded in one of the kitchen walls. Facing north and seated atop his rat, a symbol for conquering desires that are never satisfied, Ganesha's gaze was wise yet indifferent. As tradition ordained, a tray of food, wholly vegetarian, was placed before him. Whatever the household consumed was first to be offered to God through one of His representatives. That which was left over from the offering–probably the entire lot–was then mixed back into the rest of the dishes being prepared for the meal, making the entire meal prasadam, or blessed food. More than an empty gesture, this ritual served as a reminder that food and the family's other good things were not to be taken for granted. They were gifts of grace from the Divine for which one was grateful.

"How is your vacation going, my dear?" asked Abhaya's mother while mixing ingredients for the chapatti dough. "Did you have a nice time with Janaki this morning?"

"It was…okay," answered Abhaya, peeling potatoes for her mother's famous aloo gobi dish. Mom knew how to make the most delicious traditional foods while keeping her kitchen strictly vegetarian.

Though some Hindus these days freely consumed meat, her parents held firm to the time-honored belief that, as her father often said, "by following a vegetarian diet, one minimizes violence to living beings and advances spiritual growth. Nonviolence is the highest duty and the highest teaching."

Abhaya heard this so many times as a child that she could recite it by heart. Dad was accustomed to making such reminders to his wife and daughters during mealtime, either quoting his guru's teachings or from the holy scriptures, The Mahabharata. "And besides," he would add with a grin, "who needs to tear animal flesh when your mother makes such tasty vegetarian food!"

Those were the good old days, Abhaya reflected, when her father was in a good mood, joking around and smiling a lot. It seemed like a lifetime ago.

"What's wrong?" her mom asked, pausing her work and looking at Abhaya.

"Nothing, really. Everything is fine," replied Abhaya. Then she added as an afterthought, "Can I invite Janaki for dinner tomorrow evening?" Though the question had escaped her lips without planning, Abhaya's mind was quick to applaud–yes, that would be a good way to reconcile whatever happened between us earlier today.

"Yes, of course," replied Mom. "It would be nice to see her. It has been a long while since she last came over for dinner." She then returned her attention to the dough.

Abhaya suspected that her mother knew something was wrong, but she wasn't going to say anything about it. She would solve the problem on her own.

Yes, thought Abhaya, I haven't invited her in a while. That'll make this invitation even more meaningful. Once we're happily stuffed from dinner, I'll get her to spell out what's on her mind.

When they were kids, Janaki used to come over all the time. Back in those days, Abhaya did not need to ask permission to have her friend over. But times had changed. Whether it was because she and Janaki had grown up and were now young adults or money for food became tight or the mood at home had changed, Abhaya did not know. One day, just over a year ago, her dad commented out of the blue that it would be more proper if Abhaya asked permission to invite friends over from now on. His solemn demeanor imprinted that comment in her mind. She had hardly asked Janaki to join them for dinner ever since.

Silence lingered between mother and daughter with only sounds of cutting vegetables, mixing ingredients and moving pots around. From its vantage point, it seemed to Abhaya that Lord Ganesha was observing the scene, his broken tusk a reminder that wisdom allows people to see everything as an integral part of the whole.

Concerned that her mother might again raise Janaki as a topic of conversation, or worse, question why she's spending so much time online these days instead of going out, Abhaya went on the offensive.

"How are things with Father?" she asked. Her simple strategy was to change the focus of the conversation. "He seems to be more on edge than usual these days."

"Nothing is wrong with your Father," replied her mom too quickly, her calm voice suddenly unsettled.

Abhaya, surprised by the undertone, sneaked a glance at her mom.

Mom kept her head down, focused on her work. Her hands kneaded the dough, pressing harder and faster than she needed to, sinking the heels of her palms into it like an angry toddler in the middle of a tantrum stomping the ground with his tiny feet.

"Mom? Are you all right?" asked Abhaya, hoping to lighten the mood. It was one thing to change the focus of the conversation, but another altogether to watch her mother lose her cool.

Mom did not respond.

"Come on, Mom. I'm not a little girl anymore. I can see there are issues."

In the pause that followed, Mom's kneading sounded even louder.

Desperate and trying to make herself sound as grown-up as possible, Abhaya asked, "Are you and Father... splitting up?" She did not imagine this to be the case, yet she had to shake her mom into responding.

"Abhaya!" snapped her mom, halting her work and glaring at her daughter. "Your Father and I will never 'split.' It is not our way."

"Sorry," whispered Abhaya. Seeing her mom's face as red as chilis, Abhaya was uncertain whether it was a sign of anger or just the combination of the heat in the kitchen and the effort her mom exerted on the dough.

Mom began to knead the dough a little more gently, and Abhaya seized it as an opportunity to continue.

"But seriously, Mom," Abhaya went on, "I see what is going on. Father is super tense. And he's taking it out on all of us. Every small thing makes him go ballistic."

Her mother did not answer. She focused on the dish she was preparing.

Abhaya noticed a buzzing fly that became entrapped between the kitchen window and the screen. She bent over, opened the screen a notch and swooshed the winged creature free. Closing the screen allowed Abhaya a sideways glance at her mom working the dough. Despite her head being half-turned away, Abhaya could swear she saw something glitter under her mother's eyes. Were those tears?

She decided to keep quiet. Enough had already been said. Hurting her mom was the last thing on her mind. The two continued to work in silence, which seemed to stretch a while.

Abhaya noticed when Mom started softly humming a song, a lullaby she often sung when Abhaya was young and had difficulty falling asleep. It was the tune of 'Twinkle, Twinkle Little Star.' Mom did not know the English words. She was in the habit of either humming it or making up words as she went along. Grown up and familiar with the tune, Abhaya wondered how her mom, a traditionalist, adopted this Western lullaby. She doubted Mom realized where this song originated. Abhaya remembered asking her mom about it, questioning her where she picked it up, but her mom had no clue, claiming she heard it as a child herself and it stuck. Still, her mother's melodious voice carried the tune so beautifully that Abhaya found her own face softening in recollection of sweet childhood memories.

Echoes of kids playing down the street invaded the kitchen, breaking the monotonous sounds of chopping and kneading and stirring. The outside noises seemed to break the silent shroud around her mother.

"I guess you are all grown up, almost fifteen," she said with a heavy sigh. "You have the right to know." Weighing her words carefully, her voice soft and low, she continued not timidly or secretively, but burdened. "There is no problem between your father and me. His company lost their largest account some time ago, and there has been a lot of uncertainty since then as they were unable to find new clients of that magnitude. There have been talks about taking a cut in the paycheck and even of letting people go. As it is, we are hardly making ends meet. I trust you guessed that much." She paused as if mulling over her next words.

Abhaya kept quiet, her eyes locked on the cutting board, her hands still moving but slower, gentler, slicing potatoes into small cubes.

"This is why your father allowed Jee to drop out of college and go to work in that godforsaken place," she murmured, sighing heavily again. As if speaking to herself, her mother whispered, "Not Jee. I meant to say Jane."

She opened the tap and washed her hands. "After only six months at her job, Jane is making almost the same amount that your father makes, despite being twenty-four years at the same workplace."

A kitchen timer rang, startling both mother and daughter. Mom let it continue a few extra moments before shutting it off. She lifted the lid off of a heavy pot on the stove and stirred its content. Warm scents of onions, peas, tomatoes and spices tickled Abhaya's nostrils. Mom then picked up a cauliflower and started rinsing its white florets. Abhaya picked up another potato and started peeling. "You have no idea how much grief this caused your Father that his daughter, a promising science major at college, top of her class, is now working in that place." Mom pursed her lips, chewing on them. "To add insult to injury," she added, "your father takes half her pay for rent."

Distracted by her mother's agony, Abhaya let the peeler she was using slide off, grazing the knuckle on her thumb. She bit her lips, shutting off a cry of pain, and then brought her bleeding thumb to her mouth, her tongue wrapped around the injury.

Her mom had not noticed. No longer aware of her daughter's quiet presence, Mom freely let her fears pour out. "What will come next? I just know it. Next, we will have to sell the old dining room table, and after that will come the rest of my heirlooms. Your father didn't bring it up yet, but it is only a matter of time. Once he loses more of his salary, or, God forbid, his job, there will be no other way to pay for the rent. If it comes to that, we will have to move out of here." Her voice's thinned to a whisper. "My God, what have we come to?" She turned her head away, but Abhaya glimpsed that her mother's eyes and cheeks were unmistakably damp with tears.

"Excuse me, dear," her mother muttered, suddenly aware that Abhaya was watching. "This onion is…" she seemed to be searching for the right word, then uttered, "impossible. I must rinse my eyes." With that, she rushed out of the kitchen.

Abhaya removed her thumb from her mouth. The cut was still bleeding profusely. It may have been deeper than she realized. She raised her head and stared at Ganesha who was staring right back at her, his expression seemed to be saying, "You reap what you sow."

CHAPTER 16

NEW DELHI

"Fancy running into you!" exclaimed Jeevana, smiling widely at her old friend Prema. The morning was exceptionally pleasant, and the two were seated at a public square, shaded by trees. A chai wallah — tea steward — was serving them Masala chai, its scent promising a drink both sweet and spicy. The passing years hadn't changed Prema's appearance one bit. She still looked much like the teenager Jeevana remembered, except for how she dressed. Jeevana suspected she was wearing her work clothes. Jeevana was more casually dressed since her schedule called for an afternoon shift that day. She had the morning off. The two had a chance encounter at the bank, Jeevana on her way to withdraw money, and Prema to deposit checks for her company. While the two were waiting in line for a teller, Prema told Jeevana that she was fortunate enough to find a good job at an accounting firm, serving as an assistant to the office manager.

"Nothing too fancy," Prema quickly explained, "it's not like I have any education or real training with finances, just answering the phone and running errands."

Jeevana raised her eyebrows.

Prema said, "It's my personality. They hired me because of my charm." She winked at Jeevana.

Jeevana smiled warmly.

Prema suggested they sit down and have tea.

"But wouldn't you be missed at work?" said Jeevana.

"Nah, they won't expect me in the office for at least another half an hour."

"How come?" asked Jeevana.

"I was smart about it," said Prema smugly. "You see, right from my first day at this job when I was sent to deposit checks, I took more time than needed, justifying it with long lines at the bank. This way, I established what is an acceptable time for the task, and now, even if I finish the deposits quickly, as was the case today, I make sure not to rush back to the office. It gives me time to take a breather and... have chai with my old friend!" She giggled.

Jeevana remembered that lovely laugh framed by perfect teeth. She used to joke that Prema should model for a toothpaste company. That very moment, Jeevana realized she felt happy. It was the first time in a long while that she felt that way. With a light sunny breeze, low humidity and work being several hours away, the tensions of home rolled out of her mind. She was here with her dear old friend, enjoying the morning and having chai.

Prema was Jeevana's closest childhood friend, but the two had not seen each other since their high school days. It was more than just drifting apart, even if this was how Jeevana would have preferred to remember it. Jeevana did wrong by Prema, and shortly after, Prema and her family left the neighborhood. No one knew where they went and Jeevana had never had a chance to patch things up.

I wonder if she'll bring it up, thought Jeevana, the "it" being the friction that caused their relationship to sour. I surely won't.

Their encounter at the bank could have gone very awkwardly if it were not for Prema and her outgoing personality. She responded in the friendliest manner as if nothing bad had ever passed between them.

"How did we lose touch?" Jeevana wondered aloud, regretting the words the instant that they left her lips. She knew the answer all too well, an answer she did not want to recall.

"Well you know, smart alec, your brain was no match for my mouth, and you answered to a higher call," Prema said, still smiling. "How's college going? If I remember correctly, you were pre-accepted to a special program even before high school was over?"

"For those who attend, it's probably well," replied Jeevana flatly. "Me, not being one of them."

"What?" cried Prema. "You dropped out? What happened? It couldn't have been your grades."

"Long story," said Jeevana. "Let's just say that the 'higher call' ended up being me needing to help my family as a first priority."

"Oh," said Prema.

The chai wallah stopped by and refilled their tea cups from his thermos. He was a small man in what must have been his late sixties. His skin was deep reddish-brown, rusted from long exposure to the sun. On his head, he wore a colorful pagri, a sort of a turban that had definitely seen better days. He smiled a kind smile, revealing several missing teeth. Prema put several coins in his hand. The little man bowed, turned, and went back to his tricycle cart. Soon he was pushing it slowly forward, his eyes searching for new customers.

Prema turned back to Jeevana, "So you dropped out," she said. "I'm so sorry to hear this."

"Yes," replied Jeevana. "It was the right thing to do."

"I understand," said Prema. "It's just that I always thought that at least one of us was going to make it big. Now, hearing that you, too...." She didn't finish her sentence, letting the words fade into oblivion.

They sipped their chai silently.

"I wonder," Prema said after a spell. "Your father? How did he allow this? As I recall, he was a man of such...." She was searching for the right word: "conviction. Conviction and tradition." When Jeevana did not answer immediately, Prema jumped in: "Oh my God! How insensitive of me, especially me. Did he...did he... pass away?"

"No, no. Not him. He's a tough cookie." Gathering her thoughts, Jeevana said, "To answer your question, for him, it ended up simply being a matter of necessity. Dropping out of college and going to work was the lesser of many evils." She sipped her tea. "Yes, me working was the one bitter cup he had to swallow."

"What other options were there?" asked Prema.

"Let's just say that my mom finding a job was not an option, not for him," grinned Jeevana.

"Oh, that figures," said Prema. "So, what do you do? I mean, what line of work?"

Jeevana placed her cup down and straightened her skirt. "I..." she started, somewhat embarrassed, "I... I work for a help desk center."

"Ha!" laughed Prema, "that's all? By the color on your cheeks I thought you took to working the streets." She winked at Jeevana whose blushing became even more fierce. "Just teasing," added Prema, noticing her friend's unease. "But really, that's not so bad, is it? I mean, working at a help center? I heard the pay is decent."

"No, all in all, not too bad, and yes, the pay is decent," replied Jeevana.

"So that's why you're here this morning–you work shifts?" said Prema.

"Correct," replied Jeevana. "My shift today starts this afternoon."

"Hmm, must be hard to have a social life," Prema asked before reconsidering. "Or have you met some nice guy at work?"

"Ugh, I only wish I could," said Jeevana. "With my luck, all I have is that jerk of a supervisor, who also happens to be the boss's nephew."

"Come on, that's perfect! Your prince on a white horse as in all those fairytales. Go out with him and you could be the boss's nephew's wife. Aim high! Marry up!"

Shocked, Jeevana shot a glance at her friend. Often a sucker for Prema's dry wit, she burst out laughing when she realized that she'd been had.

Jeevana had a wonderful laugh when she was surprised, like bells in light wind, her mother told her. That laugh had always sent Prema into a giggling fit.

The two nearly fell over themselves, eyes streaming and holding their stomachs. Passersby eyed them strangely, but Jeevana and Prema could not have cared less. Right now they felt as if they owned the square, the trees and even the skies above.

CHAPTER 17

NEW DELHI

Janaki's phone buzzed. It was a text message from Abhaya.

"Janaki!!!"

To heck with you! I'm not going to answer this, thought Janaki. She was still upset by what had transpired between them when they last met. She did not enjoy Abhaya's sense of superiority at all, now enhanced by her newly found financial freedom. I'm not going to answer this.

Twenty seconds passed, and the phone rattled again like a persistent child throwing a tantrum at an inattentive parent. It was another message from Abhaya.

"Janaki Janaki Janaki Janaki Janaki Janaki"

Go on, try me. See if I care. Janaki was not sure if she thought these words or actually spoke them out aloud. She stared at her phone disgustedly.

Abhaya didn't give up. "I know you're reading this. Come on Janaki, I know you too well. You can't resist temptation when the phone buzzes. Answer me, darn it!"

Darn you, thought Janaki, still thinking you know everything! But in her heart of hearts, she had to admit her friend was right. The temptation was too great.

Abhaya wrote, "It's okay, my friend. Don't answer. I just wanted to apologize. I'm sorry. I'm not sure how exactly I offended you when we last met, but apparently, I did. There's a lot on my mind these days. Maybe I said something insensitive. If so, I'm sorry. Please forgive me?"

Janaki read the message and suddenly felt her eyes tearing. This was most unusual for Abhaya, these words, this tone. Maybe I'm wrong. Janaki thought. Maybe Abhaya was not so arrogant after all. Maybe she really is going through a lot. And if so... If so, I must support her. After all, what are friends for? With that, Janaki decided to answer. "Apology accepted, moron. But u owe me 1."

CHAPTER 18

NEW DELHI

In her room Abhaya exhaled, not realizing that she had been holding her breath. She still did not know how she had upset Janaki. Despite the fearless image she enjoyed projecting to the world, she felt alone. With Janaki turning cold on her, she was fragile, as fragile as an ancient vase.

"Agreed! How about you come to dinner tomorrow at my place? It is for the start of Durga Puja. My mother is preparing a special meal–you know how my father is with this holiday, and I know you love my mom's cooking and we can chat after the meal and work things out."

"I don't know... I still have that math test next week 2 prepare 4, and we have school homework."

Abhaya texted, "Please?"

Several long moments passed by before Janaki answered. "Okay. I guess taking 1 evening off wouldn't make much of a difference. If I'm going 2 fail."

"u won't! Gr8! See u 2morrow!"

Abhaya consciously altered her texts to include the shorthand she knew Janaki adored though she herself was not a fan. She preferred clear writing, surprisingly a traditionalist on this matter.

Janaki texted, "G'nite"

"u 2"

Alone in her room, Abhaya found herself drawn to the fictional Facebook page she created for Abby Smith. She even posted occasional updates, just to make it more real. "How would you have handled this?" she asked her avatar. "You probably would have told Janaki to go to heck with her childish behavior. You're so much stronger than me, and," she added, her body flopping over her chair, "prettier."

CHAPTER 19

NEW DELHI

"Wake up, lazy bones!" Jeevana tore the blanket off Abhaya's bed. "Time to get up!" Her voice though sweet, carried an edge. "Brush your teeth, princess, pamper your royal nose and face the music of a brand-new day!"

"How come you're in such a cheerful mood?" retorted Abhaya, removing sand from the corners of her eyes. Early rays of sunlight invaded the room through the half-opened window, setting Abhaya's bright red nightgown on fire. Her untamed locks of jet black hair surrounded her face like the many hands of the Goddess Durga, the warrior-slayer of the demon king Mahishasur.

"What?" replied Jeevana. She did not expect her sister to have her wits about her first thing in the morning.

"You're so joyful," spat Abhaya. "It's almost like you're going on a date instead of to your lousy job." She pulled her blanket back up but did not even try going back to sleep.

"A date?" mumbled Jeevana, her voice suddenly tired. "I wish. More like a tryst with hell. Now be a good girl and get up. I promised Mom I would wake you up this morning and I can't be late for work. My freaking supervisor would...." She cut the sentence short, her face distorted as if she had tasted milk gone bad. Jeevana grabbed her purse and left the room, not uttering another word.

As soon as Abhaya heard the apartment door close shut, she leapt out of bed and onto the computer. She had to get ready for school, but unable to resist temptation, she quickly logged into her account. The night prior she completed and delivered another phase in the project. To her delight, she found that her New York client, John, sent another payment, which was deposited to her secret ledger. A big smile on her face, Abhaya rushed to the bathroom to get ready for school. Every payment, she thought, brings me a little closer to my sweet 16th birthday departure date. Ten minutes later Abhaya left her room.

About to grab a quick breakfast from the kitchen, Abhaya heard low whispering. It seemed that her dad was still home, atypically late for him. He usually left for work very early in the morning. Old school, he believed that being at his office long before anyone else would show his dedication and loyalty to his employer. Abhaya, tiptoeing, put her ear against the mostly closed kitchen door and listened. Out of view, she could hear every word, however quiet the conversation.

Devidas's voice sounded grave. "I don't know what to do," he told her mother. "They let Amit go yesterday, and he has been with the company for almost as long as I have."

Abhaya felt her throat constricting, stout arms clutching her chest like the embrace of the naja naja's cousin, the infamous Indian python snake. She couldn't recall ever hearing him like this before.

"And then," her father continued, his voice shaken. "They gathered all of us, all twenty-four remaining employees, and announced that if we do not want to see anyone else being let go, we will all need to take yet another cut in our paychecks until things are better."

In the silence that followed Abhaya held her breath. If my father finds me eavesdropping, she thought.

A moment later he continued, "With the money we have left, between the little savings, my salary and what Jeevana is bringing home, I am afraid that...."

Abhaya's phone buzzed softly. Because of the exchange with her sister earlier, fortunately she had forgotten to turn the ringer on as she usually did after waking up. Did Father hear it? she wondered. She knew he had the sharpest pair of ears. She held her breath again, her mind racing through excuses to make up, in case she got caught.

"It is very likely that we will need to sell some of your heirlooms," Dad said. He paused for a moment, allowing his words to sink in. Resembling a condemned man whose appeal had been rejected, he groaned, "I know we kept them all these years under lock and key for the girls' dowries, but what else can we do?"

Abhaya did not hear her mother respond, not even the tiniest squeak. She knew how her mom felt about the heirlooms, about the few treasures that Abhaya's grandma, Kamalakshi's aristocratic mom, had left her daughter. Abhaya could imagine her mother's conflicting emotions, her unquestionable obedience to her father colliding with her own wishes. But still, her mom uttered not a word.

"I am sorry," murmured her dad so softly that she could hardly hear. "I know it is quite a shock. But for now, who knows? Maybe I am ahead of myself. Maybe things will still turn around in time. Why don't we start with selling just one item, one piece of furniture? That should suffice for a couple more months. I... I will consult my guru about it. He doesn't usually give material advice, but maybe he will make an exception."

Abhaya could hear a chair being pulled and a body dropping onto it. She heard the kitchen tap opening and closing. "Drink this," her father told her mom. Remembering the alert from earlier, Abhaya checked her phone. The text message that arrived was from her client, John:

John: Well done!

Abhaya smiled despite whatever else that was going on. A warmth radiated throughout her belly, a feeling of... Of what? She asked herself. Love? Is that how love feels? Whatever it was that warmed me deep inside, it feels good—good and wrong all at the same time.

"There is another option," her mother's voice finally broke the silence. "You know there is." Her weak voice grew a little stronger, word by word until it was a wave gathering strength. With these words, the warmth that Abhaya had felt began to slip away like a crack in a dam leaking a little narrow trickle at first, but growing rapidly, threatening complete and imminent collapse.

"No! No! No!" Her father's voice shattered the calm that fell in the wake of Mom's impassioned plea. "I will not hear of it! You will not go to work. It is not honorable! Not as long as I am alive."

"But it will solve the problem!" her mother protested. "I can get a respectable job."

"There is no respectable job for a woman — not in my book — except for taking care of the house and family!"

"And what honor is there in having your daughter drop out of college to go to work, of selling the dowry, of...." Abhaya was surprised how her mother didn't let go, atypically challenging her father.

"Enough!" shouted her father, stamping his foot.

Abhaya quickly took her cue. If she knew her father at all, he would soon burst through the doors and run out of the house. She retreated softly toward the apartment's outer door, shutting it behind her as quietly as an autumn leaf floating from a branch. Heading down the stairs, she felt her heart heavy, her limbs cold. Any warm and fuzzy sensation from John's message was all but gone.

CHAPTER 20

NEW YORK CITY

John's heart was beating fast. He could feel his blood pounding, gushing through his arteries, pulsing violently in his chest like the large kickdrum in the set he had loved playing during his teen years.

It's Rachel, his mind whispered. She's coming. My heart knows it. That's why I feel what I do. But where is she? He felt like he was looking through a thick fog. Was he even inside his apartment? It felt as if he had tunnel vision. He could see the door and then heard the horrible screech of that doorbell he had vowed to replace but never did. The rest of the space he called home dissolved into a dark mist. The door opened. Strange, he pondered. I always keep it locked. It is New York, after all.

"Ra--?" He stopped mid-sentence.

The figure that stepped in was Abby.

John held his breathe. God, she's beautiful, much more than the image on the freelance website, he thought. Her blonde hair, strands of gold woven throughout, floated around her figure as if blown by a soft breeze. There was only one problem: he felt no breeze. Where was the wind coming from? It hardly mattered.

She smiled at him.

"I came for you," she said with a honey-deep voice.

John's jaw drop. His heart pounded even harder. She stepped closer, her scent like a sunset over an orange grove in full bloom.

The part of his brain that was still functioning shouted, But what about Rachel?

John knew that something was terribly wrong about all of this, but he could not detach himself from the sudden desire that gripped him tight.

"I came for you," repeated Abby in a velvety voice, all the while stepping slowly, dangerously, closer.

Except she wasn't stepping. She was floating. Closing in on him, John noted her voluptuous rose-red lips that, right before his eyes, were morphing, growing humongous, hungrily parting in slow motion. Her snow-white teeth, her mouth, her tongue, all inviting him. His eyes began to close in anticipation.

His eyes flew open.

Out of the corner of his eye, he saw a dark figure moving through the open door. The dark silhouette burst into a flame that produced the woman he loved. Or did it?

"John?" Rachel demanded, her tone as sharp as a dagger. "Who is this woman!"

Abby turned to Rachel and continued to move slowly, majestically. She was a queen at ease in her royal palace. With a smile on her face, Abby said, "John is mine. You can leave now."

Rachel's temper kicked in. The fire that created her out of darkness just moments earlier had returned, engulfing her frame. "No!" cried Rachel. "John is mine. He has always been mine. Leave now, whoever you are." Turning toward John, she spat, "Who is she, John?"

John was about to respond, but it was Abby who said, "I'm Abby, his talented programmer, the only one he can really trust, his true love. Just ask him." Smiling, she looked at John and said, "Tell her, darling."

John opened his mouth. He wanted to deny everything, but found his mouth was too dry to speak. No words would emerge. He could only mutter, "abd, danb, gong..."

"John, is that true?" demanded Rachel.

No! shouted John's mind, but his voice did not comply.

"It's no use trying," Abby said in a whisper that only his mind could hear. "I wrote a short programming routine—a bug, you might call it—that temporarily disables your voice." Her smile was both hypnotizing and tantalizing. She was a goddess of desire incarnated. He wanted her, he feared her, and he was completely lost.

Rachel, fists on hips and fuming, turned to leave. John tried to run after her, but his feet would not respond.

"No, no, no," Abby echoed again in his head, "you're mine."

Tess, John's cat, hissed, baring teeth and claws, arching her back, and readying herself for battle.

Abby jerked back, her face contorting into a demonic shape, a repulsive, fierce-looking and humongous creature. She–it–suddenly had two long fangs protruding down the sides of her mouth. Her eyes flamed red, hair shimmered blue fire. Abby, or what used to be Abby, pointed a long and twisted clawed finger at Tess and shrieked in horror, "Take this beast away from me or I shall destroy it!"

At that, Tess leaped off her favorite chair, aimed at the monstrous Abby but somehow landed on John's chest.

John awoke with a start. It was 5 a.m. Tess was on his chest, curled into a little ball and purring softly. He blinked several times as if expecting Abby and Rachel to still be there. John reached out and petted the cat. He sighed in relief.

"What's up, Tessie?" He used the quiet moment with his only constant companion to calm his nerves.

Tess meowed, jumped off the bed and went to her bowl. It was empty.

"Sorry, Tess," he said. "I guess I fell asleep last night and didn't feed you." Slowly, as if rising from a grave, John got up. It took him a few moments to find his footing before heading toward her empty bowl. I may as well stay up, he thought. In an hour, I need to get up for my shift. He filled the bowl with dry cat food and then turned back, longingly. Or should I go back to bed? God, I feel so exhausted.

CHAPTER 21

NEW DELHI

Abhaya rustled around her mother's dresser drawer, looking for a headband. Her hand fell on a bundle of papers at the back of the drawer. Furrowing her brows, Abhaya pulled out the bundle. It was a stack of letters tied with a piece of string.

Peeking behind her to see if anyone was there, she shook her head. Of course no one is here, she thought to herself. You're being silly. Mom is at the market and Dad and Jee are working.

She turned back to the stack of letters and untied the string. Sliding the first letter off the top, she used just two fingers to pull back the flap and remove the yellowed paper inside. She opened it gingerly, afraid it would crumble.

Her hands shaking, she began to read.

"Dearest Kamalakshi,

Lotus eyes, reddest petal, light of my life, my heart is filled with joy!

Our little plot worked!

My aunt will approach your parents this weekend and arrange for our families to meet. I am so happy that my heart is bursting out of my chest.

May Parvati Devi, Goddess of love, continue to guide us.

Forever yours,

Devidas"

Abhaya's heart seized in her chest for a moment. This was her father talking about…her mother? "Lotus eyes, reddest petal, light of my life?"

Did her uptight father really write this to her mom so many years ago, while they were courting? Abhaya would not have believed it if she had not seen it with her own eyes.

"Devidas-ji my love,

Seeing you yesterday was both exhilarating and disheartening. Your smile, your voice, your presence all brightened my day to no end. But my father's insistence that your future holds no financial security for me broke my heart. It hurts me to know that is why he cut the meeting short. God knows I don't care about your 'lower class.' People have no classes, just hearts. And mine yearns for yours."

"Devidas-ji, what shall we do if our parents do not come to arrangement about our marriage? We worked so hard to bring them together while making them believe this was all by chance. I find myself shifting from hope to despair, back and forth like a ship on turbulent seas. As you suggested, I hold to faith, praying daily to Parvati Devi, oṁ bhagavatī parvatyai namaḥ.

You are always in my thoughts, my one true love.

Forever yours, Kamalakshi"

Abhaya felt embarrassed. She knew reading these letters was inappropriate, an intrusion into a very intimate exchange, yet another part of her was fascinated. Her mind went round and round the knowledge that they had courted before the marriage. Their marriage had been arranged by their families, as any honorable family would. It was slightly nauseating to think of her parents being romantic with each other, but at the same time it made her feel happy. It was a joy to know a side of them she had never seen.

On a whim, she pulled out her phone and snapped photos of the letters. She did not really know why she felt she had to do this, but she did, as if bewitched. A quick glance at the clock on the wall told her time was running out. Her mother would be back soon and so would her dad. She flipped through the remaining letters, taking photos of each one. Once done, Abhaya went back to reading the next letter in the pile. Just one more…The rest I can read later on my phone, she told herself.

"Dearest Kamalakshi,

Hearing you sing at the temple yesterday made my heart leap and dance to the rhythm of your musical voice. I could swear I was seeing Saraswati, the dear Goddess of music herself, there by your side, smiling at you and winking at me. Your radiance bedazzled everyone watching you. You are so beautiful, both inside and out. I feel ashamed that my father, his ears deaf to anything lyrical, would insist that once we are together you shall abandon your music. It is too bad that his very ultra-orthodox upbringing made him view artists as shams."

Abhaya had to stop. Repeating the last line, she read aloud, "very orthodox?" She had no recollection whatsoever of her grandfather from her father's side. He had passed away when she was a baby. From little comments made through the years, she knew that he was very strict and religious. How had that affected her father? She thought, now this was something I would love to share with....

Share with who? My sister? She would have wanted that, but their connection was not one of friendship and trust. Realizing that made Abhaya sad.

It's not right, she thought. One day their parents would pass on and Jeevana would be the only close family she'd have left in this world.

There must be a way for Jeevana and me to become close again, she thought. They had been close once. When they were small, Jeevana would take care of her and play with her.

Her face darkened. How much things had changed. She shrugged then, gathering her strength. Things had changed from good to bad, so maybe someday they will change back, from bad to good.

Her mind returned to the conundrum at hand. I must share this with someone now. But who? The only person who came to mind was Janaki.

But wait, her brain told her, this is such private information–her parents' love letters, for God's sake! Should I share this with a friend?

No! a voice in her head called aloud.

But how can I keep this to myself? For Abhaya, it was enough to carry Abby's secret life, and this would be yet another burden.

Serves you right, the insistent little voice called. You should not be going around, digging in other people's drawers.

"I was not!" replied Abhaya aloud, feeling indignant.

She felt annoyed and confused. To share or not to share, that was the question.

But if your father ever finds out... It was that other voice again.

Engrossed in this dilemma, Abhaya did not hear the apartment door open and close. She almost missed hearing the heavy footsteps coming down the hallway. At the last moment, she shoved the bundle of letters back where she had found them and closed the drawer. Concentrating to keep her knees from buckling, Abhaya turned around to face her mother as she entered the room.

"Abhaya? What are you doing in here?" In their household, the parents' bedroom was strictly off-limits to the children.

"Oh, I was just looking for a hairband," replied Abhaya breezily. She was hoping her mom would not notice the color rising in her cheeks.

"What happened to yours? I just got you a package of five last week."

"Ask Jeevana," replied Abhaya, biting her upper lip. She did not favor lying but in this case, she was speaking the truth. Her sister was known for losing hairbands and "borrowing" hers.

"I don't know what I will do with her," sighed her mother. "Sometimes I just don't understand how she can manage in life with all this lack of organization. Here," Mom said, opening the drawer Abhaya had just closed. She noticed the bundle of letters and snuck a glance at Abhaya.

Abhaya held her breath.

Her mother said nothing. She tucked the letters further into the drawer. Finding a hairband, she reached over and said, "You can use this." Mom smiled a tired smile at Abhaya. "Now off you go," she said. "And don't you have homework to do?"

"I already finished it during the break at school but," Abhaya swiftly tacked on, "I do have some research to do online."

Abhaya left the room but stayed in the hallway, close enough to still see her mother but far enough away not to be noticed.

She watched her mother open the drawer wider and take out the bundle of letters. She sat on the bed and started reading. As she flipped through the pages, her face became animated with joy, pain, mischief and nostalgia.

Abhaya moved away noiselessly before she was discovered again.

Back in her room, Abhaya sat on her bed, staring at her phone. Images of the letters she secretly snapped were staring right back at her. The burden on her chest, which was forgotten while evading being caught, returned. Again, the little voice in her head reproached her for what she did.

Too late for that, part of her said, while a Pinocchio's Jiminy-Cricket-type figure replied, no, it is not. Just delete them!

But Abhaya wanted to read those letters. Erasing them was not an option. Besides, it was now part of her own heritage, part of her history, part of her making. If her parents had never met, then she, Abhaya, would never be. Or would she?

It was all too confusing. She shushed the chirping cricket, and let the images stay.

Yet she could not carry such a weight alone. Again she wished she could have shown them to her sister.

No, she concluded. They simply did not have that kind of relationship.

Out of curiosity she pondered, what would Jeevana do if I showed her the letters? Snitch on me?

No, probably not, she reasoned. More likely, she would use it in the future if ever she wanted me to give her something. Despite sharing the same room for years, or perhaps because of that, the chasm between them seemed to have grown as unbridgeable as the highest peaks of the Himalayas.

Abhaya was left with only one other person. But can I really trust her? Maybe yes...maybe no. Making a decision, she pulled her phone closer and opened a chat. "Janaki?"

Second thoughts gripped Abhaya. You're making a mistake, the inner voice called for the last time, but she went ahead and typed, "Unbelievable discovery to share."

Moments passed. No response. Good, thought Abhaya, I'm almost glad Janaki didn't answer. It's a sign this was not meant to be. I shouldn't share this. Then her phone buzzed. It was Janaki.

"What's up?"

"Never mind."

"Don't you dare tease me and back off. Now out with it!"

Abhaya felt apprehensive, her mind and heart out of sync.

"I'm waiting………the clock is ticking………"

When Abhaya didn't answer immediately, Janaki continued. "And besides, who else can you share it with but me?"

It seemed that as much as Abhaya thought she knew Janaki, Janaki had the same advantage over her. "You swear by all that's dear to you that you will NOT share with ANYBODY what I'm going to share with you?"

"Of course."

"Not a word, not ever."

"Ugh. Enough with the drama already. I haven't all day."

"Ok, ok. I'm sending you an image. You're not going to believe it."

Abhaya selected one of the letters and send it to Janaki, her fingers feeling jittery as she pressed "Send". Time seemed to be standing still.

Janaki texted, "What the F?"

CHAPTER 22

NEW DELHI

"Let's go, Chetan!" Arjuna's voice thundered across the schoolyard, causing several kids to turn their heads in alarm. His call made Chetan leap out of his hiding place behind the tree. He had been secretly observing Abhaya from afar. He rushed to get out of Abhaya's line of sight, feeling his face flush hot. While he was quite certain that she did not notice him, he wanted to make sure and turned his head mid-stride. The move nearly made Chetan trip every which way, much to Arjuna's absolute delight.

It didn't matter. The important thing was that Abhaya hadn't seen.

No, he concluded, she did not notice me. Thank Lord Hanuman, Jai, whispered Chetan, a prayer to the Hindu deity who guarded him.

"Well, well, well!" Arjuna's wide square jaw made his smile stretch like Gandiva, the indestructible God-forged bow of his warrior namesake. "Spying on your sweetheart again?" he said humorously but without the slightest trace of malice.

"I should have never mentioned Abhaya to you, moron!" said Chetan, his lips drawn into a tight line.

"Come, come now, relax, chill out. Actually, maybe you can keep some of this anger for Taekwondo. It'll do you some good, keep me from smacking your pretty face for a change... haha!"

Chetan had to give his close friend credit. Arjuna knew how to amuse himself. He seemed to be always happy-go-lucky, even after receiving a low grade on a test or being refused a date. Unlike Chetan, what Arjuna lacked in appearance, he made up for in confidence. That poise allowed him to approach girls and ask them out. Little good did it him, but that did not deter him.

"How does he do it?" wondered Chetan time and again. For Chetan, everything in life was a puzzle, a problem to be solved. While this approach proved handy in academics, in real life, it deprived him of the joy Arjuna seemed to experience effortlessly.

"Just wait," replied Chetan without conviction. "Today is my turn to knock you out."

"Okay, okay, my friend," called Arjuna, his voice as loud as ever. "I see you're having a not-so-good day, so I may go a little easier on you."

By now, the two were outside the school walls, heading to their Taekwondo studio. They took the shortcut. It was not a road Chetan would have chosen to go alone. Known for its rough-and-tumble crowd, most people chose the longer path. Not Arjuna. Towering over the average New Delhi resident by a foot and boasting the body of an Olympian weight lifter, few wanted to challenge this giant of a young man. Walking close by, Chetan sneaked nervous glances right and left along the narrow lane. His lips moved, repeating a prayer to Lord Hanuman, his favorite deity. Believed to be an incarnation of Lord Shiva, Hanuman was a brave warrior. He was the monkey king, who was instrumental in helping another Hindu deity, Lord Rama, in his war against the demon king Ravana. But the alley was mostly deserted this time of the day.

Just as Chetan was starting to relax, a loud bang and a screech came from their right. Chetan's heart rose to his throat. He turned sharply toward the source of the sound, dropped his bag, assumed a martial art pose and held his breathe. His eyes opened wide with terror.

"Hahaha!" Arjuna cried aloud. "Just a cat jumping off a trash can... But a nice front stance! Six years of practice, and you learned something after all. You even managed to scare the poor cat!" Arjuna started laughing so hard that he had to stop walking. He bent over, his large hands cradling his stomach.

Chetan scowled. Anger, shame and irritation at himself roiled up for being so easily frightened. "Have we had enough?" he asked, forcing the words through pursed lips. A bull about to attack, he breathed heavily through his nose.

"No, not really," Arjuna said between short, almost painful bursts of laughter, trying hopelessly to regain control. "You're one of a kind! No wait, no!" Arjuna was giggling so hard that tears welled up his eyes. "I now see two of you.... Hahaha!"

Chetan picked up his bag gruffly, dusted it off, and stomped away, fear all-but-forgotten.

"Wait, wait!" trumpeted Arjuna, "I'm coming, too! Haha! Wait, oh Chetan, the Mighty Cat Slayer! Ahaha!"

CHAPTER 23

NEW DELHI

Tuesday late afternoon, Abhaya wandered around the kitchen like a headless chicken. Her mother was on edge as was often the case when preparing an important meal. The usually calm Kamalakshi, whom family and guests alike declared an excellent cook, still felt uncomfortable in her own kitchen, at least when it came to major holiday feasts.

Abhaya hated being around her mother when she was in this mood. If she could, she would have found an excuse to be out of the house until right before the meal. But her mother would not hear of it. She wanted Abhaya to learn culinary arts. Until she was ten years old, Abhaya found this exciting, but the fun part was gone.

Yet this time was different. Abhaya knew her mom had been trained in singing, typical for many proper young ladies raised under Colonial British rule. Her own mother, an aristocrat, never coached her daughter in matters related to food preparation. And while that may have been one reason she wanted her daughter to have proper training, it was a letter in the bundle that Abhaya recently read that left an unforgettable impression.

The letter was sent from Abhaya's mom to her dad mere weeks before the wedding, shortly after the marriage was miraculously approved. Young Kamalakshi was challenged with preparing her first meal for her future in-laws. Tasting the soup that young Kamalakshi labored for hours to make, her future mother-in-law whispered amusingly to her son in a voice just loud enough for everyone to hear: "Devidas, it looks like I will be seeing you back home quite often for dinner, after all." She then looked patronizingly at Kamalakshi, whose face flushed red. She smiled pleasantly but underneath the façade she felt like she was dying.

Abhaya realized that her mother had mastered the culinary arts over the years, but deep inside she still carried that hurt. She was like an old pot that remains favored for cooking, but with a charcoal spot from the time it was left standing for too long on the stove that no amount of scrubbing could ever completely erase.

Abhaya watched her mom slaving away in the kitchen and felt sympathy rather than annoyance. It was as if she was seeing her the first time, seeing her for who she had been. A young woman trying to please, trying to prove herself worthy.

She wanted to tell her, Don't worry, Mom, you passed the test. It's all good. You can relax.

"Abhaya, out of the way!" called her mother. "Can't you see I am carrying boiling soup!"

Abhaya's sense of irritation came gushing back.

"Quickly, quickly!" came her mom's voice again, "fetch me the spatula!"

As Abhaya was handing it to her mom, her phone buzzed.

It was Janaki. "What time?"

Abhaya replied, "6pm. And Janaki–6pm *sharp!*"

"OK, OK, chill out. I'm the last 1 who wishes 2 get in trouble with ur dad."

"And dress a little more traditionally."

"ur not really expecting 2 c me in a sari"

"Stop it, you know what I mean. Wear a dress, not pants. Something low-key."

"All right, no Beyonce-style get-up 4 me"

"And Janaki?"

"What now?!"

"I'm really glad you're coming. Thanks."

"yw :-)"

"Are you done entertaining yourself on your phone?" cried her mom, still melodic despite the tinge of anger. "Can her ladyship find time to help her mother, like right now?"

"Coming…" Abhaya held her tongue, determined to remain sympathetic to her mom's stress.

"Your father will be here shortly, back from the puja at the ashram, and he will rightfully expect us to be ready on time."

"I know, Mom," replied Abhaya, "and I'm here to help."

"I am glad you remember this. Now please start with the food offering to Lord Ganesha. And don't forget also to Durga Devi."

"Of course," replied Abhaya, picking up the offering tray and dishes.

CHAPTER 24

NEW DELHI

By six o'clock that evening, sitting at the large ancient dining table, Abhaya was wearing a colorful modern sari for the occasion. To her left was Jeevana, still dressed in her work clothes since she had been kept late at the support center and arrived home at the last minute. That nick-of-time entrance, topped by her Western clothing, earned her a scornful look from her father although he said nothing. To her right sat Janaki whom, Abhaya noticed, kept her gaze low. There was a sense of tension in the air. Opposite Janaki and Abhaya sat Abhaya's mom closest to the kitchen's entrance.

Father recited a traditional blessing, droning:

Ya Devi sarva bhuteshu Matri rupena samsthita…
Ya Devi sarva bhuteshu Shakti rupena samsthita…
Ya Devi sarva bhuteshu Shanti rupena samsthita…
Namestasyai Namestasyai…
Namestasyai Namoh Namah.

In the ancient Sanskrit language, the prayer to Durga meant:

The goddess who is omnipresent as the personification of universal mother…
The goddess who is omnipresent as the embodiment of power…
The goddess who is omnipresent as the symbol of peace…
I bow to her, I bow to her, I bow to her.

Janaki had once told Abhaya that it would have sounded so much better if her mom were chanting instead of her father, but Abhaya was relieved that she kept her mouth shut now.

Once the prayers were said, her father gave a short lecture about the holiday as was his custom. Abhaya remembered a brief argument she and Janaki had about this. Janaki claimed this was her dad's way of asserting his religious supremacy over everyone else present. Abhaya, on the other hand, accustomed to this ritual since early childhood, always thought of it as her dad's way of assuring that the context of the meal was not forgotten.

"The feast we are holding today is, of course, in honor of the blessed Goddess Durga," he said. "We are celebrating Durga Devi's glorious victory over the demon Mahishasura, who appeared in the form of an evil buffalo." Father nodded his head toward Mom, signaling that the meal may be served. "Therefore, this Durga Puja celebration symbolizes how ultimately through faith, Good will always prevail over Evil...."

Abhaya was only half listening. She had heard all of this several times before. A good portion of her attention was dedicated to digging into the delicious aloo gobi dish she had helped her mother prepare. It was made of aloo (potatoes), gobi (cauliflower), turmeric and other undisclosed ingredients. The original recipe was passed along from mother to daughter over many generations. Maintaining the family tradition, her mother kept it a secret from all but Abhaya. Whether Jeevana knew of it as well, Abhaya could not tell. Her mom could be evasive when she wanted to, and given Jeevana's disinterest in the art of fine cooking, she was not sure at all to what extent their mom had shared her other secret recipes.

"Even, and maybe more so, when facing times of hardship," continued her father. Abhaya, detecting an unusual self-reflective tone in her father's words, paused from serving herself and stared at him. "Faith shall prevail," he continued, unaware of the sudden attention his daughter gave him. To her, he sounded as if he were desperately trying to convince himself.

Her father's own gaze was directed at the image of the deity, Durga, which was lovingly placed in the center of the large dining room table and decorated with flowers. Abhaya followed her father's stare and looked at the Goddess. She remembered how, as a child, she was in awe of the deity. Now, the sculpture representing Durga seemed suddenly meaningless.

How did this happen? she found herself wondering. Is this all just a figment of my imagination, the result of overhearing Father telling Mom of our dire financial situation? Is this why I see no more salvation in faith? That I no longer wish to believe?

Abhaya felt a sudden chill, as if the temperature in the room had dropped by a good twenty degrees. Looking around the table, she surveyed the participants at this holy feast. No one else seemed to have noticed what she sensed. They were all busy eating, as if nothing had happened. But there was no doubt in her own mind that the room was colder; the skin on her arms turned to goosebumps.

Abruptly, Father's mind snapped out of the dark place. He turned and looked at her mother, who was just sitting down by his side after bringing yet another set of dishes from the kitchen. Abhaya noticed that his face softened, as if he were, once again, a young man on a date with his beloved young bride. She felt her ears burn, reminded of how she had invaded their privacy by reading the letters.

Lowering her eyes, Abhaya's gaze wandered back to the table itself. She noticed the many small chinks and crevices that adorned its surface. These were, according to her mom, mementos of Jeevana and Abhaya's baby days when the two knocked their spoons against the tabletop, either playfully or angrily. Surprisingly, her mom actually loved those marks. For her, it made the table come to life and be a part of the family, a living member whose surface bore affectionate scars of its shared past. Of all their possessions, Mom may have valued this piece the most.

"Are you going to eat the entire bowl, or can you pass along the aloo gobi?" asked Janaki, humorously. She startled Abhaya, who was deep into her memories and thoughts. She realized the serving bowl was still by her plate.

"Sorry. Here you go."

"Are you okay?" asked Janaki, concerned. "You look like you just saw the demon Mahishasura in person."

"Yes," said Abhaya mindlessly, then, "No! No, of course not. It's just that... my mind was wandering. I'm okay now."

Janaki had just opened her mouth to ask further when Mom broke in. "How are your preparations for the mid-terms going, Janaki?"

"Splendid," answered Janaki, but Abhaya thought she could detect an air of sarcasm in her friend's reply, as if she were really saying, if you expect me to be as smart as your daughter, you're gravely mistaken. But her mother did not notice, nor was Abhaya sure that the snark was real or imagined.

"Wonderful!" replied Mom, smiling.

Janaki's undertone, real or imagined, added just enough steam to rock Abhaya on edge. Her emotions had already been strained. The buildup started earlier when Abhaya first became the recipient of her mother's venting during the meal preparations, then her father's dark mood, and then the compounded guilt from reading the letters. She thought, now Janaki, too? Taking a bite from the freshly baked puffed naan that her mother had prepared less than thirty minutes ago, the bread seemed to her to be oddly stale.

For a while, the only sounds heard were of dishes being passed around, clanking forks and knives, mouths chewing, a baby crying from a neighboring apartment, and city ambience noises sipping through the open window. Above that cacophony, another neighbor's TV screamed continuous gun shots, no doubt from some gangster show. Each set rattled Abhaya as if the bullets were tearing through her own flesh. The jolts made her feel as if a fuse had blown in her head. She could take it no more.

"I wish the Chopras would lower their TV," hissed Abhaya. Her boiling rage was barely contained beneath her skin. "Every evening it's the same story, no matter how many times we have asked them to be more considerate and lower the volume!"

"Abhaya, you know they have a son who is hard of hearing," said Mom, her calm voice conveying a silent warning, the way that only a mother could.

"Yeah, they also have a tiny brain, short on memory!" charged Abhaya, no longer able to contain her fury.

"Abhaya!" growled her father.

"What?" cried Abhaya. "What did I say wrong this time?"

"You are mocking another person, and a person with a disability!" her father snapped impatiently. "You should know better. I am very disappointed. Very disappointed."

Abhaya's face turned red. She mumbled fiercely to herself, but so low that only Janaki who was seated beside her could make it out. "God, I wish I could leave this stinking place already," she snarled under her breath. "I hate this."

"What was that?" her dad said. He could not make out her words, but his daughter's attitude did not sit well with him.

Abhaya gritted her teeth and said, "Nothing."

Father stared harshly at his daughter.

No one moved. The stillness was broken by a flower that, for no apparent reason, fell off the statue of Durga and sailed onto the table. Its carefree tumble caused everyone to redirect their attention back to the goddess, as if she were about to speak.

Janaki shifted in her chair. She seemed disconcerted. She looked at Abhaya whose face clearly showed distress, and then, as if finding approval in her friend's furious expression, Janaki opened her mouth to speak.

It looked to Abhaya as if Janaki had been waiting for the right moment, but when such an opening did not present itself exactly as she had hoped, she decided that now was as good time as any. Despite her obvious discomfort at the situation, Janaki steadied her voice and said, "She just wishes that she could live somewhere else."

Abhaya's jaw dropped.

Father, who had until that moment regarded Janaki with as much attention as a fly buzzing against a window screen, swiftly turned his harsh gaze to her. Astounded at her boldness, he said coolly, "What was that?"

"What are you doing?" a terrified Abhaya hissed to Janaki. "Shut up!"

"It's okay," answered Janaki, "I'm helping you out."

All eyes turned to Janaki.

A pomegranate flush colored her cheeks, but she held her ground. In a voice strong enough to be heard, she became Abhaya's attorney making her case: "You see, it is very difficult for Abhaya sharing a room with Jeevana and maintaining her high grades in school, and all the while," she further volunteered, "trying to do some work online–she needs her own space."

Silence erupted. Only a female singer's melodramatic Bollywood solo blaring from the neighbor's TV pierced the quiet. Abhaya's blood drained from her face, her color changing in an instant from a cheeky, rebellious red to a ghostly ash. In less than thirty seconds, her best friend had just revealed all of her best-kept secrets. Well, almost all of them, she thought. One remained: her parents' love letters.

Oh God, she thought, Janaki might spill that next! What can I do to stop her? Abhaya felt frozen in time; glued to her chair, terror engulfed. Why? Why is she betraying me, my best friend! Her mind raced and roared.

Cocking an eyebrow, speaking very slowly and enunciating each and every syllable, Father asked, "What, exactly, do you mean by 'trying to do some work online?'" His inescapable stare locked onto Janaki.

Taking a deep breath before speaking, Janaki was cut off by Jeevana. "She means for school, Father, for school. No need to get all worked up." Quickly eyeing Janaki, her voice tinged with a touch of threat, "I'm sure this is all you meant, right Janaki?"

Taken by surprise, Janaki blurted out, "Yes! Yes, of course! Homework." Turning to Abhaya, she said, "Really, I only wanted to help."

Jeevana held Janaki's eye contact as if she were a street performer charming a cobra. "I'm sure you had nothing but the best of intentions. Yes, I'm quite sure of that. And I'm sure that enough has been said, and it may be best to leave it at that." Jeevana remained measured and yet commanding. "I myself also have the best of intentions for you," Jeevana added, "more than you may realize."

As if acting under a spell, Janaki got up. Still held by Jeevana's gaze, she said, "I'm sorry. I just remembered I have to get back home." She grabbed her purse and backed away, turning around at the last moment just before colliding with the door. Then she was gone.

At the table, confusion ensued. Abhaya, still terribly pale, sat examining her hands under the table.

Father, looking severe yet puzzled, turned to Jeevana once it was clear that Abhaya was not going to say a word.

"What was that all about?" he asked, unsure whether to be upset or bemused.

"Janaki is going through a difficult period," said Jeevana, her voice steady and reassuring.

"Will she be all right?" asked Mother. "Maybe I should call her mother to make sure she made it home okay...."

"Good idea," said Jeevana, "but let's finish eating first and I'll take care of the call."

CHAPTER 25

NEW YORK CITY

Late Sunday morning, John waited at Jose's Place for Rachel to show up. His patience was running out. Jose's was his favorite neighborhood restaurant. Serving Mexican style breakfast any time of the day, huevos rancheros was his favorite dish. If he had his way and money were not an obstacle, he could have ordered this same plate every day of the week.

It was yet another fault Rachel found with him. The usual conversation they had ran through his mind.

"You always order the same thing," she would tell him each time they met for brunch at Jose's. "Try something different for a change."

"Like you do?" was John's rushed reply. "For you it's always sausage and egg tostadas," he would point out. "Oh! And let's not forget the spicy home fries on the side."

"Up yours," Rachel would flare up. "I do change my order. Just last week I had the guacamole salad!"

"Right," replied John, "which you returned claiming it wasn't spicy enough, and then asked for, hmm… let's see…sausage and—"

"Shut up!" Rachel said, attracting some attention from nearby diners.

As usual, they would follow this outburst by sitting silently like two disagreeable children. Once the food arrived, they would focus on their entrée until John would find a way to apologize, somewhat, and get their conversation back on track.

Despite repeating this strange ritual all too often, John never got the notion in the moment that he should simply pause before responding. Upon reflection, he would make a mental note, realizing that arguing with Rachel never ended well. She simply hated being put on the spot. Yet by their next get-together, that mental note was all but forgotten, and the ritual would be repeated.

Once, when they had another one of their typical little fights about some trivial thing and Rachel stormed off to the restroom, an older gentleman sitting at a nearby table caught John's eye. He smiled, nodded, leaned over and whispered, "Never argue with a woman, young man. Life has taught me that it's best to keep your mouth shut." The stranger added, "The sooner you learn to nod your head, the faster the storm will blow over."

John's expression was doubtful.

The older man responded, "Trust me. This way you'll live a longer, happier life."

Yet, as much as John loved Rachel, he lacked the ability to hold his tongue. That, or he just had not yet matured enough to realize the simple truth.

Where the heck is she? John wondered. She's never this late.

Rachel was all about precision, but with John she allowed herself to occasionally be "fashionably late." That, she explained to him once, was a delicate art of being just late enough to give the impression of having a lot going on: five to ten minutes.

"But you don't have to impress me," John complained.

Another mistake–questioning Rachel. His "reward" for the rest of that particular get-together was that Rachel went on and on about how challenging it was for her to be late, and how only with him she can explore such attempts.

Five to ten minutes passed about twenty minutes ago. "Still waiting?" asked the young server, looking as if to say, if you will wait any longer, your hair will turn gray. "Would you care to go ahead and order?"

John had never seen this waitress before. She must be new, he thought, or at least new to the days he visited Jose's. She's cute, he thought, but aloud, he said, "I'm sure she'll be here any minute now." He squirmed uneasily in his chair.

"All righty!" said the waitress. Her eyes said, "Listen buddy, you're not the first guy I've seen sitting here that got stood up, and you're taking valuable table space on a busy Sunday morning. You better tip me big time when all this is over."

At least, that is what he imagined her to be thinking. She turned and headed away.

"No, wait!" John called out after her, his stomach growling demandingly. "On second thought, let me order already."

The waitress turned and came back, trying very little to hide a self-satisfied smirk. "Yes?" she said, more as a matter-of-fact than a question.

John browsed the menu, his eyes trying to skip over his favorite dish. As much as he tried, he found himself being drawn back almost compulsively like his cat Tess eyeing each wayward pigeon from her window ledge.

"Yes?" repeated the pitiless pretty tyrant of a waitress.

"I'll have... I'll have..." mumbled John, hearing Rachel in the back of his mind, saying, the same thing? Again?! "The... well, the..." he coughed, trying to spit out words stuck in the back of his throat, "huevos rancheros!" He said it so fast that the words jumbled out his mouth as "waybos-ranchos."

The waitress nodded her head, faked a smile, scribbled something on her small notepad and took off, without uttering another word.

Just as she turned away, John noticed her name tag for the first time. It had been partially hidden by a wrinkle but now glittered in the sun: Rache. Great, he thought to himself, just what I needed–another Rachel to humiliate me. He felt heat radiating from his face, a sure sign of a blush in progress.

Taking a long sip of water, John looked at his phone's screen for the twentieth time. The clock on the phone showed she was now forty minutes late, and there was an unread text message. John figured that he must have missed it when he was busy chatting with the server. He guessed that it was probably Rachel, letting him know she was running more than fashionably late:

Hey Long John, I was just thinking about you! -Abhaya.

It was sent five minutes ago. Who the heck is "Abhaya"? thought John. The number was of his programmer Abby.

John: Who is this?

A moment later came the reply:

Abby: What do you mean? It's me, Abby.

John: So why did you sign your earlier message with Abhaya?

Several minutes passed by with no reply.

Abby: Oops. My mistake. My name is Abby but because I'm now in India, some locals decided to call me Abhaya which is an Indian name :-)

John: Oh, I see.

Abby: It means "fearless." Like the Goddess Durga.

John: Durga?

Abby: Oh, you're not very familiar with Hinduism?

John: Not really. What would they call me if I were to live in India?

Abby: Hmm, let me think.

A couple of moments later–

Abby: John–isn't that from the Old Testament? From the language the Israelites spoke? Jonathan? Meaning, God has given?

John: You know, you're right! I have never really given much thought to the origin of my name. I'm impressed!

Abhaya offered a silent prayer to the god of Google: Thank God for being able to quickly search name origins online! She smiled, self-satisfied, and wrote:

Abby: :-) If so, maybe they would call you Datta.

John: Datta?... Like Data in Star Trek: TNG?

Abby: Star Trek?

John: You mean to tell me you're a techie and not a fan of Star Trek?

Abby: Oh, that Star Trek. Haha! No, Datta in Hindi means given.

John: I see. Cool. By the way, you seem to know a lot about Hinduism for a Brit.

Abby: Well, you know. I live here. It is important to know as much as possible about the people and culture around you.

The waitress, Rache, arrived with his order. John's hunger reached new heights. His mouth was watering. The phone buzzed softly as a new text message came in but he ignored it. His focus was solely on his plate.

"Still not here?" asked Rache, smirking slightly as she placed his order on the table.

John's hunger turned into a burst of anger. "Let me ask you something," he growled. "Are you nasty to all your customers, or is there something in me that makes you try extra hard, Rache?" John rolled her name off his tongue as if it were bile he was trying to spit away. The moment the words had left him, he already regretted it. He was so very hungry and now he feared they would kick him out of his favorite eatery. The phone by his plate buzzed again. John was looking Rache in the eye. Her expression, hurt at first, softened.

"Eat," she simply said. "As that commercial goes, 'When you're hungry you're not yourself.'" She smiled pleasantly and turned to go.

"I'm sorry," John mumbled after her, "and thank you." He turned to his meal. Luckily the dish was boiling hot or John would have vacuumed it up in three seconds. Between bites he checked his phone. Several messages came through. Two from Abby and one from Rachel. He opened Rachel's.

Rachel: So sorry. got this really nasty stomach virus. throwing up all night. finally fell asleep at 5. Just woke up.

John rushed to answer, but the tomatoe sauce coating fingers smeared the keys.

John: Don't worry. Sorry to hear you're not well. Can I do anything to help?

Rachel: No. thx. prob a 24-hour thing. def stay away until it's over. let's reschedule. next Sun, no good. got something. next Sat OK?

Another message showed as coming from Abby, but John ignored it. He quickly texted Rachel.

John: Sure. Feel better & don't hesitate to lemme know if u need me to drop by or bring u anything.

Rachel: thx

Shortly afterwards came another note:

Rachel: you're a darling.

John wiped both his fingers and his phone's display with a paper napkin. He took another big bite from his breakfast and turned his attention to Abby's messages. There were three in total.

Abby: John? You still there?

Abby: John did I say something wrong? I'm sorry if I did.

Abby: I hope you're okay. I have to run. Have a dinner I need to attend. TTYL. xoxo.

John stared at the messages. Dinner? he thought, and then remembered that New Delhi was nine and a half hours ahead of New York. Nine and a half hours. What an awkward time difference. A moment later his mind was already elsewhere.

Poor Rachel, he reflected, feeling awfully guilty about being so upset at her. And that waitress, Rache? She didn't mean any harm. I was just so hungry. I'll give her a nice tip.

CHAPTER 26

NEW DELHI

After Janaki's rushed departure from the Durga Puja, Abhaya's family ate in silence. The neighbors' television set continued its noise pollution, but no one seemed to notice.

Excused from the table, Abhaya and Jeevana went back in their room. As soon as the door closed behind them, Abhaya paused in her tracks, staring in amazement at her older sister. On the wall above Jeevana's head, a pair of large yellow cat eyes stared right back at her. A relic from the big sister's teenage years, her "Walk on the Wild Side" 1962 movie poster featured actress Jane Fonda standing stridently in front of those eyes, dressed in a slinky lime-green gown and holding a thin cigarette. The image caused much grief to their father, who protested loudly and furiously when fifteen-year-old Jeevana first brought it home. He eventually allowed it to stay, attributing the provocative action to Jeevana's rebellious age. Abhaya remembered the conundrum.

She also remembered something Jeevana never knew. One evening during that turbelant event, young Abhaya went to her parents' bedroom to ask something of her mom. Through a crack in the door, she could hear her mom defending Jeevana. Turns out that behind the scenes, Mom had convinced her dad to turn a blind eye. "Devidas-ji," she told him, "this Jane Fonda in the poster is much like a modern Durga—fierce and commanding with her tiger-like cat." Abhaya recalled how awekward it was to hear her mom calling her dad by his name. A traditionalist, her mother preferred to use the honorific Ji, and would rarely called her husband by his first name. When she did, it was only in moments of great empathy or to dig in her heels in for a worthy cause. Needless to say, Dad lost that fight. Abhaya never shared that tidbit with her sister. She was afraid her parents would find out she was eavesdropping and there would be ramifications.

Jeevana smiled back at Abhaya. "What?" she said, her tone whimsical. "Do you really believe that I share a room with you, share the same desktop computer, and I would not know about the sort of work you do online?" Jeevana started undressing, removing her work uniform.

Abhaya's eyes grew wide and her cheeks turned deep red. "What work online?" she stuttered, trying very hard to sound innocent. "You did? I mean, you do?"

"Of course," grinned Jeevana. "Boy, you are so naïve. You may be the computer genius in this house, but I wasn't exactly born yesterday. And I work with computers all day long."

"Ok," murmured Abhaya, beginning to digest the fact that her secret online activities were not so secret as she had thought them to be. "But why, I mean how...?"

"Why didn't I bring it up before?" volunteered Jeevana, undoing her bra–she and Abhaya always felt comfortable being naked in front of each other. "Because there was really no point. You see," she explained, "I learned a while back that information is an asset. When you learn of some secret knowledge, there is no need to rush and divulge it for no good purpose." She smiled mysteriously, "You never know when it may come in handy."

"Actually," said Abhaya, who stood by the closed door as if rooted to the ground, "that was not what I meant to ask though what you said is good to know."

It was Jeevana's turn to feel outwitted.

"I meant to ask how you pulled that trick on Janaki. It looked almost as if you were hypnotizing her."

"First things first," Jeevana said, folding her clothes. "I still didn't hear you say thank you, and one you actually intend, for a change. I saved your arse big time."

"Thank you," said Abhaya sincerely, twirling her hair. "Yes, that you did."

"Second," continued Jeevana, examining her nude body in the closet door mirror, "I want an apology for mocking me all this time for my Western name."

"What?" asked Abhaya, completely taken by surprise at the seemingly off-topic request.

"You heard me, Abhaya," smiled Jeevana, "or should I start calling you 'Abby?'"

Abhaya's jaw dropped.

Her sister knew more than she realized.

"I'm waiting," said an unflinching Jeevana.

"I'm sorry," said Abhaya, her gaze lowered like a child caught not only with her hand in the cookie jar but with cookie crumbs all over her face. She had never felt so embarrassed in her entire life.

Jeevana let a few moments pass, enjoying the sweet taste of her little victory, before saying, "Now, regarding Janaki, there is a very old trick a dear friend of mine once taught me." She paused, her eyes sliding to an old photo by her bedside, carrying her to a different time.

"What trick?" asked Abhaya, puzzled yet again. "Can you please teach it to me?"

"Well," smiled Jeevana, "I don't know. It's risky and may end up hurting you, as well as your friendships–more than you may intend. It reminds me of a saying: 'The greatest enemy of knowledge is not ignorance but the illusion of knowledge.'" Jeevana was fond of quotes.

"Why hurting?" asked Abhaya, ignoring her sister's quote. Abhaya cared little for pearls of wisdom by long forgotten people.

"Because of the second rule of friendship."

"Friendship has rules?"

"Of course!" Jeevana countered.

"Okay. So, what is the second rule of friendship?" Abhaya reconsidered. "Actually, no, first teach me the trick!"

Jeevana cocked an eye as if considering.

Abhaya fluttered her eyelashes pleadingly, an old sisterly joke between them.

Jeevana sighed. "All right. Just watch out and don't use it often, if at all," she said. "Have you heard of the card game called poker?"

"Of course!" Abhaya said.

"Wow!" "You sound like you more than just heard of it," Jeevana said.

"No, no, I never played. But I certainly know of it. Please go on." Their father would not tolerate his girls gambling or doing anything of the sort. The thought horrified Abhaya.

"Well, poker is as much about pretending and being really confident as it is the cards you hold." She quickly added, "at least that's what I heard since I never really played it either. The idea is to show that you have a strong hand, even if you don't, and to make your opponent believe it. My childhood friend and I practiced that, playing another game, an imaginary one she invented when we were kids. She always said it would come in handy one day, and it did–today!"

Abhaya nodded, "Oh, I see…. So you actually had no real dirt on Janaki. You just pretended you did?" Still, something did not make sense to her. "But if so, why did she fold so quickly?"

Jeevana smiled. "Everyone has dirt," she said, "and I have no doubt that your friend, Janaki, has hers. Pretending to know is what matters. Let your opponent's imagination do the work for you."

"First of all, don't call her my friend," Abhaya said bitterly. "Not anymore, not after what she did this evening. But secondly, boy, you're good! You definitely could have fooled me. I was sure you knew some stuff about her that she didn't want to be known!"

"Which brings us back to the third rule of friendship. Never dig into your best friend's dirty little secrets, especially the ones she's decided not to share with you."

"As I just made clear," Abhaya hissed, "Janaki is no longer my friend."

"Not now she's not," agreed Jeevana. "But let me remind you that you two go back a long way. I won't be surprised to see you together again sometime in the near future, that is, after all the dust has settled."

"Never," Abhaya said.

"'Never' when you're a teenager is often much shorter than you may imagine, little sister. You'll see. It's because of the fourth rule of friendship."

Abhaya did not know if Jeevana was serious or having fun at her expense. Nevertheless, she decided to play along. "More rules? Okay, what is the fourth?"

"Whatever it was that made you two become such good friends for so long will bring you back together again when the storm passes." Jeevana paused to consider what she had just said, and then added a clarification: "That is, of course, unless the special 'something' has fundamentally changed."

"Deep…" Abhaya said, all-but-mocking. "Have you been reading Deepak again? I thought only misguided Westerners read that crap."

"Which, to remind you, I am one now."

"I dare you to let Father hear that!" Abhaya retorted. If only she could see 'Abby Smith,' Abhaya thought.

Jeevana picked up a towel and started heading toward the bathroom.

"By the way," asked Abhaya, "out of curiosity, you mentioned rules two, three, and four. What is rule number one?"

Already half way through the door Jeevana turned, looked her sister in the eye and said, "the simplest but most difficult thing to accomplish: forgive."

"Wow," Abhaya teased, dripping with sarcasm. "Now you really sound deep."

"You don't know the half of it," she said, far more seriously than before. Her eyes locked onto Abhaya's.

Abhaya flushed and looked away.

"I've learned this lesson the hard way," Jeevana said, her eyes drifting yet again toward the photo by her bedside. In it, two cheerful teenagers were posing, one of whom was a younger Jeevana. The other was a friend that Abhaya only vaguely remembered. Maybe her name was Prema? But before Abhaya could ask anything else, Jeevana, looking again at her younger sister, said, "Forgiveness does not change the past, but it does enlarge the future."

"Another Deepak quote?" teased Abhaya.

"No," replied Jeevana, "this one is actually by a little known Western fellow, an American. He was all but forgotten until the Internet popularized his quotes, years after he passed away. His name is Paul Boese."

Abhaya looked at her sister with some admiration. Jeevana did know her quotes.

"You didn't pick this up in school?" she said.

"No," replied Jeevana. "You know how much I like quotes. But it doesn't matter who said it. Just think about it the next time you take a break from mocking almost everything around you. One day this rule might, just might, make sense to you. That may be the day you start to grow up."

With that, Jeevana left the room.

CHAPTER 27

NEW DELHI

"Janaki dear, are you okay?" asked Janaki's mom, gently knocking on her daughter's closed door.

"Go away!" Janaki replied. "Leave me alone." Janaki buried her head in the pillow and cried softly. *I was only trying to help.... I was only trying to help,* she repeated silently to herself in between muffled sobs.

"But Janaki, what happened at Abhaya's?" persisted her mom. "I saw you coming home all upset."

I was only trying to help.... I was only trying to help. True, Janaki had prepared ahead of time for her little dinner speech in advance. She did not study her lines as an actress would, but rather a stage director preparing for an improvisation and rehearsing in his head. Throughout dinner, she had a general notion of what she would say and how, but not when. She did not entirely know why, either. Her motivation for acting was not completely clear. She did not ponder it much. An opportunity came along, and she took it.

The truth was that deep down inside, Janaki was envious. There was a part of her that wanted to embarrass Abhaya. Yet Abhaya was also her best friend.

Janaki refused to accept the truth of her jealousy. After all, Abhaya and she had grown up together. They were best friends. Best friends do not envy each other. Ever. That was a value her mother instilled in her.

Yet here she was, envious and denying the truth.

When a powerful stream gets blocked one way, the laws of nature dictate that it will find another path to release its surging energy, and that path for Janaki turned out to be an excuse, albeit a poor one: she was not trying to hurt her friend. Janaki began to feel better. She sat up.

On the contrary, she told herself, she was only trying to help. It was so clear to her now. Since Abhaya could not have said to her family what she really felt, Janaki, her best friend, did it for her. After all, wasn't it Abhaya who said the other day she would love to have someone else tell her family about it rather than having to face the wrath of her father herself?

I was only trying to help. It wasn't easy. I was brave to stand up to Abhaya's dad.... I should get some credit for my courage!

That she spilled her friend's secrets did not even occur to her now. It did not fit the do-gooder story she told herself, a tale repeated enough times that she now fully believed it. She was in the clear. How could she have known that Devidas would react the way he did?

"Janaki!" her mom shouted once more. She tried to enter her daughter's locked room, turning the doorknob to no avail.

Janaki took a deep breath. Until she gave a satisfying reply, her mother would not relent. She lifted her head, focused on her breath, and tried to relax her abdomen as the yoga teacher had demonstrated, the one her mother hired privately for her.

"Janaki, open up!" her mother pleaded through the door once more.

Janaki drew another deep breath and said, "I'm okay mom. Really." Janaki fought to make her quivering voice sound steady. "Nothing happened, It's just that...." Her mind was racing. What can I say that she would believe? "I got my period."

That wasn't true, but it would suffice. Her mother knew that her first day of the period was very challenging for her.

"Oh," said her mom, "I understand. Should I fix you a special chai to help with the cramps?"

"No, but thank you. I'll be okay. I just need to rest."

"Okay dear, you do just that. Let me know if you need anything. I love you."

"Love you too, Mom." Janaki could hear her mother's footsteps walking away from the door. She exhaled.

Janaki considered for a moment whether to bury her head back in the pillow and resume her weeping but decided that she had shed enough tears.

She also had something troubling to think through.

What secrets did Jeevana know about me? Janaki wondered, her skin crawling.

Maybe she saw me smoking in the street the other day. Is that what she meant when she said, "I also have the best of intentions for you, more than you may realize?" Janaki cringed. My dad would kill me if he found out.

Her phone buzzed. She picked it up.

"Janaki, it's Chetan"

"Of course it's you, dummy. I can see it's your number," she murmured to herself. She was in no mood for people who stated the obvious. What did I ever find attractive in this idiot? Oh yeah, I thought for a whole quarter of a second that he actually liked me. She wrote, "What's up?"

"Sorry to bother you so late. Just wanted to check if there is any progress with you-know-who."

Idiot, thought Janaki. What? Are you afraid to text her name? "What news?"

He deserved to be played with a bit, she thought, smiling for the first time since being home.

"So sorry to bother you–"

You already said that!

Chetan continued. "I was wondering, you know, if you and Abhaya, you know, if you spoke?"

"Of course we did. We speak daily." Janaki was now grinning widely. This is fun!

"So sorry. You know what I mean, if you spoke with her about me?"

Janaki paused. How should I handle this? What do I really want? Do I still want this confused boy to like me? Do I want to hurt Abhaya, who does not seem to understand why I only wanted to help? She needed time to think this through. She was not going to act on a whim, twice in one evening. She was smarter than that.

I'm a... a... I'm a movie director! she realized. If that's the case, then I need to study this screenplay and put on a show that no one will forget.

Janaki texted, "Listen, I really have to go. Let's continue this another time. Good night."

Right after she hit "send," Janaki turned off her phone without looking. She was sure Chetan would reply, but she had had enough drama for one evening. Without showering or even brushing her teeth, she turned the lights off and went to sleep.

CHAPTER 28

NEW DELHI

"What's up, Cat Slayer?" grinned Arjuna, holding a punching pad between his massive hands. "Just moments ago, you were fierce and focused, and now, all of a sudden you punch like a kitten!" His voice thundered across the dojang, the training hall where the two practiced.

Chetan stopped punching and stared at Arjuna without blinking.

No one else in the practice area seemed to notice. No doubt because of Arjuna's loud voice, Chetan knew.

"Come on," Arjuna encouraged him, "I'm just having fun. As you heard me say before, I really do believe you come from a lineage of Kshatriya, the warrior caste." Chetan made a face at him.

"Yes, it is true, Chetan," Arjuna retorted. "I have no doubt that if you ever face that moment of truth, you will have your martial arts skills to defend your life. Or maybe," Arjuna winked, "save a damsel in distress? You will have what it takes. Now go on, warrior, punch like you mean it!" He shook the punching pad in front of him encouragingly.

"Quite a speech," said Chetan, "but it isn't that–whatever you were just blathering. It's just that something popped into my head that confused me."

Arjuna inspected Chetan's face for a moment, narrowing his eyes as if to read Chetan's thoughts. He sniffed the air around Chetan as if he were a bloodhound tracking a fox. "I smell love in the air!" he announced to the world.

Chetan blushed again. He glanced out of the corner of his eyes to see if anyone noticed. No one had.

"Look, official practice time is pretty much over. Let's wrap it up and you can tell Arjuna what aches your heart." Arjuna smiled in the friendliest manner. He headed off the dojang floor, performing the traditional bow as he exited.

Chetan followed on his heels, somewhat dazed.

They changed out of their black and white practice uniforms and exited onto the street within minutes. Moments later they were headed toward their favorite park by the river. Chetan still did not utter a word.

Arjuna, for a change, did not rush him or make any sly comments.

Chetan began. "You see…" He stopped and looked his friend straight in the eyes. "This stays between us, Arjuna," he said, deadly serious. "You cannot say a thing to anyone else–no one!–about it."

"Me?" responded Arjuna innocently, his voice peculiarly high-pitched. "My lips are always sealed!"

"Right." Chetan half-chuckled. "As tightly shut as your father's fishing nets."

"Hey!" thundered Arjuna, "don't get my father involved! He has enough problems with the fishes without you adding more holes!"

Chetan laughed.

Arjuna's dad was an artisan. While he struck gold with his handwoven rugs, which sold for outrageously expensive prices at Western-themed galleries across India, his fishing hobby was a complete disaster and a source of endless amusement between them.

"Your big mouth knows no limits," argued Chetan. "All I'm saying is just that you must keep this to yourself."

"Alright, all right already!" called Arjuna. "Get on with it. Tell Arjuna, the love expert, what is on your mind."

"Since when have you become a love expert?" said a bemused Chetan.

"Ha!" replied Arjuna. "Don't get me started or else we will never get to hear what is bothering you. Now, are you going to tell me or not?"

Chetan took a deep breath and started. "I told you already that I really like Abhaya."

Arjuna nodded his head.

"And that I asked her friend Janaki to help me approach her."

"I still don't understand why you can't just go up and speak with Abhaya directly. If I were you…."

"That's exactly it," Chetan interjected. "I'm not you. I'm… hm… well… more reserved."

"Reserved?" cried Arjuna. "That's an understatement. You're shy. No wait, shy is too outgoing of a word to describe you. You're a picture on the wall... No! Not even that! A picture is going to be noticed on occasion. You're more the wall behind the picture, a...."

"All right! Enough already! I know what I am," Chetan said, raising his voice. "I know what I am. Can we please move on?"

"Okay, my friend," Arjuna nodded, "please do go on. I'm all ears," he said, flapping his large ears as if they were butterfly wings.

Chetan rolled his eyes. "The thing is," he said, "Janaki promised to help me with this, but I don't think she's really doing anything. In fact, I think she's just stalling, and I can't figure out why."

"How come?"

"Here. Let me show you my texts with her from only last night." The friends found a nearby bench and sat down, Chetan pulled out his phone and handed it over to Arjuna, who browsed the texts:

Chetan texted first. "Janaki, it's Chetan."

"What's up?"

"Sorry to bother you so late. Just wanted to check if there is any progress with you- know-who."

"What's new?"

"So sorry to bother you, I was wondering, you know, if you and Abhaya, you know, if you spoke?"

"Of course we did. We speak daily."

"So sorry. You know what I mean, if you spoke with her about me?"

"Listen, I really have to go. Let's continue this another time. Good night."

"xoxox"

The final message was Chetan again. "?"

Arjuna returned the phone to Chetan, brought his hand to his chin, his index finger tapping his lips. "Hmmm," he said, "did she reply to your question mark at the end?"

"No," said Chetan. "She may have turned her phone off since it was marked 'undelivered.'"

Arjuna pondered some more. "Very curious," he said.

"What is?" Chetan was even more confused than before.

"First off, my friend," said Arjuna, sounding fatherly, "you apologize w-a-y too much."

"I'm sorry," said Chetan, "but I'm not following you."

"There you go again!" cried Arjuna. "What are you sorry for?"

"It's just a manner of speech," protested Chetan.

"No, it is not," Arjuna pointed out. "It's an issue with you. It's a matter of attitude, a mindset. You need to toughen up. Learn to take what you want. Be a man."

"What does being a man have to do with being polite?" objected Chetan. "I was brought up with good manners."

"You're completely missing the point," said Arjuna patiently, as if explaining to a child. "This isn't about being impolite. Have you ever seen me be crude?"

"Well," replied Chetan smiling, "now that you bring it up, yes! Most of the time. You can be quite the arse..."

"Not true!" opposed Arjuna. "I'm an arse only to people who deserve it! And, unfortunately, there are quite a few of those around." He burst out laughing the way only Arjuna could: with short bursts furling into each other, rising and falling like ocean waves.

Chetan waited, knowing there was no point in saying anything until Arjuna calmed down. Anything else would have been as useful as yelling into the wind.

When Arjuna took a long breath, Chetan broke in, "Okay, so, what is your point?"

"My point, my friend, Chetan, the fierce Cat Slayer, is that you're a spider when you should be a feline."

"I don't follow."

Arjuna continued. "Have you ever seen a cat planning a trap and waiting for a mouse to fall in? A cat is patient, but not for long. He strikes hard and quick if he wants to avoid remaining hungry. But you're a spider weaving a web and.... No! Not even that! You don't even weave your own web. You wait for others to do the work for you. And because of that, my friend, you may starve before anything happens." Arjuna paused. "There. I said it. Nothing else to add. My job here is done."

"You?" chuckled Chetan. "Nothing else to add? That will be the day!"

Arjuna burst into his rollicking laughter again. "That, you're right! But this is beside the point. You'd still stand there drooling while others feast. What'll it be, Chetan?"

"I don't know," said Chetan in a low, sad voice. "I'm just not like you. I can't bring myself to go to a girl I like and spill it all out."

"You want me to do it for you, my friend?" ask Arjuna.

"No! Don't you dare!" replied Chetan, half terrified at the thought. "You promised this stays between us!"

"All right! All right!" giggled Arjuna. "Remember? My lips are sealed like my father's fishing net," he winked.

Chetan shook his head.

The two sat in silence for a while.

"Also," added Arjuna abruptly, making Chetan jolt.

"Yes?"

"I'm not sure what to make of this Janaki. My gut feeling, seeing this exchange between you two, is that...." Arjuna's sentence faded away. "You know what?"

"What?" asked Chetan, getting agitated.

"Can you show me another exchange between you two?"

"Hmmm," said Chetan. "I guess so." He took the phone back from Arjuna and scrolled through messages. "Here," he said, as he handed the phone to Arjuna.

"Sorry to disturb you, Janaki, it's Chetan."

"Here!" exclaimed Arjuna, victoriously.

Chetan almost jumped out of his seat. "What? What?"

"You see!" pointed out Arjuna. "You apologize! Again! Why do you do that?"

Chetan moaned. "You almost gave me a heart attack!" He placed a hand on his heart as if to check whether it was still beating. "We have already been through this," Chetan continued. "Let's move on."

"All right, all right," moaned Arjuna. "Let me look into this. Now sit still and don't disturb the master at work."

Chetan rolled his eyes but said nothing.

Janaki texted, "Well, hello."

"Hmmm," said Arjuna.

Chetan replied, "Just a quick check if you had a chance to speak with Abhaya?"

"No, not yet. Been very busy."

"Okay, I see. Sorry, I don't mean to be pushy."

"Another sorry," whispered Arjuna disparagingly. "Idiot," he muttered as if to himself but loud enough for Chetan to hear.

"I heard that!" said Chetan, flushing.

"Oh!" replied Arjuna, as if surprised. "It wasn't you. I was just thinking about someone... someone else." He smiled.

"Sure you were." mumbled Chetan.

"Now be quiet. Do you want me to analyze this or not?" asked Arjuna.

Janaki texted, "U aren't being pushy, but maybe it's better u & me meet 4 updates in person?"

Chetan replied, "Sure, we can meet at school during break, that is when you're not with Abhaya."

"I'm not with Abhaya all the time u know. I have a life of my own."

"Sorry, I didn't mean to suggest that."

"That's okay. I'm not angry with u. I don't think I could be really angry with u. I meant out of school?"

Janaki's second message came through before Chetan could respond. "Listen, have to run. Another time? Xoxox"

"Okay."

"Hm," hammed Arjuna again. He handed the phone back to Chetan and scratched his head. "Yes," he finally said. "This Janaki—a little fiery, isn't she? Yes... I think she may have the hots for you. Maybe that's why she's stalling."

"Janaki? For me?" protested Chetan, but his cheeks betrayed pinkish coloring. "No way. She's the wealthy snobbish type. That's why it was easier for me to approach her. I knew she wouldn't care for me. A different class, you know what I mean?"

"You just wait and see," smiled Arjuna, a twinkle in his eye. "The Love Doctor has spoken. Now, I'm hungry. So much talk always makes my stomach rumble. Let's go have some yummy chole bhature."

"You don't need to talk for that to happen," commented Chetan as the two friends started walking again. "Your stomach always rumbles."

"True, true," agreed Arjuna. His laughter engulfing the air around them, setting it on fire like the late afternoon sun.

CHAPTER 29

NEW DELHI

Sitting on a bench by the river, Jeevana, dressed for work, was watching the reflections of the late afternoon sun bouncing off the water.

If she had not known how polluted the Yamuna river was, a fact she heard her dad protest a thousand times, the scene could have been perfect. The river's surface glimmered with golden feathery shapes, as if the precious stones and metals that were said to once decorate the Taj Mahal had melted onto the great stream, adorning the goddess Yamuna herself.

Jeevana's mind wandered to scenes from her childhood. The wonderful times she spent with her best friend Prema; the sense of anger she felt when she thought Prema was eyeing the boy that Jeevana liked. How one fateful day years ago, Jeevana watched from afar while Prema was being brutally bullied and did nothing. Jeevana didn't even call for help. She could have run and called friends to intervene, a teacher, anyone, but she just stood there, watching from afar. In retrospect, she realized that all the anger that had quietly boiled inside her had made her halt, watch, and remain an onlooker while a group of nasty seniors at the far-end of the schoolyard verbally humiliated her best friend and physically abused her.

Somehow, despite the distance, Prema had noticed Jeevana on that fateful day. She saw her standing aloof, not running to call for help.

Prema knew. Yet she never blamed her friend. Never.

But Prema changed. After that incident things were never the same. The warm Prema that was always laughing and hugging soon folded inward and shut down, a beautiful flower denied sufficient light.

A complaint was filed by Prema's mother, but the school did nothing to address the situation. The administration cited no reliable eye witnesses, and with the seniors barely a month away from graduating, no one wanted to rock the boat. Prema's parents decided to take action and moved away. It seemed to happen overnight and without warning.

Jeevana had had plenty of time to reflect upon this. Time and again she told herself that she was simply immature. Time and again, she regretted her actions as well as her lack of action. But deep inside she knew there was no excuse.

I wronged her, she thought. I do not deserve forgiveness.

It seemed a lifetime ago even though it was just a few years. Jeevana felt she had grown since then. Dropping out of college to assist her family, letting her own ambitions die, feeling abused by her supervisor at work. And Prema, good old Prema, how much she loved having her as a friend.

Jeevana had been devastated by the loss of their friendship. She had tried in the past to locate Prema but to no avail. And then that chance encounter just a week ago, Jeevana thought to herself. How wonderful!

But where is she? Jeevana suddenly snapped out of her meditative state of mind. As usual, she's late, she thought.

Her frown turned into a smile when she heard a familiar voice say, "There you are! I walked by and almost missed you." Prema, dressed in a pretty flowery dress that enhanced her charm, reached out to embrace her friend.

Jeevana got up and returned the hug. She was holding Prema close, as if afraid to lose her again.

"It's so good to see you," said Jeevana as tears flooded her eyes. "I'm sorry," she added and searched for a handkerchief to wipe her eyes. "I don't know what's come over me."

"Nah," said Prema nonchalantly, "you're just being your old self... that is to say, a sentimental cow."

The two friends burst out laughing and sat on the bench, watching the sunset.

"This river is so darn dirty," commented Prema. She nodded her head in the direction of a group of sadhus, holy men, some dressed only in white, some simply in orange in loincloths, and all about to bathe. "These fools really believe that by simply bathing in the Yamuna, they can diminish the reactions for their sins," she groaned. "Ugh!"

"I wish it were that easy," replied Jeevana, her mind wandering again to the way she wronged her friend. Silence settled until Jeevana broke it.

"I realized after seeing you last week that I never apologized for the wrong I did you."

Prema turned to Jeevana somewhat surprised.

Unsuccessfully suppressing a sly grin stealing over her face, she said, "Right, and I must tell you that for the past nine years there hasn't been a day that's gone by when I hadn't been contemplating how to punish you."

Jeevana, oblivious to the slight smile on her friend's face, said shakily, "Really? I'm so, so sorry." Tears once again welled in her eyes.

"Get out of here!" shrieked Prema, elbowing her friend. "I already forgave you years ago. Even without an apology. Even without you being around."

Jeevana wiped the wetness from her eyes with the back of her hand and looked quizzically at her friend.

"Yes," Prema clarified, "you did not call for help. You probably didn't want to be known as the snitch... but what else was there to be expected from the most snobbish pupil in school?"

"No, I was not!" protested Jeevana.

"Of course you weren't!" called Prema. "You were just Ms. Perfect, turning in a perfect grade on every single test. Though I dare say, at current, you can only claim the title of Ms. Past Perfect." The two friends were laughing again. "I even remember a chemistry test where you scored a hundred and ten!" reminisced Prema. "I flopped that test and you got better-than-perfect for answering a bonus question. God, how I hated you then," she said half-heartedly, smiling affectionately.

"We had so much fun," smiled Jeevana.

"We still do," commented Prema, "and now that we've reconnected, we will!"

"By the way, how's your mom?" asked Jeevana turning serious.

"It was tough," replied Prema. "My dad, as you may remember, was already ill. He died a year after we moved."

"I'm so sorry," said Jeevana, "I didn't know."

"Of course you didn't," smiled Prema weakly. "My mom was so very much connected to him." She paused for a moment. "But in a sense, our poverty was our salvation. Mom had no time to mourn herself to death. She had to go out and work to feed the little ones. And me? I dropped out of school in my senior year and joined the workforce. Who said being poor can't be a good thing?" she laughed. "Just imagine: if we'd been wealthy,

Mom would have probably sunk into depression and secretly drunk herself into the grave. At least, that's what I hear some rich folks do."

"I always admired your sense of humor and ability to find the positive in the darkest of nights," commented Jeevana.

"Yeah, yeah. That's what caused me grief in high school. Everyone loved me except those witches that figured out I was the source of their misery."

The two sat in silence for a spell.

"Oh well," said Prema, "as I always say, humor is the underprivileged's medicine, the last resort, the only affordable weapon at their disposal."

Jeevana nodded and asked, "Who are you quoting? I have not heard that one before."

"Ha!" Prema guffawed. "Are you still collecting quotes?"

"Yes," admitted Jeevana, her cheeks flushing.

"Well," Prema said, straightening her posture as if she were a famous person about to receive the Noble Prize, "chalk that one up to me."

"Really? Good one," mumbled Jeevana.

Prema giggled even harder, seeing her friend's amazement.

"Speaking of quotes and memories," asked Prema, "it occurred to me to ask you, did you ever watch the film of that poster hanging on your wall? What was it called? Something with 'wild?'"

"Walk on the Wild Side with Jane Fonda–meow!" replied Jeevana with a smile. "No, I have not. God, that was a long time ago. My dad gave me such grief over that poster. I just really liked it, and I'm not even sure why. There was so much provocation in that image, so much strength. There was something for me to aspire to."

"It's been this long, and you've never seen it? These days, with the Internet, I'm sure you can find it online," Prema said. "How about it? Maybe you and I can watch it together sometime?"

"I'm sure we can," replied Jeevana, "but you know what? I would almost rather not. I have such a specific image of that character in my mind that I'm afraid that no film would be able to match it. I'd rather keep the symbolism, even if it's not real and the movie theme is completely different."

"I like that!" Prema clapped her hands, "Yes, this also applies to some men I know. They look good and then they spoil it by opening their mouths." Her smile widened. "Speaking of which," Prema posed another question, "what's new on the romantic scene? How's your love life, Princess Damayanti?"

Jeevana blushed. She had not heard this nickname in years. It was one that Prema had given her when the two were very young, named after the mythological princess whose beauty and grace made even the gods admire her.

"I'm doomed," Jeevana replied, "much like Damayanti."

"Not true," replied Prema. "Damayanti did find her true love and ultimately lived happily ever after."

"Right," responded Jeevana, "I'm not at that part of the fairytale just yet. I'm still living the crappy portion, all the various miseries she suffered before the happy end."

"I see.... Go on," Prema encouraged her friend. "Tell old Queen Tara all about it."

"Ah!" laughed Jeevana, "so you still remember the nickname I gave you."

"But of course," said Prema, pursing her lips. "How could I forget? A queen who was the daughter of a monkey."

"Stop, stop," Jeevana laughed. "You know that's not why I named you Tara. It was because she's revered for her wit and devotion."

"Right," responded Prema, "but she was still the daughter of a monkey. A physician ape, mind you, but still...." Prema imitated monkey sounds while moving her arms, scratching her head and armpits.

"Hahaha!" Jeevana laughed so hard that her eyes were tearing.

Passersby turned their heads. Some looked bewildered. Others gave them a disapproving glance.

With the sun just beginning to set along the horizon, some street lights started to come on. In this area of New Delhi most of the public lighting was working, which was a rarity. The two were walking through a neighborhood where the wealthier people lived. Jeevana took a look at her wristwatch. "I have to head to work soon," she said.

"Aren't you all excited about it?" asked Prema. "What's up with that?"

"There is this guy," stated Jeevana.

"You see!" Prema jumped in. "I knew it! You always had some guy wrapped around your finger."

"No, no," protested Jeevana, "it's nothing like that. Remember last time we met, I told you about the boss's nephew? My supervisor who bothers me all the time?"

"The guy that wants to take you out on a date?" asked Prema.

"Yes, though a date would be too generous a term for what this creep probably has in mind."

"Go on," poked Prema.

"Well, it's just getting worse. I don't know what to do. It's like I either have to leave this job or go out with him. And finding a new job is not that easy, not that easy at all."

Prema stopped walking and folded her arms, thinking. Jeevana looked at her, hoping for way out.

"Tell you what," Prema said after a few moments, "this is what I would do if I were in your shoes. I'd tell that jerk that I'd agree to see him, say, two weeks from now. This will buy you time. If he believes you'll go out with him, he'll be less likely to bother you. And then I would use that time to look for a new job."

Jeevana looked dejected.

"Now, don't get discouraged," Prema continued. "There is work out there. And you're now an experienced help desk assistant. Good people are always in demand. Your English, if I recall, is very good. Almost no accent."

"But I'll have no references," protested Jeevana, "and no chance of getting one if I walk out."

Prema pondered this and then her face lit up. "Leave that to Queen Tara. Let me see what I can do for Princess Damayanti. I have some contacts in high places," she winked.

Jeevana looked at her friend. "You sure?"

"Of course! Just do as I say, and it will all work out."

"Right!" laughed Jeevana. "I still remember the last time you said that, just before skipping school and getting caught. We both got punished."

"Hahaha!" cried Prema, loud enough that the seagulls nearby fluttered and took off.

Jeevana's face relaxed somewhat.

"It will be all right," Prema repeated, smiling faintly.

An hour later, Jeevana was at her desk, ready to take on support calls. Eshaan strolled by and came up behind her. Creeping closer, he placed his hand on her right shoulder.

Jeevana felt sick. His presence alone was enough to make her nauseous.

"So, what do I have to do to make you go out with me?" Eshaan purred, his fingers now caressing her shoulder.

Jeevana's skin crawled. "Please remove your hand, right now," she demanded, but did not wait for him to comply. She shook her shoulder free.

"You know I won't stop until you say yes, right?" He placed his hand back on her shoulder.

Jeevana cringed as she thought, in your dreams! She said instead, in a voice as poisonously as she could muster, "I know."

"Tell you what," Eshaan said. "Come with me to a movie just once, and if after that you don't want to go out with me, I won't bother you ever again." He tried to sound sweet, but this only reminded Jeevana of those cutthroat open-air market hawkers offering a "special deal," one that would sour in ten minutes flat.

"Okay, okay," she replied hurriedly, not wanting to miss a golden opportunity to shake him off for good. Remembering Prema's advice, she added, "but not before the end of next week, about ten days from now."

"Oh?" Eshaan had not expected her to agree.

Mistaking his reaction for resentment, Jeevana felt compelled to add, "I have a family event coming up, and then, there's work. Next weekend would be my first availability." She hated lying, but anything said to this creep should be excluded from that category.

Only upon seeing Eshaan nodding absentmindedly did she realize his response was delight, not anger.

That made Jeevana emphasize once more, "But remember, ten days from now, and you're not to bother me until then or this deal is off."

"Very good!" exhaled Eshaan, rubbing his hands together as if he were just about to throw the best loaded dice in his life.

Mission accomplished, he left her to her work.

Now what am I going to do? wondered Jeevana. Look for a new job as Prema suggested, or just take my chances, go out with him once, tell him off afterwards, and hope that he keeps his word? I'll need to ask Prema what she thinks.

"Hello. Thank you for calling Over the Rainbow customer support," Jeevana found herself saying, answering a customer call. "How may I assist you?"

CHAPTER 30

NEW DELHI

Abhaya's phone buzzed. It was 10 p.m. Only one person would text her that late. Janaki.

"Abhaya? r u still angry at me?"

Abhaya ignored the message.

"Abhaya, I know ur up. I know ur seeing this. Please answer me."

When pigs fly I will, thought Abhaya. Even Janaki's text abbreviations, which she usually tolerated, annoyed her.

"I was only trying 2 help. u have 2 believe me."

Abhaya's thumbs tapped on the keypad. She was eager to send a nasty reply but held back.

Janaki didn't give up. "If I really wanted 2 hurt u, I would've told about ur parents' love letters, but I didn't, did I?"

Is that a threat? thought Abhaya. Is she making a threat? Why was I so stupid to send her that letter?

"I didn't tell because I'M UR friend. I'm sorry I said what I said. It was in the heat of the moment and & I felt like standing up 4 u. That's what friends are 4, isn't it?"

Abhaya still didn't budge though after reading these words her fury began to subside.

Janaki pleaded. "Abhaya, please, ur my BEST friend, my only real friend. Please 4give me if I have done u wrong, please, please, please?"

"Very simple," Jeevana's words rang in Abhaya's ears. "Rule number one of friendship, very simple but most difficult to accomplish: forgive."

Abhaya stared at the last message from Janaki and felt the last of her anger dissipate like air seeping from a punctured balloon. She felt tired. Tired and drained.

"Okay. Good night," Abhaya replied.

With that, she turned off the phone. She didn't want to see Janaki's reply. She headed to bed.

CHAPTER 31

NEW YORK CITY

John groaned.

The espresso machine at the East-West Café was broken. Someone must've messed it up the previous evening.

Or maybe the Coffee Gods did not look favorably on me, John thought, since he was working the morning shift that day. Perhaps they decided to punish me.

Punishment it was. From 7:00a.m. to 9:00 a.m. it was always the busiest time of the day. A line of Manhattanites seeking their morning fix starting at the café's counter, stretched out the door and snaked around the corner well onto the sidewalk. To an out-of-towner, they would have resembled a line of vampire zombies. If it had been that simple, John would have complied already, rolling up his sleeves and offering a bite. Anything to make them go away.

Unfortunately, this bunch fed on caffeine, not blood. They wanted a specialty joe — a skinny cappuccino, a dirty chai, a soy latte, a doppio espresso, etc. — all drinks that required the machine, the same machine that was not working.

Best of all, none of them seemed to have noticed the handwritten sign in big block letters that was loosely taped to the door: ESPRESSO MACHINE BROKEN. Or maybe they noticed it and thought it did not apply to them. Or that the machine would be miraculously fixed by the time they reached the counter. Or maybe, imagined John, they did not realize that a latte required an espresso machine, a working espresso machine.

For the hundredth time that morning, John said, "Sorry, the espresso machine's broken." He was rewarded with harsh stares, as if the situation were entirely his fault.

God, I hate this job, he thought. Just a few more weeks and my app will be ready to launch–and then, who knows? Maybe on to easy street!

"Really?" snarled a fragile-looking woman in her mid-thirties, her blond hair neatly done, her mascara thick, her makeup a mask for her furious face. "I have been waiting in line for fifteen minutes, and now you tell me?!"

"I'm sorry," repeated John, pointing at the sign on the door, a sign, he now realized, that was mostly hidden by the people in line. Apologetically he added, "We did put a sign up."

"Right," cried the woman. "A sign! How, just tell me how, am I supposed to start my morning without my cappuccino!"

John was amazed. Here was this elegant woman, one he would never have imagined behaving the way she did. But then again, looks are deceiving, and New Yorkers are known to have split personalities: one before their morning coffee, another one after.

"How about regular coffee?" John offered, weakly.

"Really?" she said without any hint of smile on her face. She stormed out the store, steaming. No coffee in hand.

Thus it went, on, and on, and on. At 9:00 a.m., the line dwindled. "Where is the broken machine?!" thundered the espresso machine repairman.

"Now you get here!" cried John.

"Watch it!" warned the husky mustachioed guy. "Be thankful that I came at all. This time of the day, traffic is a nightmare."

John held his tongue and pointed at the machine.

Ryan, his fellow worker and supervisor, tapped him on his shoulder. "Good job holding the fort, John. I know it was rough this morning. Go take a thirty-minute break and I'll cover for you."

John looked at him, relieved and grateful. He always thought Ryan was a decent guy, and this proved it. "You're sure?" he asked.

"Yeah, yeah," laughed Ryan. "Get outta here."

John took off his apron and collected his bag. He never took his own breaks at the café, if he could help it. Funny, he thought as he stepped out, I used to love sitting here before being behind this counter. It was here, he recalled, that the idea for his mobile app first came to him.

Crossing the street, he entered a Starbucks. He preferred his local East-West Café, but strangely enough, the ambience here was so different from the more bohemian East-West that it made him relax. He felt compelled to buy something though he knew that no one would kick him out, even if he sat empty-handed for thirty minutes. "Grande chai latte," he murmured to the barista.

His phone buzzed softly in his pocket: text message. John ignored it, paid and went to wait by the counter. Some minutes later, sitting at a corner window table with his latte, he watched the neverending stream of people passing by.

What strange creatures these New York crowds are, he thought. Living dead, if there ever were. His phone buzzed again. Another message. Reluctantly, he pulled out his phone. His face lit up. It was Rachel.

"What's up? just got into the office."

The second message was from Abby. Strange, John thought. It's kind of late in the evening, even if she's in India. What is she doing, working so late? Doesn't she have a life?

A second thought occurred to him. Look who's talking: a guy with no social life, a stupid day job and a mobile app pipe dream. He smiled, remembering what his friend, Chris, had once said: "In New York, everyone has a day job and a business idea."

Abby texted, "Hey, John. I'm working and was thinking about you :-)"

John went back to Rachel's message and typed. "On a break from work. Espresso machine was broken this morning. What a total nightmare."

Then, switching to Abby's message he replied: "Good to hear you're working! How's the progress?"

The phone buzzed and a message came from Rachel. "Sorry to hear. deprive NYers their cup of joe and & you're as good as dead"

The phone buzzed with a new message, but John was replying to Rachel. "Tell me about it! It was a war zone out there. I barely survived."

He then turned to the message from Abby.

Abby wrote, "Very good. I'm glad to make you happy! :) :-) :-D"

What's up with all these smiles? thought John. What are you? A teenager? Instead, he wrote, "Great! I'm happy that we're on schedule and even a little ahead."

Phone buzzing, he switched to the message thread with Rachel.

Rachel replied, "well, ur a tough cookie. no, scratch that. ur a pumpkin! ;-)"

A pumpkin? thought John. Rachel had not called him by this affectionate nickname in a year, maybe more. It was an old joke between them, he being the pumpkin, she being Cinderella or the Princess, depending on the context.

The phone buzzed again, and mindlessly, he switched to Abby's message.

"You're okay? I'm about to log off and call it an early night. I need to have my beauty sleep! :-)"

Something seemed odd about this message, but John's mind was still on Rachel. He typed, "Sweet dreams, my princess."

Thinking of Rachel with a smile on his face, John tucked his phone away and headed back to his coffee shop, just shy of his thirty-minute break.

NEW DELHI

The following morning, Abhaya was sitting on a bench under the pipal tree in the schoolyard. Every few minutes she would pull out her phone and look at John's last text message from the night before. A smile would spread over her face. "Sweet dreams, my princess."

Her heart felt as if it would overflow at any moment. It's true! John is in love with me! That's how she read him calling her a princess. What else could it mean? She kept the phone by her bedside at night, afraid that if she put it away, the magic would be gone. Having it nearby also made her feel as if John himself were lying there, right by her side.

She even dreamt that much at night. The phone materialized and became her Long John. He hugged her while she slept, his hands tracing the back of her head, caressing her hair, her shoulders, and back and holding her gently, but holding her tight. She dreamed of kissing his lips. Her skin turned to goosebumps, recalling how real that dream was. It was simply wonderful!

Abhaya was still beaming at the small screen when she realized that someone was seated by her side, watching her with intense interest. Feeling invaded, privacy all but gone, Abhaya turned her head sharply. Her gaze met Janaki's long eyelashes. Underneath were the pale brown eyes that often seemed a bit eerie to those meeting her for the first time. But not to Abhaya. Those eyes were as familiar to her–maybe more so–than her own. Until recently, she had loved Janaki more than her own sister.

"What's up?" asked Abhaya, tucking her phone into the safety of her bag.

"Nothing much," answered Janaki. Nodding toward the now-concealed phone, she asked, "What was that all about?"

"What?" replied Abhaya, trying to sound indifferent.

"Well, you were staring at the phone so intensely, for a moment I thought you were expecting it to turn into a prince!"

Abhaya, despite her attempts at self-control, felt her face flush. Her mind was racing with excuses, although she was well aware she had already lost. Janaki knew her all too well.

"Come on, come on," cajoled Janaki, "out with it."

This, thought Abhaya, is not how I imagined our first encounter after that miserable dinner would go. Abhaya had a score to settle. How did Janaki, that little weasel, suddenly become my interrogator? That was too much for her.

Easy Abhaya, easy, she reminded herself. You already decided to make peace with her. Don't let your temper get the best of you. Biting her lips, Abhaya slowly pulled the phone out of her bag.

"It was John," she murmured, as if admitting to cheating on a test. Why do I find it so hard not to answer her?

"John, who?" asked Janaki.

"John? My New York client?"

"Oh," said Janaki, recognition settling in. "That John."

"Why? Did you think I meant John Travolta? Do we know any other John?"

This time, it was Janaki's turn to blush.

Abhaya could feel the tide turning. If this were an arm-wrestling match, now was the point where the underdog flexed hidden reserves of power. She tucked the phone away, all the while maintaining eye contact with Janaki. Her expression turned accusatory.

Janaki shrank back, as if unwittingly touching a hot pot.

"And besides," said Abhaya, not missing a beat, "before we poke further into my business, we still have much to clarify."

"Clarify... yes. Yes!" said Janaki, hanging on to that word, somewhat relieved that her friend had not chosen a different, much stronger term. "Listen Abhaya," Janaki blurted out, before Abhaya could say her piece, "I'm really, really sorry."

To Abhaya, the next few minutes felt as if Janaki had prepared a speech in advance and rehearsed several times over. Abhaya took this as a compliment. Janaki revered this moment so much that she prepared for it. That meant that their relationship was still important to her.

"...and so you see, I really just wanted to help. You know me," Janaki pleaded, "I would have never done anything like this, and especially not in front of your dad."

Abhaya made a mental note that Janaki hadn't belittled her father at all–another good point scored for her.

"...But I really felt I needed to stand up for you." She paused. "That's it," she said, sounding like a train that ran out of steam more than one that reached its final destination. "I'm done." She added, "I'm at your mercy."

Abhaya felt the speech's conclusion could've been less melodramatic. The cynic in her was about to comment, but she held herself back, true to her decision that unless some horrible hidden secret were to be revealed, she would forgive her friend and they would move on. As her sister was fond of saying, "No need adding oil to a flame."

Despite herself, Abhaya smirked, and that did not go unnoticed.

Janaki raised an eyebrow.

"You know, as my father often says," Abhaya rushed, hoping to cover up her unintended reaction, "'There are a lot of ugly things floating in the Yamuna river, but the stream carries them away and the waters are still sacred.'"

Janaki watched her, feeling like a defendant awaiting her fate at the judge's hands.

"Our friendship is the river, Janaki," Abhaya said. "Let us put that miserable evening behind us, good intentions or not." She smiled at Janaki.

Janaki relaxed her shoulders and smiled back timidly. Just then the school bell rang.

Perfect timing, thought Abhaya, concerned that with one battle down, Janaki might bring up John's text message again.

Abhaya was not quite sure certain that she was as ready to share new secrets with her old friend. *Janaki will need to regain my trust before that can happen.*

CHAPTER 32

NEW DELHI

Ten past noon on a Friday, Devidas removed his shoes and entered his guru's little ashram, a space slightly larger than Devidas' own living room. This was where his revered teacher lived, taught and worshiped. The abode, unnoticed by most passersby, was located at the end of a narrow alley within a short walking distance of the sacred Yamuna. Its interior was simple. It had a straw mat at the far end of the room and an altar with several deities including Ganesha, Durga and Kali on the other side.

Once inside, Devidas was hit by the familiar strong smell of incense, almost too powerful to bear. For him this was the scent of faith, the perfume of aspiration, a symbol of a different and greater sort of love and devotion. In addition, the ashram was very hot and humid, much more so than outside, where a light breeze made the mid-day air tolerable. A born and bred New Delhi native who was used to the heat, Devidas still felt sweat breaking out, a narrow stream creeping down the back of his head along the length of his spine. Was it just the heat? he asked himself, or was it also a sense of awe for his master?

The guru, a small dark man, was wrapped in orange clothing that threatened to swallow his thin frame. Always orange, thought Devidas, signifying the purifying power of Agni, fire, and the illuminating quality of the sun, driving away the darkness of ignorance. The guru sat on a small cushion on the floor, legs entangled in a classic lotus pose, feet on opposite thighs. Despite years of attempts, it was a posture Devidas never quite mastered.

As soon as Devidas entered the space, he bowed and knelt down, bringing his forehead to the ground. First, he faced his guru and then the altar with the deities. He mouthed a prayer expressing his thanks and obedience to his master, the remover of darkness and ignorance. With his eyes closed and his posture quiet, the guru did not seem to notice his disciple. His thick white beard covered dried lips that seemed to be repeating a mantra, a sacred prayer, over and over again. Devidas sat back on his heels, keeping a distance from his guru but watching him intensely.

He took a quick peek at his wristwatch: twenty past noon. Devidas asked for and was granted a longer than usual lunch break, but time was running out. If he were to be back at the office in time, he would have to leave the ashram by 12:50 p.m. at the latest, only thirty minutes from now. A horrible thought crossed his mind. Who knows if the guru will acknowledge me at all?

Another thought, even worse than the first: What if the guru grants me an interview mere minutes before I need to head back? After all, the disciple cannot be rude to his guru and just get up and go. Once the interview gets started, I will need to wait it out patiently, no matter how long it takes.

If Devidas was sweating before, the trickles turned into a steady stream. Anxiety creeped from his belly into his chest. Did he remember to take the aspirin his doctor friend prescribed for him a few weeks ago?

That was after he started experiencing occasional chest pains. He was almost sure he took it with his tea earlier this morning. By the grace of my guru, he told himself, this will all work out. The guru will acknowledge me shortly, he will inquire why I came, he will guide me with his wisdom, and I will be back at the office in time.

Another glance at the watch. Can it be twelve thirty-five already? Why does time flash by so fast when one is in a hurry? All this, he decided, was just another teaching his guru was imparting onto him: the merits of patience and trust. Trust my guru, trust my guru, trust my guru, Devidas kept repeating to himself, as if it were a sacred mantra.

Five minutes later the guru opened his eyes, as if waking from a trance. He turned his head, seemingly surprised to see Devidas, and smiled.

That was when Devidas realized he had not brought his guru any offering. Tradition had it that a disciple always brings something to offer his holy teacher. The wealthy bring valuable possessions, but the poor are still expected to bring something: a piece of fruit, a flower, a leaf, anything.

It was too late.

The guru must have noticed the look of terror on Devidas' face as his own expression twisted with compassion. He indicated that Devidas may approach.

Devidas rose, walked the short distance, and then knelt down again, sending a hand to touch his guru's feet. This was the tradition, acknowledging his master's divine nature. The old man gestured for him to sit, and Devidas, a small part in the back of his mind counting off the passing minutes of his lunch break like grains in an hour glass, sat crossed legged where instructed.

"What is on your mind, my dearest Devidas?" asked the guru.

"Guru," started Devidas. He tried again, "Guru-ji, I humbly seek your advice on a rather earthly matter." He hesitated, voice weakening. Up until now he always approached his guru only on matters of spiritual guidance, never for anything materialistic. Yet today he was about to break that convention and he did not even bring an offering for his teacher. How foolish.

His guru did not reproach him. Instead, he raised an eyebrow and said, somewhat puzzled, "Continue."

"You see, guru-ji, my family... I... we have fallen on hard times." Devidas thought he noticed a slight change in the guru's face, but he was not sure what to make of it. Is my guru upset? Should I stop? Nevertheless, he continued: "At work, people are being laid off or fired. For me, they reduced my salary. My older daughter went to work...." Devidas was certain he noticed an expression of disapproval on the old man's face. He quickly added, "I didn't want this to happen, but what was I to do? It was either her or sending my wife out. I am at a loss as to what to do. I beg you, please, guide me."

The guru furrowed his eyebrows, looking sharply at Devidas.

Devidas lowered his head, gazing at the guru's feet. Some time passed by, and Devidas did not dare, nor much cared, to look at his watch. He knew he would have to work out some lame excuse for his tardiness when he got back to the office. That may cost him his job. Today might be his last day.

How ironic, he thought. Here I am, coming to seek my guru's advice about what to do with the little I have left, and now it might cost me all that I have left.

The guru remained silent. Sometime later when Devidas did finally dare looking up again, he saw that his holy teacher had closed his eyes. The guru's lips went back to mumbling whatever it was before his arrival. Devidas watched him, fear mixed with anticipation.

No doubt I upset him.

Devidas reproached himself. He knew his teacher was superbly traditional and did not view women in a household as workers, that is, aside from being homemakers. "The Vedas, our holy scriptures," he had lectured to his disciples, time and again when the topic came up, "indicate that a woman's main role is to help her husband perform his duties. Otherwise a woman's ultimate function is childrearing, raising children and bringing them up to be obedient followers of the divine. Not dressing up as in the West to go to work. Tsk."

Long moments passed. A chai wallah announcing his offering of hot tea could be heard from down the main street. A sneak glimpse at his wristwatch told Devidas that if he left right now, he would already be ten minutes late. His guru maintained his posture, eyes closed, lips moving silently.

Is he praying for me? Or what else is he is trying to teach me? Devidas struggled helplessly. He could take it no longer. Like it or not, he realized nothing else would be said. His audience with the guru was over. Devidas bowed his head deeply to his teacher and backed out of the room on his knees. Glancing at his guru one last time before exiting, Devidas saw the holy man he admired so much as still as a statue, enwrapped in his orange solitude. A little man. Then another horrible thought crossed Devidas's mind: What if the guru is just an ordinary man? A man just like me, lost without a clue?

This notion was too much to bear. Devidas quickly wrote it off. He put on his shoes and started running toward his office, almost knocking down the chai wallah as he entered the avenue from the narrow street. His breath short and choppy, he felt the pressure growing heavy on his chest.

CHAPTER 33

NEW DELHI

Feeling conflicted, Janaki stared at her computer screen, determined to do right by her friend. It was Friday afternoon, a day after she and Abhaya had reconciled. Now Chetan's face was staring right back at her from his Facebook page, good-looking Chetan in his Kung Fu uniform. Was it Kung Fu, Karate, or another martial art that he practiced? She could not tell the difference. Kung Fu seemed to stick with her because of that funny animated movie. She had already decided to give him up and do whatever she could to make good on her word: introduce him to Abhaya.

But why did he have to be so darned handsome?

Two sides of herself were at war with each other.

"To heck with him. I hate him!" Jealous Janaki raged and pouted.

"No, wait...I also have a crush on him," said Loving Janaki.

Janaki put her hands to her face and pressed her palms into her eyes.

So confusing, and no one to ask. Usually, she would have consulted Abhaya, but she couldn't figure out how to do this when her friend was also her competitor.

Or was she? It was not Abhaya's fault, thought Loving Janaki, and Abhaya was not even aware of Chetan's crush on her.

"Why does Abhaya need to be so pretty?" Jealous Janaki was at it again. "And so smart? I hate her, too!"

Loving Janaki stepped in. "But she's my only true friend."

Janaki typed "Abby Smith" in the Facebook search bar. Too many results came up. She narrowed the search, and the picture Abhaya selected for her avatar popped up.

Was this Abby pretty? Janaki wondered. She presumed she was, at least to a Westerner's eye. To Janaki's eye, the woman in the picture had a mouth that was too small and eyes that were too narrow. Her hairstyle was out of fashion, and… her skin was too fair.

That last item was a bit of a touchy subject for her. Some years ago, around the time that Janaki reached puberty, she became aware more than ever of her appearance. She realized in a new way what she had not fully comprehended: that her skin was two shades darker than that of the average New Delhiite.

Color mattered, and that darker brown put her at a disadvantage in a society in which lighter was idealized as "better." Born to a father whose shade was deep, and a mother whose skin was bright, Janaki seemed to have inherited more of her father's genes. For a while Janaki, who had her mother's silent approval, obsessed over expensive skin-lightening products. She thought those had helped a bit, but as time went by, Janaki realized it was a losing battle.

Luckily for her, Janaki also inherited some of her dad's wits. All of a sudden, one bright morning, she had a change of mind, a perspective she voiced out loud to just about anyone willing to listen. Her message was that people should be proud of their brown skin, and not ashamed. "The contemporary caste system," she explained after researching the topic extensively, more than any other topic she had ever studied at school, "evolved from the ancient Vedic tradition, a system that was based on social groupings related to occupation and not to skin tone."

From that point on, Janaki ignored references to colorism, and sometimes showed outright disdain for any related bias, especially if a person's skin tone was lighter than her own. She realized she was a bit of a hypocrite, but so were those with lighter skin shades who claimed colorism made no difference but still were snobbish when dealing with darker people.

In that respect, Janaki had mixed feelings about Abhaya. She knew Abhaya adored Westerners, admired them as a model to be emulated, and that their fair skin was part of the deal.

Yet at least her friend did not try to pretend that skin color did not matter. To her it did. Abhaya, she knew, was no hypocrite. She spoke her mind. As far as Janaki could tell, Abhaya never looked down on others, even if she herself did idealize lighter shades.

Jealous Janaki huffed and switched to Abhaya's own Facebook page. She looked at Abhaya's photo, an image that Janaki herself took of her friend, laughing delightedly at some foolish thing she had said several weeks ago. Abhaya loved that photo so much that she instantly made it her profile picture, a fact Janaki enjoyed tremendously. So pretty and so not aware of it. Janaki sighed.

All at once she felt immensely sad, tears clouding her eyes.

What is wrong with me? Why am I crying?

She tried to stop the tears from becoming a stream. She imagined her mother's calming voice saying, "It's okay. You are going through hormonal changes and your brain is rewiring itself. This is all normal for your age."

"No, it is not!" she could see herself screaming at her mom. "It is not okay! It is not normal! I hate it! I hate you!"

But her mom would just smile and hug her.

At the time, Janaki cried and cried and when she thought she was done crying, she cried some more.

Looking back, she was reflective. How lucky I am to have such an understanding mom.

A second thought followed quickly. How lucky I am to have Abhaya as my friend.

Resolved, she pulled out her phone. "I'm better than this," she said out loud. "I can do the right thing." She opened a message thread with Abhaya and typed, "Abhaya, next week we're done with school. How about a film Sat eve?"

CHAPTER 34

NEW DELHI

Friday afternoons, Chetan worked at the fish market. It was a job Arjuna's dad arranged for him. It wasn't the sort of work he aspired to do the rest of his life. Yet it paid fairly well, and the fishmonger that employed Chetan, a large bustling man named Bhima, was kind to him.

Chetan did not have to deal with customers. That was a big plus since it involved haggling, a skill Chetan was far from mastering. He cleaned the fish, organized them neatly on trays, refilled ice to preserve their freshness, and, when there was nothing else to do, used a fan to scatter the never-ending stream of flies constantly buzzing around the fresh kill.

Chetan did not mind hard work. His parents raised him to be unspoiled, but he found this particular job challenging for other reasons. The market's loud noises–sellers announcing their wares, merchants haggling with customers, motorcycles passing by, and young kids wailing–all combined into a cacophony that Chetan found hard to bear. Worst of all were the smells. They would stick to his clothing and skin for days.

He still recalled how he had asked Bhima what he could do to rid himself of the distinctive stench at the end of his first day on the job.

"What?" replied Bhima loudly, theatrically sniffing his own palm while staring at Chetan quizzically. "You don't like it?"

Chetan, embarrassed, started stuttering. "It's... it's not that I don't like it...."

A wide smile spread over the fishmonger's large face, and akin to someone sniffing the perfume of the love of his life, he stated loudly yet dreamily, "It's just w-o-n-d-e-r-f-u-l!"

To this day, Chetan was not sure if Bhima was poking fun at him, or whether the merchant really was that much in love with his trade. Either way, Chetan never dared broach the topic again.

Luckily there was the Internet. Chetan did his research the first chance he had. He found several tricks to help keep the stench to a minimum. Rubbing his body with lemons worked miracles. When those weren't available, he used a piece of stainless steel "soap" he'd purchased online. Strangely enough, that seemed to do the trick. He taught his mother to add baking soda to any laundry that included his work cloths. That helped, too. It's enough, he thought, that I have to deal with my acne. Hanuman, be my helper if my friends ever get wind of this smell. I'll be the laughing stock of the entire school until my graduation!

Yet he had to survive this job. It paid well. Knowing his family was too poor to spare him any spending money, Chetan saved his earnings, rupee by rupee, for the day that he would be able to take Abhaya out on a date.

My girlfriend, Abhaya. The thought passed uninvited through his mind. He felt his face redden and butterflies in his stomach. Then another thought flashed by. What am I to do with her once we're finally on a date?

He knew nothing about girls. His parents were very conservative and such topics were never discussed at home. He tried to read about it online but what came up in the search results was either porn or suggestions too daring for him.

"Chetan," thundered Bhima out of nowhere, "what are you doing?"

Chetan jolted from his daydreams. Oh boy, he thought, this is exactly what I do not need right now: angering my boss.

"Good job," called Bhima, examining the neatly organized pile of surmai and kingfish. "You can take twenty minutes off, but make sure to be back on time!"

"Are you sure, Sir?" asked Chetan.

Although Bhima always treated him well, rarely did he give him a break. "Get out of here!" cried his boss, smiling. "Now!"

He must be up to something, thought Chetan, as he collected his bag and headed toward the tea stall. Bhima, Chetan suspected, had some shady side dealings with black-market money launderers. As much as he trusted Chetan, that trust did not extend to such dealings. Chetan was not offended. Some things he preferred not knowing.

Finding the chai wallah, Chetan paid the tea preparer six of his precious rupees and watched patiently as the old man boiled the water and tea leaves in front of him and added spices and milk. He then strained the pot into a plastic cup and handed it to Chetan. Just then Chetan's phone rang once: a text message. He found a place to sit by the curb, and careful not to spill the hot liquid, pulled out his phone. It was from Arjuna.

"How's it going, my friend?"

Chetan placed the cup between his feet and typed. "How do you think it going? Stinking fish… I don't know if I should be thankful to your dad for arranging this job, or hate him."

The phone buzzed again. To Chetan's surprise it was Janaki. He opened her message, excitedly.

"Hi. Busy?"

The phone buzzed yet again with a message from Arjuna, but Chetan had answered Janaki's first. "Kind of. I'm at work."

He bit his lips. He should not have said this. She did not know he worked, and he did not want her to learn the sort of work he did, for fear that Janaki might tell Abhaya. He then switched to the message thread with Arjuna.

Arjuna wrote, "Well, you know what they say–better one fish in the hand. Hahaha!"

Chetan smiled and quickly replied, "that's a bird in the hand, dummy!"

The phone buzzed again. A message from Janaki.

"I didn't know u work. What sort of work do u do?"

That was exactly what Chetan feared.

While he considered a reply, another message came from Arjuna. "I know, I know, you're a fish out of the swimming pool! ;-)"

Chetan grinned. "That's out of the water, you imbecile!"

He was well aware that Arjuna was doing this on purpose to amuse him. Yet this game, which they played on occasion, gave Chetan the strange satisfaction of proving his intellectual superiority.

The phone buzzed again.

Janaki texted, "I'm waiting. Actually, never mind that right now. I have some good news 4 u re: Abhaya."

Holy crap, thought Chetan, good news! He hastily looked at a new message that just came from Arjuna before replying to Janaki.

Arjuna wrote, "I understand. You're a big shot now and have bigger fish to fly."

Chetan giggled and was about to hit reply when the next message came from Janaki. Too curious to wait, he switched to her message screen.

"Are u ignoring me?"

Chetan nervously clutched his jaw. He pondered what to answer. A car, passing by a little too fast and a little too close, hit a mud puddle and splashed residue into Chetan's tea cup. He looked at it, confused, amazed and irritated. Six rupees down the drain. Absorbed by the mud in his tea, he typed to Janaki the answer that his mind had prepared for Arjuna. "Bigger fish to fry, not fly."

Then he noticed the time on his phone. It was several minutes past the twenty given him for his break.

"Holy crap! Crap!" he called aloud, attracting a harsh glare from an older woman passing by. Pressing "Send" as he got up, Chetan knocked over the chai he never had a chance to drink and rushed back to work.

In her room, Janaki stared at the screen: "Bigger fish to fry, not fly." What in the world does that mean? Is this jerk toying with me? She finally managed to set up a situation where she would be able to get him to meet Abhaya, and this was her reward?

"Good thing that I don't care for him anymore," she declared. And besides, he's too tall for me, and also too thin, not to mentioned too quiet. She smirked. And probably too poor. This princess needs someone with the means to take care of her! Yet her pride did not allow her to send him another message, asking for clarifications about his awkward text message. She would corner him about this another time. The new Janaki, she told herself, controls and leads the situation. She does not let others play her.

CHAPTER 35

NEW DELHI

Jeevana and Prema were having an early lunch at Padma Taalaab, The Lotus Pond, a vegetarian restaurant of Prema's choice in southwestern New Delhi. Prema was dressed in a tight stretchable outfit, the sort Western women wear for yoga practice.

"What's up with these pants and the tank-top?" asked Jeevana, raising an eyebrow. She was not the only one; quite a few other locals were staring openly at Prema.

"Oh, I don't think I mentioned it to you," replied Prema while considering items in the menu. "I now teach yoga, and I recommend the chole biryani. Also their rice rava upma. It's simply delicious. Actually, everything here is yummy. And," she added, lowering her voice, "quite affordable."

"Wait! Wait a minute," cried Jeevana, looking up from the menu and gaping at Prema. "First you tell me you turned vegetarian, and now you tell me you also teach yoga? What other surprises do you have for me?"

"None," replied Prema. Without looking at Jeevana, she reconsidered. "Well, almost none, but can we first order, please? I'm famished. I don't eat a couple of hours before the yoga class and by the time the practice is over, I could eat a cow. That is, if I were no longer a vegetarian." She smiled meekly.

"Okay, okay," replied Jeevana and waved for the waiter.

Lunch order placed, Prema became more aware of the stares she was receiving from the other guests. She covered herself with a shawl that she pulled out of her bag.

Jeevana was still unsatisfied by Prema's short answer earlier. "To the best of my recollection–and not that I practiced yoga myself but my mom did years ago–all she wore was a casual sari. I went with her to class once when I was very young. And I remember that most other people there were wearing either a plain sari or track pants and a loose t-shirt."

"Well," replied Prema, "you see, you're thinking traditional Hindu yoga. I teach near where the Western Help Desk centers are, probably very close to where you work, and it is Western style yoga. They expect me to dress up in this way."

"Western-style yoga?" wondered Jeevana, her puzzlement showing on her face. "I thought that yoga was yoga. What is Western style yoga?"

"Ha, ha, ha!" Prema cackled, "you don't know the half of it!" The waiter came by and brought several appetizers served in small dishes, which Prema ingested whole.

"Sorry," she said, her mouth full, "I'm soooo hungry. I really should eat slower. Eating fast is really bad for digestion." Moments later with the appetizer dishes empty, Prema seemed a little more settled.

"You were saying?" poked Jeevana.

"Saying?" replied Prema. "Oh yes, yoga. You see, in the US and elsewhere in the West, yoga is a big industry. It's not like here, where it is part of a spiritual and religious practice. There, it's all about fashion and showing-off, like who's most flexible and who's cool."

Jeevana's shock must have shown on her face as Prema smiled. "It's still yoga but with a twist. First, the people in the West have multiple types of yoga, some you probably never heard of."

"Such as?"

"Such as Nude Yoga," grinned Prema.

"Wait, wait!" Jeevana's voice rose to almost a shout, "I consider myself quite progressive but," eyes looking around to make sure no one was listening and dropping her voice to a whisper, "what exactly is Nude Yoga?"

"It is exactly what it says," replied Prema smiling. "People who do yoga in the nude."

At that moment, the waiter came by bringing more dishes. Overhearing Prema saying the word "nude," he snuck a quick glance at her. Atypical for Prema, she blushed.

Jeevana, noticing all this, whispered to her friend once the waiter was gone, "it's okay, he's kind of cute…"

"Oh hush up!" called Prema, her cheeks reddening even more.

"Haha!" laughed Jeevana. It felt good to laugh. She had almost forgotten how good it felt to laugh. Prema smiled, too.

"You were saying?" prodded Jeevana.

"What can I tell you?" said Prema in between bites into of the newly arrived dishes, "They're strange in the West. They have "Doga" which is yoga for dogs and their owners...."

Jeevana, her mouth full, burst into laughter, spraying food all over the table. "I'm so sorry, I just couldn't help it." She bent to wipe it up, still apologizing. "What else did they come up with?"

"There is 'aerial yoga' where people do yoga hanging from the ceiling in anti-gravity silk hammocks, 'paddleboard yoga,' which is yoga on a flat board on the water. There is 'mommy-and-me yoga' for mothers and their toddlers, and many other sorts."

"What?!" exclaimed Jeevana.

"Yes," replied Prema, "if our yoga forefathers could ever hear of this, they would no doubt come back, reincarnated, to take charge of this circus. But this is how it goes in the West."

"How do you know all this?" wondered Jeevana.

"I heard about all this from my Western students."

"Were they pulling your leg?" Jeevana could not believe such things actually existed, no matter how much she trusted her friend.

"Not at all," Prema countered. "I looked it up online afterwards. Like I said, Westerners can be weird."

Digesting all that she just heard, Jeevana fell silent for moment. "Okay," she said, "but none of this explains how you got into this yoga-teaching business in the first place. I don't recall you being much into the physical aspects of the body, or even spirituality, when we were growing up."

"True," replied Prema, wiping her mouth with a napkin. "This all began sometime after my family moved away. I was very much alone and was looking to make new friends."

There was no accusation in her voice though Jeevana felt a tinge of guilt.

"Someone was giving a yoga lesson in my new neighborhood, a traditional yoga class. Nothing crazy like I just told you. I took it and it clicked. You know how it is in life. Sometimes it's all about timing, and yoga was right for me at that time. I learned to listen to my body. Yoga has been, at least for me, a wonderful unexpected gift. Looking back," she reflected, "mostly good has come out of that horrible incident and the move that followed."

Jeevana flinched at her mention of that event.

Prema did not seem to notice. "As you're fond of saying, 'Everything happens for a reason.' I didn't use to believe it, but now I do."

They were quiet for a while.

"Is that also when you became a vegetarian?" Jeevana asked. "I do recall you devouring your mom's chicken tikka masala when we were kids. That was," she added dreamily, "among the few times I was able to taste meat, you know, given that our household is strictly vegetarian."

"That was a great dish!" agreed Prema as the memory caused a soft smile to spread across her face. "But no, that didn't happen immediately. It was a few years later," she said. "You see, I was dating this guy...."

"Dating a guy?" exclaimed Jeevana. "I knew there was more you didn't tell me."

"It wasn't that serious, though at the time, I thought it was," responded Prema. "Anyhow, he was a yogi and a vegetarian, and I was a young woman in love. I took to avoiding meat, all types of meat, and my body seemed to agree. This was, oh, maybe five years ago."

"And you have never had meat since?" wondered Jeevana, still baffled at how her friend the carnivore was a carnivore no more.

"No," replied Prema. "I just didn't care for it anymore."

"That explains the vegetarian part, but not how you became a yoga instructor, and for Westerners, of all people," said Jeevana.

"It's a long story," replied Prema, "and we're short on time. Wasn't there something you wanted to discuss with me urgently? What's up? When you called me last night asking to meet for lunch today, you sounded as if you'd just discovered you'd grown another head."

Prema's reminder of the purpose of their meeting pulled Jeevana right back to reality. The color drained from her face. She felt her tongue stuck to the roof of her mouth and terror took hold.

Prema jolted, shocked at her friend's sudden transformation.

Taking a deep breath, she narrowed her eyes and took Jeevana's hand. "Okay," she said softly, "I think I can guess. It's that jerk at your workplace, isn't it? I almost forgot about the advice I gave you. I guess you took it, and your 'date' is coming up. That's it, isn't it?"

Jeevana, still frozen, slowly nodded her head for yes.

"Did you try to find another job as we discussed?" asked Prema still holding Jeevana's hand, stroking her forearm.

Jeevana nodded her head again.

Prema, maintaining eye contact with Jeevana, pinched her arm.

"Ouch!" cried Jeevana, pulling her arm away. Shock and then anger replaced the horror on her face. "What was that for?"

"Snap out of it, girl." laughed Prema, "It's not the end of the world! How did the job search go?"

Jeevana, rubbing the reddening spot quipped, "Well, I thought it went pretty well. I interviewed with two places. Both seemed to like me, but they have no immediate openings. They said they'll contact me once something opens up. The thing is, I need a job, like right now. I cannot go even a week without bringing in some money." Jeevana shook her head and stared at the ground, her thoughts turning to her family's dire situation.

Prema looked at her friend thoughtfully yet said nothing.

Jeevana continued. "It is so unfair. I gave up an academic career. I could have been someone, maybe a famous researcher, a science professor, but now I'm stuck in a lousy call center with someone who harasses me. It's just not fair."

Prema listened.

"Well?" prodded Jeevana, "say something!"

"Hmm..." replied Prema.

"That's all you can say?" questioned Jeevana.

"Nooo," responded Prema, extending the vowel. "I can also say Ommm...and Emmm... but it would all mean the same."

"Which is?" demanded Jeevana. The joke was lost on her.

"It means, 'really?'" said Prema, as if talking to a child.

"What do you mean by that?" Jeevana folded her arms, clearly insulted.

"It means that you had a choice," said Prema.

"What choice? I had to do it, I had to drop out of college so I could help support my family."

"No, you didn't." Prema pointing a finger at her friend. "You were the top of our class. The top of our entire school! A rising star. You were accepted on full scholarship, including room and board, to a prestigious college. You could have stayed there."

"But my family...," protested Jeevana.

"Right. Let me tell you something," said Prema. "Your family could have managed. One way or another, they could have managed. Dropping out of college was your choice. Trust me, I know all about choices."

Jeevana felt hurt. Her hands dropped to her thighs and she found herself looking anywhere except her friend's eyes.

Prema glanced at her wristwatch and then flagged the waiter to bring the check. "I'm sorry," she told Jeevana. "I didn't realize the time. I must be leaving very soon. I need to change for work since I have another gig this evening."

"Another gig?" asked Jeevana. "Doing what? I thought you worked in an office."

"Yes I do, five days a week. But I also have the yoga thing going on, and some evenings I also tend bar at a pub that serves Western workers."

"You what!?" cried Jeevana, shocked, forgetting her earlier anger.

"Never mind that now," said Prema, taking the bill from the waiter and pulling out her wallet.

"Here," said Jeevana reaching for her own, "let me pay."

"No way," responded Prema, placing her hand on the check to hide the amount. "This one is on me. I'm so sorry, but I really have to go. I'll call you tonight and we can continue this over the phone."

"I'm working tonight."

"What time are you off?" asked Prema.

"It's the late shift, one I particularly hate," answered Jeevana. "It ends at midnight."

"You know what?" said Prema, "I'm done at the pub at one. Why don't you stop by on your way back home and we'll finish this chat in person?" She rose to go.

"Me?" responded Jeevana. "A pub? My father would skin me alive if he ever found out. It's enough that I work at the help center and wear Western clothing!"

"He doesn't need to know. I'll text you the address. I'm sure it's close to where you work."

"I don't know...."

"Come on!" exclaimed Prema.

"We'll see," replied Jeevana.

CHAPTER 36

NEW YORK CITY

Rachel had just entered the crowded subway car when her phone vibrated. It announced an incoming text message. There is absolutely no way I'm going to pull my phone out of my pocket right now, she thought, as she struggled to find a roomier spot. Crushed against the masses of the New York City's morning rush hour, she could hardly breath. Whatever it is, it can wait.

John sneaked one last glance at his phone. Still no answer. He was about to start his morning shift at the coffee shop, and there was a strict no phone policy during the busy morning crunch, enforced by his shift's supervisor. "Why isn't she answering?" he wondered, unaware that he was mumbling aloud.

"What's up, lover boy?" teased Latisha, his co-worker. John did not know her real age. She kept on coming up with a different figure each time someone asked, but to him she could be twice his age. "Your woman's ignoring you again? Come to mama, I'll give you some love..." and, smiling, she blew a kiss in his direction.

John felt his cheeks flush. Even in his twenties, he still seemed prone to blushing. There was no malice or truth in Latisha's comment and John knew better than to respond to her. Experience had taught him that one retort could start a teasing spree lasting all morning long. He just tucked his phone back into his bag, making sure to turn the ringer off so as to not upset his supervisor. Tying on his work apron, he stood behind the counter. His first client of the day was a pale young woman that seemed all too familiar to him.

"Abby?" he muttered.

"Excuse me?" snipped the woman. It wasn't really a question.

"I'm sorry," he said. "I must have mistaken you for someone else. What'll you have?"

The Abby look-alike huffed, "That's okay, just a cappuccino, one shot, and light on the milk." A split second later, she added, "You know what? On second thought, make it soy. I just remembered that I'm dairy-free this week." While John rang up the order, Latisha passed by and whispered in his ear, "That desperate, aren't you?"

John felt his ears burning but said nothing. He collected himself, ignored Latisha, and told the customer, "That'll be $4.25 please." At the far end of the counter, inside a bag stashed underneath a coat, his phone quivered with a new text. He hoped it was Rachel, but John would not see it for hours.

CHAPTER 37

NEW DELHI

"You!" Chetan froze.

"Yes, you! I need a word with you!"

Turning around, he saw Janaki approaching him, all business. The bell signaling the last period of the school-day rang. Holding his Taekwondo practice bag, Chetan was on his way to meet Arjuna in order to head to the studio together.

"Now explain," Janaki's voice wavering between irritation and curiosity, "What you meant by texting me, 'bigger fish to fry, not fly?'"

Chetan had no clue whatsoever what she was referring to. His dumbstruck face must have annoyed her, making irritation overcome curiosity.

"Listen, you blockhead, this is the text message you sent me a few days ago. What does it mean?"

Chetan was racking his brain, but he had no recollection of sending Janaki, of all people, such a strange text message. *Why would I do that?* he kept asking himself.

All he remembered from Friday was that when he had returned to the fishmarket after his break, a little later than his allotted time, Bhima was waiting and looking at his wristwatch. The fishmonger was not in a good mood, probably due to a deal gone bad, and he took it out on Chetan.

"I'm so sorry," uttered Chetan with difficulty, "but I truly don't remember."

"Oh, all right!" Janaki realized she was making this a bigger deal than it deserved. On top of that she was losing her temper in public, something the "new" Janaki did not want to do. She softened her voice a little, smoothed her stubborn curly hair and continued as if nothing just happened.

"So, we need to chat about my plan for you to meet with you-know-who."

"You mean Abhaya?" asked Chetan.

Two girls passed by and giggled, unrelated to the conversation between Janaki and Chetan, but Janaki looked at them and thought otherwise.

She hissed at Chetan, "Can't you take a hint and keep your voice low? Soon the whole school will know about this, and then what do you think will happen?"

"What?"

"Let's take a short walk and I'll tell you," said Janaki, heading toward the school's gate.

Chetan felt torn. On one hand, this was exactly what he had hoped would happen for so long, but on the other hand, Arjuna would soon be waiting.

"I can't," he said, his voice wavering, no longer following in her footsteps.

"You what? Seriously? I go through all this trouble to arrange this... this...." For a moment she found herself at a loss for words, "this... setup, and this is what I get in return? Is that what you meant by 'bigger fish to fry?' Is Abhaya no longer the girl of your dreams?"

"No, no, it's not that. You don't understand," protested Chetan. "I do want this to happen, very much so, but...."

"But what?" Janaki snapped. "You either come with me now or forget about the whole thing. I put too much effort into this, and I don't feel like being toyed around with."

Chetan, glancing nervously at his wristwatch, started toward Janaki.

That's better, she murmured to herself. She was surprised to find that a part of her actually enjoyed this, pulling the strings of her own little private puppet show. If I cannot have Chetan for myself, she thought, then at least I can have fun playing the director in this theatrical staging.

"Now listen," she whispered, once they were out of earshot of the other students, "Saturday evening, I don't care if you have any other plans, you drop them."

"I don't have any plans," Chetan said.

Janaki wasn't listening. "Cancel your other plans because you will be showing up, as if by chance, at the same movie theater that Abhaya and I will be going to." She halted and faced him. "Are you listening?"

"Yes, of course," he echoed. "Saturday evening, no other plans, I'm going to show up where you tell me to."

"That's correct. So this is what will happen next," she said, and she laid out her secret plan.

Twenty minutes later Janaki suddenly remembered that she had an appointment at the hair salon and cut her tale short. "You got this? I've got to go."

As soon as she was gone, Chetan ran back toward school, hoping against hope that Arjuna would still be there.

"What's the big rush?" boomed a familiar voice. "Some wildcat is chasing you, oh Lord of the Feline Species?" Arjuna was sitting atop a low stonewall, just outside the schoolyard.

"Thank God, you're still here," gasped Chetan. He then bent over double, trying to catch his breath.

"Of course, I'm here," said Arjuna. "Where else would I be? I'm not like you, oh immortal one. I cannot be at two places at the same time. I'm but a simple man. I can only be at one place at a time."

Chetan found that surprisingly funny, but still being out of air, his laughter turned quickly into a cough.

"There, there," called out Arjuna. "First, catch your breath and then laugh. You're still trying to do too many things at once." He got off the wall and tapped his friend on the back.

They began walking toward the studio.

"Now tell me," he said, "what's this? Have you got that many girl-friends all of a sudden? Is it your reputation as a cat slayer?" Arjuna turned serious. "Can you teach me how you do this thing, attracting so many female admirers?"

Chetan slowed his walk and turned to look at Arjuna who wore a very straight face. Reading no mockery, Chetan's face twisted into a question mark.

Arjuna held that face for a moment longer before bursting into laughter so hard and raucous that it seemed a sudden thunderstorm fell upon the entire city.

Caught by surprise, Chetan's face flushed crimson. Had he been a cartoon, steam would have come out of his ears.

"You--!" he protested. "You... you big piece of...!" So flustered was Chetan that he could not come up with an insult strong enough. He ended up muttering "of...of something!"

That made Arjuna laugh even harder.

Chetan's anger subsided more quickly than usual as his thoughts turned into anticipation for his dream come true: a date with Abhaya. Of course it was not really a date since Abhaya had no clue that he would be there. Still, it was as close to a date as he could have hoped for.

Chetan found himself debating whether to share the plan with his best friend. Janaki had warned him against telling anyone, and Chetan considered himself a man of his word. Though concerned that Arjuna would poke fun at the whole thing, he was dying to tell someone, and Arjuna was his closest friend.

"So tell me," asked Arjuna, just as Chetan was about to spit it out, "Who was this girl I saw you speaking with? She's not the one you're in love with, right?"

Chetan motioned to Arjuna to keep his voice low. "No, no," he replied and said no more.

Arjuna's thundering voice made him decide in that moment not to share anything with his giant friend. He imagined Arjuna unintentionally disclosing the secret just by speaking in his usual loud voice.

"She's a friend of the one I like," added Chetan, realizing that Arjuna was still waiting for details, "and she's helping me with some advice."

Arjuna was about to prod further, but Chetan was saved by their instructor who, impatiently, waved them over.

They were late.

The two rushed to change into their practice uniforms and went in.

Once inside and going through their warmup exercises, Arjuna whispered to Chetan, "I think I like that one, that girl you spoke with. She's like a hot pepper, very fiery, exactly my type." He winked at Chetan. "Maybe...do you think you could talk with her about me? You know, help set me up with her?"

Chetan's jaw dropped. "You?" he cried out loud. "You need me to help you set up with her?" Chetan just could not have imagined that the outgoing Arjuna would ever ask of him something like that. Him, of all people.

"You two," called their instructor, "give me fifty pushups right now. First, you arrive late, and now you run your mouths?"

Chetan and Arjuna dropped to the floor and started pumping.

CHAPTER 38

NEW DELHI

Abhaya felt like she was going to pass out. It was Friday afternoon and the early afternoon sun beat relentlessly against the windows, setting the humid room on fire.

Abhaya refused to let the heat get to her. She had to finish this project, and this was the perfect opportunity. Her parents were both out. Her dad was at work and her mom was at the market. No time to waste. She was to deliver the last part of the project to John tomorrow. In an attempt to further impress him, she was eager to complete it today, ahead of schedule. The few other lighter jobs she earned through the freelancing website were mostly done. She would complete those in a day or two, probably ahead of deadline. But it was John that Abhaya wanted to astound. She had already finished writing the actual code. What remained was testing and debugging.

Abhaya wiped beads of sweat from her forehead and gazed at the screen. An old Lady Gaga song play on YouTube through her earphones, masking street noises from the open window. Abhaya only dared to listen to Western music when she was absolutely sure that no one else was home. She turned up the volume on the video but her work in another window mostly obscured the video. "Bad Romance" had Abhaya tapping her toes.

Someone tapped her on her shoulder. Abhaya gasped in terror and turned around. It was her father.

Now she really was going to pass out.

"What is this?" asked Father, nodding his head at the computer screen. His voice was calm, but calm was not always a good sign with him.

"Oh, this?" stuttered Abhaya, taking her earphones off. "Nothing really, nothing, just some computer homework." Abhaya knew her dad was a complete novice when it came to anything to do with technology, but her heart was still beating fast.

"I see," said Father, again not betraying what he was really thinking.

Lady Gaga still crooned through the earphones that now rested around Abhaya's neck and shoulders. Did he hear that? Abhaya panicked. God forbid he sees the video. That will be the last time I'm ever allowed near a computer! Abhaya reached out, seized the mouse and, in a somewhat atypically jerky motion, closed the invisible tab playing the video. The singer's voice lingered for a moment in the earphones before fading away onto cyberspace.

"What was it you just did?" Her dad's tone was bland. It was a tone she had never heard before.

What's up with him? Abhaya wondered. He had never before showed even the slightest interest in her computer. In fact, as much as she could tell, her dad considered computers to be a tool of the devil, a direct path to hell. It had only been with much persuasion from her mom and sister that this desktop computer was allowed in their room.

"Devidas-ji," her mother had protested on one of those rare occasions that she dared to challenge her husband, "it is required for school. Abhaya cannot do without it. There is a letter from the science teacher asking that all parents whose children do not have computers do whatever they can to gain access."

"Tut, tut," protested her father, annoyed.

In a rare show of support for her younger sister, Jeevana said, "Father, this is different than when I was in school. All kids today use computers."

Still appalled, her dad had said only that he would consider it.

Days passed by, days of torture for Abhaya, awaiting her father's decision, yet nothing else was said. She tried to broach the topic several times but was silenced by her father's harsh stares. About a month later, without a warning, Father showed up, back from work one sunny day, carrying a cardboard box with a second-hand computer. Without a word, he handed it to Abhaya and walked away. Abhaya had no idea where he got it from.

That was nearly two years ago, and although the computer was already dated when they got it and barely compatible with the newest software,

Abhaya dared not ask for an upgrade. She knew there was no chance that her dad would approve with their current financial circumstances.

Internet connectivity at home proved to be yet another challenge, but Abhaya worked it out. Unbeknownst to her parents, she hacked into her neighbors' connection and piggybacked. She suspected her sister realized this but chose to keep quiet, enjoying the stolen web access herself as a silent partner-in-crime. Abhaya stacked up at least five different local networks so that when one was down or heavily used, she could switch to another.

Abhaya did as much of her work on the cloud during her free periods in the school's computer lab as she could, but that time wasn't sufficient.

Her dad knew nothing about this. Once he handed it over to her, he never ever asked about the computer. That is, until today.

"Oh!" said Abhaya, realizing that her father was still waiting for an answer, "This? It's just a browser tab. I noticed I wasn't using it and thought I'd better have it closed."

"A browser tab?" asked Father. "What is a browser tab?"

What is all of this sudden interest? Abhaya wondered. Janaki! The thought sprung into her mind involuntarily. It must be her again, one of her games!

But if it were Janaki, Abhaya's rational brain kicked in, then Father would not have been so calm and patient. So if this is not Janaki's doing, what is going on?

Abhaya realized that she didn't have the luxury of time to figure this out, so she answered her father's question instead. "A browser," said Abhaya, "is a computer program that you use to surf the internet. You can open more than one program at a time, and each instance has its own tab for easy access." She explained what was so obvious to her as if encountering a new student from a remote village who had never before seen a computer.

"I see," said her dad, but his voice conveyed that he had no clue. Silence lingered between them with Abhaya staring at Father and Father staring at the computer screen as if it were a tiger staring right back. Whoever blinked first would lose.

Abhaya realized her father was not going to speak anytime soon. "Father, what is this all about?"

"Oh," he said, as if waking from a dream, "yes, you see, at work, they are trying to modernize. Actually, it's a new manager they brought in to make things more efficient. So this young person, some hot-shot college graduate that came back from America, requires that we all now get an email address. A free one, he said, so the company doesn't need to pay for it. They believe that it will save money for the company. He said we can get it from something called…wait, I wrote it down." He pulled a note out of his trousers' pocket, "Gee-mail? Hot? Mail? Yohoo? I don't understand any of this." He tucked the note back into his pocket and resumed his staring contest with the monitor, his face pulled into a long frown.

Abhaya resisted a smile. Now she understood what this was all about. Her dad needed her help! And not just any help, but help with technology, computers, internet–his most feared adversaries.

She could only imagine what he was feeling right now, forced to admit defeat. A small voice inside her whispered that she was wrong to think this, but that voice was very weak. She couldn't help feeling somewhat vengeful for all the trouble he had given her before bringing this ancient piece of equipment home. And now he comes to me for help!

Still, this was her father. Abhaya pulled herself together. "Okay," she announced decidedly. "Let's start at the beginning. I need to give you a lesson about how the Internet works so you can understand what you need to know about emails."

"I don't need the whole story," he said impatiently, "just the email."

"Fine," replied Abhaya, a little hurt since she had been very well-intended. "Which of the email options do you prefer? Gmail, Hotmail, or Yahoo?"

Frustration stole across his face and into his voice. "Listen here," he said, "if it were up to me I would have nothing to do with this, but I need to show the new manager at work that I now have an email. Can you do this or not?"

Abhaya exclaimed, "Sure, I can do that!" and then she repeated her question. "I just need to know what email account you prefer: Gmail, Hotmail, or Yahoo?" She quickly pulled these three up in new browser tabs.

Father looked at the computer screen and then at her. His expression of disgust transformed into anger.

"Never mind," he murmured, turning away toward the door. She could hear him make out a few muttered words: education, silly, progress, tradition.

"But Father!" Abhaya called after him, "wait, I can help!"

Too late. Her dad was already out of her room, and, judging by the slammed front door, out of the house as well.

Abhaya thought gloomily, he's probably taking one of his chill-out walks by the river. She turned back to her computer screen, closed the email tabs and pulled up the programming code she was working on for John. She sighed. Her spirit was no longer in it.

A deep sense of sadness came over her. How come this person, my father, was so gentle and romantic when courting mom years ago but is now a bitter and miserable man?

Lingering on these thoughts, Abhaya found herself up on her feet and sneaking into her parents' bedroom. I'll finish John's project a little later, she thought. It's almost done anyway. There's not much left to do. With both her parents out, the temptation to look at the actual love letters again was irresistible. She felt it created some invisible bond between her father, mother and herself.

You shouldn't, called a voice inside her head. It's not proper, not right. It's also dangerous.

Yet before she knew it, she had left her room and headed toward her parents'. These letters were exchanged between my parents at an age not much older than mine!

Abhaya stopped at the entrance and listened. She knew all too well that her parents did not approve of her and Jeevana entering this room uninvited. That was a rule dictated since childhood. She perked up her ears but not a sound could be heard except for the city's continuous humdrum. Abhaya stepped into the forbidden space, feeling guilty, curious and excited all mixed together.

I'll just take a quick peek and leave, she told herself. I want to touch those pages again.

Never mind that she had photos of them in her phone. That simply did not suffice. The urge to hold the actual old papers in her hands, feel the roughness of the paper, the trails of ink, their tangibility, something that a digital image just could not provide, all that was too powerful. She opened the drawer, took out the first letter her hands reached, and released a breath she hadn't realized that she'd been holding.

"Dearest Kamalakshi,"

Passing her fingers over the writing, she felt how each character left an imprint. Each letter told a story. As if by magic, she felt like she was in the story. I want to know what made you change from this amazing guy to who you are today, she whispered to herself. Holding those letters could provide her with the key. Abhaya loved cracking puzzles, solving riddles and piecing together mysteries. She went on reading:

"My sweetheart, darling canary, I cannot believe you agreed to the terms of marriage that included an end to your singing. This cannot happen. I will not stand for it! Last night I had a harsh conversation with my father. He is a stubborn old conservative man, and my mother is too weak to oppose him. I know that in her heart of hearts she supports me in this argument, but she didn't utter a word. It doesn't matter. If push comes to shove I will disavow my own parents and we can run away together and get married somewhere far, far away.

You should always sing, bird of my heart.

Desperately loving you, forever yours, Devidas."

Abhaya had read this letter before on her phone, but holding the actual letter and reading her father's words as he argued with his own dad and planned to run away, took her breath away.

"Abhaya! What is this?"

Her mother's voice slapped Abhaya. Bent over the letter with her back to the door, Abhaya spun around and straightened up all at once, trying desperately to hide the piece of paper behind her back.

It was too late. The open drawer, the stack of letters on the bed, Abhaya's burning cheeks–nothing could have concealed the truth. Until that moment, she had never really feared her mom. She had always loved and respected her mother, but there was never any fear. For the first time standing before her that she could remember, Abhaya's knees felt weak and her stomach churned. Usually good at coming up with cover stories, Abhaya was at a loss. Words failed her. Her mind was racing but to no avail.

Her mom remained standing by the door, but her eyes took in everything: the drawer, the letters and, most of all, her daughter. "I am waiting," she said placidly, a calm before the storm.

"I'm... I'm sorry, Mom," Abhaya finally managed to say, her words hardly audible.

"What was that?"

"I'm sorry," repeated Abhaya, "I should not have entered here without permission. I should not have looked through your stuff. It was just that...."

"That's right," her mother said, cutting off her daughter's feeble attempt at an excuse. "You should not have. This is unacceptable." Her mother's voice, usually so gentle and welcoming, trembled with quiet anger. "This is unforgivable. You have disappointed me to no end."

Abhaya lowered her eyes and tears arose.

"Now," added Mom, "put the letter back and leave this room."

Abhaya did as her mom commanded.

"And," added her mother, "you are grounded, except for going to school. You are grounded until I decide what to do with you about this." Abhaya wanted to ask if her mom was going to tell her dad but thought better of it. She tiptoed out of the room without saying a word.

She walked down the hall but then crept back and peeked through the cracked door. Her mother was sitting on the bed, caressing the bundle of letters. Abruptly, she rose and stuffed them back into the drawer. She sat again, held her pillow to her face and wept without making a sound.

CHAPTER 39

NEW DELHI

Heading back home, Jeevana tried to make sense of the past hour. She was overwhelmed, and she needed time to process it all. Walking down the barely lit streets of her hometown, she felt nervous. Jeevana hardly ever walked alone that late at night. The darkness provided good cover for thieves and evildoers, but no safety for honest people, let alone a young woman all on her own at such a late hour of the night.

In accordance with the required safety policy, her workplace did provide women leaving the nightshift with transportation back home, but she was not coming from work. She was heading back from a pub, Prema's workplace.

Prema had offered to call a cab, but Jeevana, trying to save a few rupees, elected to walk instead. If Prema had only known the reason, no doubt she would have offered to pay for the ride. Jeevana, who felt that her friend had already done more than enough for her, explained that the walk would do her good. Jeevana was already regretting that decision.

The pub where Prema worked was a mere thirty-minute brisk walk from Jeevana's home, but with darkness surrounding her, the journey seemed to be across a haunted forest. Shadows lurked along the walls, reminding her of wicked fingers waiting to grab passersby. She looked over her shoulder often, worrying that someone was following her. The rest of the time, Jeevana lowered her head, as if that could hide her from an unfriendly world. She hastened her pace, debating whether to break into a run. She concluded that that would only attract unwanted attention.

Jeevana could not forget the fatal sexual assault on a twenty-three-year-old college student that took place right in this city not that long ago. The incident, one of many, had happened not that far from here. The brutality of the crime branded itself with a lasting mark of shame in the minds of every person in New Delhi. Jeevana tried to pull her thoughts together, but the ruckus of meowing stray cats interrupted her. She began recalling the night's events the best way she could.

Her shift ended at midnight and it was her last evening at work before the dreaded date with Eshaan. *God, did I just use that word? Date?* Atypically true to his promise, Eshaan had lessened his harassment of her since Jeevana agreed to go out with him. Only once did he stop by her station, and that was today. In an unexpectedly soft tone, he confirmed that they are still on for tomorrow. Eshaan's gentleness took her by surprise. She answered back normally rather than in the harsh tone she usually reserved for him. He smiled at her and she was unsure if the curves around his mouth showed some depth of character that she had somehow missed or a touch of concealed cruelty.

When Jeevana left the building at 12:05 a.m., she swore she could see Eshaan lurking in a remote dark corner of the office, watching her. *Or am I becoming paranoid?* she wondered. *Tomorrow,* she thought. *No, it was today.* Her stomach turned queasy. Since it was already past midnight, she figured, what was tomorrow had become today.

The pub, called by the lame moniker The Colonel's Last Stand, was indeed very close to Jeevana's workplace. It was buried in the basement level of a fancy old hotel that had recently been renovated into a new flashy Western-owned office building. As she approached the pub, she thought, *my father would shoot me if he ever finds out about this.* Jeevana had never before visited such an establishment.

When Jeevana opened the door, the blaring music nearly blasted her back out. Her traumatized eardrums entered a state of temporary deafness. Cigarette smoke snaked into her nostrils from the area designated for "tobacco addicts," a term her father favored when expressing his disgust at the habit. *Here I go again,* she thought, *thinking about my father. What's up with me?* But she knew exactly what was up with her. She felt guilty for breaking one of her dad's rules. Jeevana was visiting a forbidden institution, a place unsuitable for traditional women.

Once inside, someone grabbed her by the arm, scaring Jeevana out of her wits. "Hey doll, lemme buy you a drink," a Westerner exclaimed, exhaling his alcoholic fumes in her face. She tried to place his accent. Was he Australian? Or maybe a New Zealander? She wasn't sure. Though she was good at picking out accents, given her work at the call center, the noise and the shock of it all threw her off. She was out of her element. Her analytical mind, ignoring the situation, pitched another puzzle at her. If he's from the Down Under, why would he be considered a Westerner? Eyes wide with terror, Jeevana stared at the stranger who was still gripping her arm tightly. She did not reply, could not reply. Her tongue was stuck to the roof of her mouth.

"Let her go, Jimmy," commanded Prema amusedly. She nudged the fellow away. "Come, follow me," she told Jeevana. "I'm so happy you came!"

By the time Jeevana was seated at the end of the long-worn bar, it was twenty minutes past midnight. That corner of the pub was a little distant from the loud music and cigarette smoke, making Jeevana a bit more comfortable. She sipped cold sparkling water and surveyed the interior while Prema served beer to another customer. The bar itself was made of worn wood. The pub was larger than it first seemed, especially with the designated smoking area. They had enforced the partial ban ever since passing the law on public smoking several years ago. Thank God that despite the government being corrupt, she thought, they do the right thing once in a blue moon. Maybe this country has a future after all.

It was almost time to close and the pub was getting empty. A lone couple slow-danced on the small rectangular area to the softening music. The rest of the space was filled with tables. Jeevana found herself wondering how her friend, a woman, was allowed to work at a pub. She recalled hearing about some new law issued on this matter that forbade such things.

"Tell me," she asked Prema, as soon as her friend came back, "isn't there some rule that prohibits women from working at places that serve alcohol?"

"Oh!" laughed Prema, "are you referring to the Punjab Excise Act? Yes, you're right, but it doesn't apply to this area. This pub is located in the part of the city that belongs to the Uttar Pradesh state. Uttar Pradesh doesn't have that law, but the other parts of town do."

"Oh," said Jeevana, but her thoughts already wondered elsewhere.

"So," asked Prema, "how are you feeling?"

"Tired," replied Jeevana. "Tired and very much concerned about what tomorrow evening may bring."

"Right," said Prema. "Tomorrow's 'date.'"

"Don't dare call it a date," protested Jeevana, even though she herself had made the same slip moments earlier. "A date is when both parties consent to go out together."

"Excuse me, but Eshaan — that's his name, right? — he asked you out and you agreed," Prema countered. "That's consent."

"I didn't have much of a choice," protested Jeevana. "It was either that and continue being harassed by him or quit a job I really need."

"Here we go again," said Prema, "No choice. Let me point out that if you include the word 'either' in a sentence, it automatically makes it a choice."

"Very funny," snapped Jeevana. "Tell me," she said, eyeing her friend from head to toe, "do you have a choice when it comes to the outfit you're wearing for this job?" Prema was dressed in tight black clothing. Her low-cut shirt exposed her cleavage.

"I happen to like it," muttered Prema, caught off-guard.

Jeevana thought she noticed a reddish bloom on Prema's cheeks though in the dimly lit space, it was difficult to tell.

"But even if I didn't like it," Prema retorted, "I still would have had a choice: tell my boss how I feel or quit. There is always a choice."

Jeevana remained unconvinced.

"Listen," said Prema, "years ago when I was bullied in school, I had a choice. I could fight back, stay quiet and be abused, or move away. I made the choice: move."

"You? "exclaimed Jeevana, "I thought it was your parents."

"No," replied Prema, her voice even, "it was me. I was given options and made my choice. And no, it wasn't easy. I knew I would lose you. I knew we would be moving to a new place where I would know no one. I knew my parents were making a sacrifice for me. But I made a choice. There are always choices."

"Excuse me!" yelled a patron across the bar. "Do you serve drinks in this joint or should I serve myself?"

"Hold your horses. I'm coming." answered Prema.

Moments later Prema was back. "Look," Prema said when she returned, "maybe it was a mistake that I asked you to come by. It's late. I can see you're not comfortable here, so let's just call it a night. I have to start closing in fifteen minutes anyway. Since they implemented that other new law, the one that closes all pubs at one past midnight, the police have really been coming down hard on violators."

Jeevana met her friend's eyes. "Prema," she said, "I'm sorry about what I said before. I have no right to judge, and you of all people."

"That's okay," said Prema, smiling gently. "Trust me, I know. I may be young but with all I have been through.... Let's just say it takes a lot to shake me up." She placed her arms around her friend and hugged her.

"That's cool," came a familiar voice.

Jeevana recognized him as Jimmy, the guy that had grabbed her earlier.

"What now, Jimmy?" asked Prema. Before turning to look at him, she winked at Jeevana mischievously.

"You two making out? Can I join?" said Jimmy.

"Jimmy," barked Prema, "sit!" Jimmy immediately dropped to a nearby bar stool, opened his mouth and started panting, the obedient dog waiting for his owner to acknowledge him.

"Good boy," said Prema, picking a pretzel from some bar snacks and feeding it to him as a treat. "Now be an even better boy and leave us alone."

Jimmy gave Prema a miserable, sad, doggy look.

"Come on, let's go!"

Jimmy whimpered and took off.

"And Jimmy," called Prema after him, "we are closing in ten minutes so be ready to leave. I don't want to put the collar on you again!" Prema turned back to pick up the conversation.

Jeevana was staring bug-eyed with her jaw in her lap.

"So, where were we?" asked Prema as if nothing had happened.

"Hold on," said Jeevana, still in shock. "What was that all about?"

"That?" laughed Prema, "Oh, Jimmy is a regular here. We are actually good friends. He's a great guy. That is, when the booze in his blood is under control. In fact, he's one of the reasons I suggested you stop by here."

"Him?" Jeevana could hardly believe it.

"Yes," said Prema. "He may not look the role right now, but believe-it-or-not, Jimmy holds a senior managerial position at one of the largest customer support centers here. I believe I can talk him into interviewing you for a job."

"Him?" repeated Jeevana flabbergasted, "a senior manager?"

"I know, I know," said Prema, "but don't judge a book by its cover, especially not this late at night, and especially not here."

"I don't know," said Jeevana. "I just can't imagine...."

"You don't have to imagine anything, let alone decide right now," said Prema looking at her wristwatch. It was just about one o'clock. Most of the customers, including Jimmy, had left the pub by now, well aware of its strict closing time. The few that remained were gathering their belongings.

"That's one direction I have been exploring for you," explained Prema. "The other may be more of a longshot, so I would rather not discuss it now. But listen, I have to close and there is quite a bit of work I need to do once the doors are shut."

"Can I help?"

"No, no," laughed Prema, "I have my routine and I know what I'm doing. No offense but you will only get in the way. Now off you go." Prema interlocked her arm with her friend's and escorted her to the entrance.

"Is that how you get drunkards out?" asked Jeevana laughing.

"No," replied Prema, "for them we have a bouncer."

"A bouncer?" puzzled Jeevana.

"I'll tell you more about that when you stop by for your next lesson about grownups' nightlife," winked Prema. "Now listen: some streets here are really unsafe at this time.... Actually, not only at this time but even earlier in the evening. On second thought, let me call a cab for you," she said, dropping Jeevana's arm and heading back toward the bar. The phone sat near the cash register.

"Oh, no," responded Jeevana, thinking of the cost. "It's okay, I would rather walk."

"Walk? Are you out of your mind?"

"Yeah, walk, two feet moving? Stepping?" laughed Jeevana, and then she explained, "Really, I need to clear my head."

Seeing Prema's worried face, she added, "I know the area. It's not that far from my home, remember?"

Unconvinced yet not sure what else to say, Prema instructed, "This is the path you want to take," naming all the streets Jeevana should walk. "You know, I really don't like you walking alone," she repeated. "It is dangerous so don't dawdle. If anyone calls after you, don't stop. If need be, run."

"I know, I know," said Jeevana. "Don't forget that I was born and grew up in this area."

"Still," advised Prema, "there is a big difference between daytime and 1:00 a.m."

"So what do you do when you're done and need to get home?"

"The bouncer comes to pick me up with a car," replied Prema, giving her another hug before sending her off.

"That bouncer again," mumbled Jeevana, as if it were the name of a mysterious magician. She thought she had heard this term before but did not quite know what it really meant.

One more street and I'm almost home, Jeevana muttered to herself. She was about to relax her pace when a loud crisp bang on her left made her heart leap. A second bang followed. It sounded like gunshots. Jeevana automatically recited a quiet prayer to Lord Hanuman that her father had taught her as a child to dispel fear.

An old motorcycle passed by. She placed her hand on her heart and changed her prayer to one of thanks.

In no time, she was home. With her parents and sister fast asleep, no one noticed Jeevana's late return. She was safe, at least for now. Tomorrow, which was actually today, was a different story altogether. Eshaan, she thought, and her heart sank again.

CHAPTER 40

NEW DELHI

A loud commotion gave Abhaya a rude awakening. Saturday morning was Abhaya's favorite time of the week, a time for staying in bed. Long ago she had mastered the art of ignoring the bright sunlight sneaking through the curtain's folds, enjoying a late start to the day.

"Watch out!" she could hear her mom shouting in terror, followed by an audible bang. Abhaya rubbed her eyes, still half asleep, and slowly started dragging herself out of bed. Another loud bang followed by yet another cry from her mother, this time a "be more careful!"

Peeking out into the hallway, Abhaya saw two unfamiliar men slowly maneuvering the large dining table out of the apartment.

"How did this ever get in here?" muttered one of them.

Another bang, followed by Mom's shriek: "For heaven's sake, watch where you are going!" This table was so very dear to her. Where were they taking it, and on a Saturday morning? Abhaya wondered. She glanced back in her room to ask her sister, but Jeevana was nowhere to be found. She thought she had heard her coming in really late the night before, but Jeevana was not in her bed when Abhaya awoke moments earlier.

Father, his face worn, noticed his daughter standing at her bedroom's doorway, still in her nightgown. He squinted his eyes and glared at her fiercely. No words were exchanged but Abhaya knew exactly what he was thinking: "What's wrong with you? Put some clothes on! Can't you see there are strangers in the house, and moreover, they are men?"

Abhaya disappeared into her bedroom, leaving the door ajar. Through her mother's muffled sobbing, she heard, "Now what will I do with all those beautiful tablecloths I inherited from my grandmother? She had them made to order especially for this table." Abhaya was unable to hear her father's reply in full, just several words here and there. She knew him well enough that she could imagine what he would say to comfort Mom. "It's all right, Kamalakshi. We will get this table back" and "Now, now, you are just very upset."

Just then her sister came through the room's other entrance. Fresh from the shower and wearing only a towel, Jeevana smelled good, Abhaya thought. "What's going on out there?" she whispered, her semi-sleepy mind refusing to piece together what she had just seen and heard.

"Oh," replied Jeevana. "Didn't you know?"

"Know what?" Abhaya was annoyed. She was in no mood for riddles.

"Father had to sell the table. Actually, not 'sell' but rather 'pawn.'"

"But why?" asked Abhaya, resembling a four-year-old forbidden to watch TV.

"Let me think," said Jeevana, who was still toweling off. She paused theatrically for a moment. "Maybe it is because we don't have money, at least some of us don't," she added with a hint of resentment, "and the rent needs to be paid?"

The renegade sunbeams entering the room danced like little demons across her skin as she applied lotion.

Abhaya was silent. Noises coming off the street drew her to the window. She peeked through the curtains and saw the two men struggling to lift the ancient heavy table onto the truck. Patel–Pawn, Jewelry and Loans was painted in large golden letters on the side of the vehicle. Further down the street she could see her dad walking briskly, his wife by his side, heading toward his favorite path, the one he usually took when he had to blow off steam.

Abhaya sighed and turned back to her sister who was beginning to dress. She has a beautiful body, thought Abhaya, and she was immediately surprised by the insight. She had seen Jeevana naked plenty of times before, but this was the first time she took note of the young woman her sister had become. Another, more frightening thought crossed her mind. It's not Jeevana who's changing. It's me. Her gaze drifted toward some remote horizon until Jeevana's voice pulled her back to the present. Abhaya realized Jeevana had been speaking to her.

"Did you hear me?"

"Sorry, what?" responded Abhaya.

"I was saying that the table is just the beginning. You may want to start packing."

"Start packing?" Abhaya squealed. "What do you mean?"

Jeevana answered while putting on a shirt, "Only that pawning the table together with Father's reduced salary and some other things that are going on, I wouldn't be surprised if we'll be moving soon to the poorer part of town." Abhaya stared at her sister who now dabbed on a light layer of makeup. Lowering her voice, she asked, "What other things are you referring to?"

"I can't tell you right now," said Jeevana, adding lipstick. "I already said too much."

Abhaya made repeated attempts to make her sister talk, but all she got in return were evasive answers. Questions arose in her panicking mind like spray coming off waves hitting a rocky shore. She wanted to move but on her on terms and without her family. *If we move, will I need to change schools? Will I be able to see my friends? Will they want me to go work like Jeevana?*

Ten minutes later Jeevana was gone, and Abhaya was left home alone and grounded. She pulled out her phone and started texting. "Janaki, you there?"

"Yeah, what's up? Ready 4 our big date nite?"

"What date night?"

"Sorry, no, no date. Just u & me @ the movies this evening."

"Holy crap, I completely forgot! Sorry, but my mom grounded me."

"@$#%! What the---? ur mom NEVER grounds u. Your dad maybe, but ur mom? What did u do 2 her?"

"It's a long story. Bottom line: I'm home this evening, going nowhere."

"NO UR NOT!!! U CANNOT DO THIS 2 ME!!! I planned this evening & ur coming!!!"

"Me doing this to you? I'm the one that's grounded. You're free."

"Listen, let me think."

"Think all you want. That won't change the fact I cannot go out."

"Shh!"

Moments later, Janaki continued. "I know! I got it!"

"Yes? OK"

"Remember that funny American movie we saw a while back on video?"

"Which one? We saw a few"

"Come on–the real funny one. I forgot its name. something with a boy's name and skipping school for a day?"

"Oh, you mean Ferris Bueller's Day Off? The oldie from the 1980s?"

"Yes! yes, that's it. Remember how he faked being sick 2 stay home instead of going 2 school? U will do the same–pretend 2 be sick"

"Janaki, this is a whole different situation. This is about me going OUT Saturday night and my parents are home. Faking it to stay home doesn't help."

"Oh, right. Dang it. I thought I had it. Let me think some more."

"Think all you want, just don't think yourself to death :-)"

"Hush!"

Several minutes passed by. Abhaya waited in amusement.

Janaki texted, "I got it!"

"Yes?"

"What's the 1 thing ur parents feel is most important for 4 u?"

"Staying a virgin until they marry me off?"

"Hahaha. Very funny. Now b serious!"

"Okay — my education."

"Right! And what else?"

"All sorts of traditional values."

"Exactly, such as helping others, right?"

Abhaya wrote, "So?"

"So! We have that big math test coming up. Tell ur mom–no, scrap that. I'll come by and beg ur mom. No, not good enough."

"What? You keep on cutting yourself off! Can you please finish a sentence? I know! I got it!"

"Got what?"

"I'll speak with my mom, tell her I really need ur help with this test or else I'll fail & ur the only 1 that can help me. I'll ask her 2 call your mom 2 ask if she can let u come over & help me study this evening."

"But what about your parents? They'll notice if we go out instead of staying home and studying, wouldn't they?"

"Not unless they can b in 2 places at the same time! They have a fancy dinner 2 attend. They'll b out most of the evening & we'll b back b4 they do. It'll all look perfectly fine!"

"And what if my mom tells your mom that I can't go out and that you need to come here?"

For a few moments, there was no response.

Abhaya texted again. "Helloooooooo? Are you there?"

"I'm thinking… I know! I got it! I'll tell my mom I cannot carry all the study materials & I can't use urs. ur in the advanced section & I'm not."

"Janaki, you're a genius. You should be a politician :-)"

"So we're all set. I'll go 2 work on my mom & c u at 7:30pm @ the movies"

"OK. You got it."

Abhaya sighed. Now, I need to figure out what to wear. Abhaya looked at her closet. Nah… she decided, it's just me and Janaki. A T-shirt will do just fine. On second thought, also a sweatshirt. Some of the newer theaters have the AC on way too high. She pulled out one of her favorites–a loose white pullover with black sleeves. On the front were printed two large panda bear eyes. That will do. She smiled.

CHAPTER 41

NEW YORK CITY

"Here you are!" John said as Rachel approached his table. It was 8:40 a.m. "And five minutes ahead of time!" John further noted, "Wow! That's a first. What happened to 'fashionably late?'"

"Don't push your luck," grimaced Rachel, sitting down. "I figured I stood you up once, and then asked you to come earlier today–and on a Saturday! So the least I can do is make an early appearance."

"Yep," smirked John, waving his phone in her direction, "some whole whopping FIVE minutes early! Yippy!"

Rachel tried but failed to conceal her smile. "Okay. Let's get down to business. Can we order? Or do you have some more announcements to make?" Rachel noticed John's face turning a little pale. "What's up?" she asked, concerned.

"I actually do," he said in a feeble voice, "but you're right. Let's order first." He flagged the server and looked closer at her. Whaddaya know, he thought, if it isn't Rache, the one that gave me a hard time the last time I was here. He smiled at her, but Rache did not seem to recognize him. She just smiled politely back and said, "can I take your order, or do you need a few more minutes?"

Rachel, completely immersed in the menu, missed John's staring. Without lifting her head, Rachel said, "he'll have his favorite, the huevos rancheros, and I...."

"But wait a minute!" protested John, "how do you know that's what–"

"Oh hush!" spat Rachel like a queen expecting complete obedience at her court. "I don't have time for this today. I need to get to work, remember? That's why we are meeting earlier. Let me order for both of us so we can get this done quickly."

John could have sworn he saw a slight grin on the waitress' face. Lovely, he thought, more humiliation.

"And I'll have—"

"Sausage and egg tostadas," offered John, cutting Rachel off, "and a side of spicy home fries."

Rache raised an eyebrow and looked at Rachel. Rachel brought her head up a notch and snapped at John, "Didn't I tell you to keep quiet! I'm ordering today," and then, looking at the server said, "just two egg whites, scrambled dry, and a small house salad, oil and vinegar on the side, no bread."

John stared at Rachel. "And two coffees, skim milk for him, almond milk for me, both on the side."

Rache, the server, finished writing the order and took off.

"I eat light on workdays," Rachel answered.

For John's puzzled look, she added, "and today, as I told you when we spoke yesterday, I was asked, no, scrap that, I was ordered to go to the office for half a day because that schmuck of a client threatened my boss saying if he didn't receive the design by Monday first thing in the morning, he'll be taking his business elsewhere. God, I hate this job!"

John's phone buzzed but he ignored it. He was texting with Abby earlier while waiting for Rachel to arrive. No messages of any real significance. It seemed Abby was bored and was looking to strike up a conversation. He had no time for that right now. This was his big day.

Practicing for two weeks, he decided that this morning he would finally tell Rachel how he felt about her. He was taking a big risk. She could snub him. And if that happens, he thought, I'll not only lose the love of my life but also my best friend.

Yet he couldn't wait anymore. He had already made up his mind. It was now or never. Besides, he further contemplated, with my–no, our–project so close to launching, God only knows what the future holds for me. Maybe in just a matter of weeks, he fantasized, I'll find myself relocating to Silicon Valley where all the tech action takes place. I'll rent offices and make it big, like Zuckerberg. Maybe, yet maybe, and this was an option that John definitely did not want to think about, but the thought floated stubbornly in his head, what if the project tanks? I'll find myself poorer than ever. Who the heck would look at me then, a failure? Then, there was the job offer that Rachel mentioned, the one from the West Coast. She did not elaborate on it since dropping that bomb. But what if she decides to take it and move away? Today must be the day, he told himself.

"So what is the big announcement?" asked a curious Rachel. "It must be serious. Your face went stark white."

John felt his heart kick into high gear. He could not tell if sweat was dripping down his forehead or if he imagined it. He didn't dare check. Right as he cleared his throat and prepared to speak, their server, Rache, came back with a pot of coffee. On edge as he was, John instantly lost his courage. He could not say what he had to say when a stranger, and that particular stranger of all people, could hear. Rache poured coffee carefully into Rachel's cup, and then John's.

As she turned to leave he thought he saw her winking at him. Did she just wink at me? he wondered. Last time I was here, he thought, this server was giving me such a hard time. Now, all of a sudden, she winks? Is she making a pass at me or just mocking? God, women can be so confusing.

Rachel got up.

"Where are you going?" asked John, "you just arrived."

"Well," replied Rachel, "if you do want my full undivided attention for your important announcement, then I better head to the john. Mother Nature's calling." She grabbed her purse, and in a moment, she was gone.

John picked up his phone and browsed through the messages. He was right. The messages were indeed from Abby. First, she informed him that the project was completed, to which he replied with plenty of smiles and a raised thumb. Before long the thread started to take a weird turn.

It began normally enough with how sorry she was that the project was coming to an end, how much she enjoyed working with him and how much she was hoping to keep in touch and maybe work together again soon. But then it turned strange when Abby started asking if he ever planned to visit her in India, or would he fancy her visiting him in New York. He was contemplating an answer when Rachel came back. Maybe he could consult with her about the meaning of this. It made him again wonder how women's minds worked. He just did not seem to get it.

CHAPTER 42

NEW DELHI

Jeevana was almost late to the cinema. Ahead, she could see Eshaan waiting impatiently. He was dressed like a 1940's Mafia don out for a night on town. He wore a garish light striped suit, white and blue button-down shirt, and a loose grey tie. All that was missing were the overcoat and a fedora.

Eshaan took a puff from his cigarette and blew a perfect smoke ring. He took a step forward.

He had spotted her.

"I thought you chickened out," he called out like a boss scolding a procrastinating employee.

Jeevana, dressed in a dark high-neck loose-fitting sweater, bristled but refused to speed up. "I'm not on the clock, remember?" she blurted out, barely containing her irritation. "I don't have to be on time or else be fired."

"Don't be so sure," asserted Eshaan, "If the boss's nephew–that's me, in case you forgot–isn't happy with this evening, I'm not so sure you'll have a job to get back to."

Jeevana stopped cold in her tracks. "What's that? That wasn't our deal! We said that I would go out with you tonight, and regardless of the outcome, you would get off my case at work."

"True," agreed Eshaan, taking Jeevana by the elbow, which made her cringe, "but I see no contradiction. If you no longer come to work, there would be no more me being on your case." He smirked, satisfied with his wittiness. Glimpsing her furious expression, Eshaan softened and said almost apologetically, "but let's not be so negative. In a voice sweeter than honey, he added, "The night is still young and I'm all yours."

Jeevana felt bile rising up her throat. She swallowed hard, suppressing it. *What was I thinking? That suddenly he would be nice? That this would go smoothly? He's a wolf in sheep's clothing.* Watch out, a small voice in the back of her head called, Watch out! Better still, it's not too late to back out. You'll have no work to go back to, but maybe that's for the best. Jeevana pushed the thought aside. She could hear Prema in her mind, telling her that she always had a choice, but she just couldn't believe that.

Janaki was waiting for Abhaya to show up. Dressed in a bright red top that exposed a little too much of her small bosom, she was standing right in front of the cinema's entrance. Pacing back and forth nervously, she felt like a theater director on opening night. Her plan, so far, was working perfectly. Her mother called Abhaya's mom and the latter agreed to let Abhaya come over. Janaki's parents left on schedule, and then Janaki had texted Chetan to be sure he would arrive as planned and on time. "Not a minute earlier, not a second late!"

It was all about timing. *I am indeed a genius!* She thought. Turning to walk in the other direction, Janaki almost bumped heads with Jeevana. Both stared at each other in surprise.

"Well, hello Janaki," muttered Jeevana as Eshaan pulled her along not-so-gently.

Janaki just nodded her head, thinking, *What is she doing here? And who's this guy she's with, looking like some idiot gangster. Abhaya didn't tell me her sister was dating someone. I'll give her a piece of my mind about that! This is just the kind of juicy news I would have expected her to share immediately.* Then she thought, *I just hope this won't hamper my plans.* She turned to look at Jeevana and the unfamiliar guy again, but by then, the two had already entered the cinema.

As she turned again, Abhaya showed up.

Inside the entrance, Jeevana and Eshaan were standing in line to buy tickets.

"There's this new Western that just started playing," said Eshaan excitingly. "I want to see that."

"Really?" snapped Jeevana. "That's your idea of taking a girl out?"

"What's wrong with that?" protested Eshaan as they made their way along the long ticket line. "Like, what would you pick? Some stupid romantic comedy?"

"Do you really want to see me walking out right now?" hissed Jeevana. No, this isn't going well at all, she said to herself. But I cannot lose my job, not yet.

"All right, all right," Eshaan said, appealingly. "Then, what would you like to see?" he added with a twinkle in his eyes. "'Fifty Shades of Grey?'"

Jeevana blushed despite herself. Even though this film was banned in India, the reference was clear. "No," she said, her eyes quickly scanning the billboard's selection of featured films. "How about 'Once Upon a Time in Bihar?'" From what she had read in an online newspaper, she knew that it was a political film. No chance Eshaan would think that she was interested in him romantically. Not even a guy as thickheaded as he is, she thought.

"What?" responded Eshaan, "not a chance. It's boring."

Of course it is, thought Jeevana. I didn't really expect you to go for it.

"How about 'The Silent Heroes?'" Eshaan suggested. "It's supposed to be a cool adventure movie." Jeevana scanned her memory for reviews about that film. Was there any romance in it? Anything that would give Eshaan the slightest chance to make a move on her?

By now they were facing the ticket agent who looked at them impatiently. Jeevana was about to suggest another historic film but Eshaan had rushed and purchased the tickets. As they left the line and headed toward the usher, Jeevana pulled out her wallet and handed Eshaan some rupees.

"No, no," protested Eshaan, "this one's on me."

"I don't want it to be on you," objected Jeevana. "Take the money."

"I will not," insisted Eshaan, pushing her hand with the money bills away as if he were a little child refusing mother's vile medicine. Ignoring Jeevana's protests, Eshaan headed to buy popcorn.

Outside the theater, Janaki's eyes narrowed at Abhaya. "Guess who I just ran into?" she said, long before Abhaya had a chance to draw near.

"Who?" asked Abhaya.

"You didn't tell me your sister's dating someone." replied Janaki, her voice sounding a tad offended.

"Jeevana?" laughed Abhaya. "She isn't dating anyone."

"Well, either you're not telling me all that you know or," she continued slyly, "you yourself don't know about her secret lover...."

"Lover? Jeevana? No way! She barely has time to breathe," said Abhaya. She soundede certain, but in her mind she wondered if that was why she got back home so late the other night.

"Well, I just saw them passing by and they were hanging onto each other like lovebirds."

Abhaya planted her hands on her hips and stared down her friend with a look that said really? "Janaki, when will you stop making up these imaginary tales?"

Right as she was about to protest, Janaki noticed Chetan standing nearby, staring at his feet.

"Well, what have we here?" Janaki exclaimed with delight. In her mind's eye, the theater curtain had just been raised and the first act was about to commence. She was the director and one of the lead actors of this show. A relative darkness covered Chetan's blushing cheeks. Abhaya started at the sight of him, looking confused.

"Chetan!" called Janaki, as if welcoming a lost friend, one she had not seen in years, "fancy running into you here. What are you up to?"

Just remember your lines, Chetan, remember your lines. Janaki had rehearsed them with Chetan over the phone hours earlier.

"Oh," mumbled Chetan, "I'm just here...here... arr..." he stuttered.

Go on! Janaki encouraged him in her mind but said, "yes, we see you're here..." making "here" sound more like an invitation.

Chetan got the hint, found his voice and continued: "Here to see a movie."

"Very good!" congratulated Janaki. "So are we. Do you want to join us?"

At that, Janaki noticed Abhaya glaring at her sideways, a harsh question mark written all over her face.

"Oh," said Janaki, interrupting Chetan as he was about to reply, "I'm being rude. I'm here with my friend Abhaya." She was speaking loudly and punctuating each word, as if talking to someone a little slow. "Do you two know each other?"

Seeing the bewilderment on Abhaya's face, Janaki rushed ahead to make introductions, "Abhaya, this is Chetan. He goes to school with us, but I don't think he has any classes with you."

So that's where I know him from, realized Abhaya, but what she said instead was, "of course, I remember him." She felt it would have been foolish, and maybe even arrogant, to admit she did not remember who he was, especially with Janaki seeming so familiar with him. Wait a minute, Abhaya further thought, does Janaki have a boyfriend and she didn't even tell me? She could not ask this, at least not yet.

"All right, then!" said Janaki theatrically. "Let's go to the movies!"

Staring at the billboard, Janaki studied the titles. "So, what should we see?" she asked aloud. The truth was that she had already checked in advance which movies were playing and had made up her mind. This public display was all part of her carefully prepared act, intending to lend credibility to the situation. "There's a new Western, a historic film, a romantic comedy...."

Janaki was a bit annoyed to see that Abhaya was totally distracted. Her friend was clutching her phone and typing short messages.

Nearby, Chetan kept quiet, a perfect extra in a film awaiting the director's instructions.

Janaki turned back to the screen. "Romantic comedy," announced Janaki. "Yaara Silly Silly! I remember reading it. It's quite good."

By now, the trio was approaching the ticket counter.

"Here," Chetan rushed forward, as if awaken by a cue, "please let me pay for this."

Janaki frowned for a moment. This was not part of her screenplay. She had imagined that they would each pay for their own ticket. Yet she saw no harm in this act, so she nodded her directorial consent, approving of her actor's surprise improvisation.

Abhaya, still absorbed with her phone, was oblivious to Chetan's gesture.

Moments later they were seated. Janaki tried to arrange it so Chetan would sit between them, but Abhaya, returning momentarily to reality, gave her a reproachful look. She maneuvered herself to sit by Janaki, placing her friend between herself and Chetan.

Never mind that, thought Janaki, I'll go get popcorn soon and leave these two alone. She rehearsed this part as well with Chetan earlier that afternoon, letting him know he would be given a golden opportunity to chat with Abhaya one-on-one. She went as far as suggesting for him a conversation starter. What is up with Abhaya? Janaki found herself wondering. She just does not seem herself this evening.

Abhaya was indeed in another world. Staring at her texting thread with John. Why isn't he answering? He did seem very enthusiastic when she wrote to him, saying that she completed the last task of the project. She felt as if this would be the best opportunity she'd ever have to see if he really shared the same feeling. In fact, after he called her "princess," she had no doubt they were. With the money she was making from her online work, she fancied herself running away from home, maybe even earlier than she originally intended, especially if her family would be forced to move away. She would find a way to get to the USA, uniting with Long John, her true love. It would be just like in the movies, she fantasized, as the coming attractions were playing on the big screen in front of her.

A new Star Wars preview came on, but Abhaya did not notice, nor was she aware of a trailer for a film starring Salman Khan, her favorite actor. She was staring at her small screen, willing John to answer. No text appeared. Despair was slowly but surely staining her picture-perfect future life. Her sensible mind flooded with unfamiliar powerful feelings. She hesitated for a short moment and then typed a text message. After reading it to herself several times with trembling fingers, as if commanding whatever remained of her life-force to go ahead, she pressed "send."

"Anyone up for popcorn?" called Janaki out of the blue, sounding very theatrical. She was getting up. "There are at least ten more minutes of previews and I really feel like some."

"Let me," suggested Chetan, gallantly rising up.

"You sit down!" glared Janaki at him, and seeing Abhaya still immersed with her phone, she nodded to him to open a conversation with the girl of his dreams. With that, Janaki walked out toward the concession stand, feeling satisfied that she had done everything she could to get the ball rolling. Now, she thought as she stood in line, I just hope this nerd listened to my coaching and does his part.

CHAPTER 43

NEW YORK CITY

On her way to the restroom, Rachel reflected on what was it that John wanted so desperately to share. She did indeed need to visit the ladies room, but she also wanted a short break to ponder this. Rachel was no fan of surprises. What would make John so nervous? What would make him literarily become so pale? She could not figure it out.

A few minutes later she walked slowly back to their table, those thoughts still on her mind. Passing by a couple seated further away who were staring into each other's eyes, hopelessly romantic, a light bulb suddenly went off, and she knew without a doubt. Oh my God! She thought, it is so obvious, how could I have missed it? Quickly…she had to think quickly. Not slowing her pace, she could already see John from her vantage point, moving uneasily in his seat, not touching his food. How would I respond if he told me he loved me? John, her best friend. How do I feel about him? She did love him, she realized, but she wondered if it was that sort of love. There was no time. Just a few more steps. Her mind felt turbulent as if a sudden thunderstorm had interrupted a perfectly sunny day. Yes, of course she loved him, but time has run out. The last grain had fallen in the hourglass. She was by the table now. He was quiet. She seated herself and looked quizzically at him. His phone, lying on the table, chirped with a new text message but John ignored it. His face was still ghostly white.

"Are you okay?" Rachel found herself asking, "you look stark white."

"Hm?" responded John, "Oh, yes, I think so."

Moments earlier, while Rachel was still in the restroom, John ran various scenarios of rejection in his head.

Suddenly it all seemed so futile. What if? he kept on asking, what if she doesn't feel the same for me? Where will that put us? I do not want to lose her. I'll take friendship over knowing that she'll never be mine. But wouldn't life like that be an ongoing torture? It would. Of course it would. Yet if I speak now, I may lose her. Is it worth the risk? Of course it is! It's now or never, he decided.

Just as he was about to open his mouth, Rachel said, "do you need to get up and walk around a little? Maybe splash some water on your face?" She was clearly concerned. "It might do you some good."

"Yes," responded John instantly. He felt as if he were a drowning man, holding onto her suggestion as a way to delay his fate, should the worse come to pass. He got up and headed to the restroom.

Rachel was about to dig in when John's phone buzzed yet again. She found herself wondering, who is texting him so feverishly and this early on a Saturday morning? Curiosity got the best of her, and she picked up his phone. The screen was locked. His password, Rachel guessed correctly, was Tess, his cat's name. Rachel knew many of John's little secrets which he always enjoyed sharing with her.

She glanced in the direction of the restrooms with a fleeting twinge of guilt. John had just disappeared into the narrow hallway. She calculated that she had a few minutes before he returned. If I put the phone back exactly where I picked it up, he won't notice a thing. No harm done. That is, after I check who's been messaging him so many times. Pulling up the text app, she saw that the ones marked as unread were all from Abby.

A wave of resentment rose up in her, bubbling briefly in her belly before shooting to the top of her skull. Why am I feeling like this toward a woman I don't even know? she asked herself. After all, John and I are not romantically involved, she thought, at least not yet. She opened the last message John had read. Abby was letting him know she finished the project. John replied cheerily. Innocent enough. In the next message Abby was asking him about coming to visit her in India. Hmm?... And then, Abby went on about coming to see him in New York? What was going on? The pretty face of the British programmer floated into Rachel's mind. Now, she was pissed off. It seemed as if these two were having a virtual affair.

In the final text, Abby wrote, "John, I have very strong feelings toward you, but I trust you already know that. To put it even more clear–I love you. I'm sitting with friends at a movie theater, waiting for some romantic comedy to start, but all I can think about is you, my love."

Rachel felt her cheeks burning, her blood pulsing. Raising her head, she still did not see John rounding the corner, returning from the restroom. Control yourself, she commanded her body. Here I was, a fool, thinking he was going to tell me how much he loves me, while in fact he probably wants to tell me about some freaking programmer he fell in love with online. With my luck, he's probably planning on going to India! What a joke. Rachel placed John's phone down where she found it. She stared at her food, which had suddenly lost its appeal, picked up her purse and left the restaurant just as John came near. Seeing his empty table, John looked up and saw Rachel outside the window, hailing a taxi from the sidewalk. She had no time to waste for Uber. Oblivious to the people sitting around him, John cried out at the top of his lungs, "Rache, wait! Where are you going?!" But it was too late. A yellow taxi swallowed her whole, and in a heartbeat, she was gone. John plodded dejectedly back to his table. The commotion his sudden yell caused was quickly forgotten as yet another "Only in New York" moment.

"Is everything okay?" It was Rache-the-server dropping by his table. She looked at John with some degree of concern, but there was no trace of mockery in her pretty eyes. He looked back at her blankly and answered truthfully, "I haven't got a clue."

"Let me know if you need anything," she said, her voice soft and understanding." She smiled at him and left. John's phone buzzed again. Another message. His first thought was that maybe it's Rachel. Maybe some emergency happened, and she had to rush and that she's texting me to let me know there is nothing to worry about. He picked up the phone and looked at the messages. There was one unread message from Abby, simply saying: "Please answer me...."

Please answer me, wondered John. He was puzzled. The other messages in the thread were marked as read. He opened the previous text and noticed that there were a few other messages since the last one that he had remembered seeing. He scrolled through them, his stomach churning the more he read. What the heck is going on? He groaned to himself. When? How? What made Abby think he was in love with her?

It then struck him. Those latter text messages, those love notes from Abby, were marked read. But he was just seeing them for the first time. Is it possible? No, Rachel wouldn't. Or would she?

As the idea took shape in his head, anger started swelling in his gut. If it was indeed the case that Rachel saw those texts from Abby, then Abby had messed up his life beyond belief. This programmer's delusion needs to stop, and stop now! he thought. Furious, he fired off a response to Abby and pressed send. He tried calling Rachel, but she did not pick up. John decided against leaving a message. He sat there staring blankly for what seemed an eternity. Rache-the-server passed by again. With effort, he signaled for the check.

Handing him the bill, she looked into his eyes. She said, "I might be off-base here, and if so, I'm sorry, but bear with me. Do you love her?"

John nodded his head. "Then what the heck are you doing, sitting here?" urged Rache. "Go! Go now! Go after her! Let her know!"

John looked at Rache as if seeing her for the first time, her words sinking like rain on desert sand. "Thank you," he whispered rising up. "Thanks so much."

She smiled to herself, watching him rush off. She felt good doing this. Little did he know that she had been in his same exact shoes a year ago but had not acted fast enough. The love of her life was gone by the time she woke up. Her smile turned into a half grimace when she realized that John had left without paying his bill, and neither of them had eaten a bite. "Darn it," she cursed softly to herself. She would have to pay it out of her own pocket. A couple of hours' worth of work down the drain. Oh well, she thought, it was still the right thing to do. She would not let a little loss of money spoil how she felt about it. Isn't this what good karma's all about?

CHAPTER 44

NEW DELHI

In the movie theater, Eshaan placed the popcorn between him and Jeevana. He offered to share it with her, but she showed no interest. That did not deter him from shoving generous portions of the crunchy treat into his mouth and chewing loudly. Jeevana found herself more and more agitated. The previews for coming attractions were just about to finish and the theater became dark as the film's opening titles spanned the big screen. Dramatic music filled the air. The person in the row in front of her was checking messages on his phone, its tiny screen projecting bright light into the dark interior. So inconsiderate, thought Jeevana.

She felt a hand on her knee. It was so unexpected that she jumped in her seat.

"Take it easy, baby," whispered Eshaan in her ear.

"Take your hand off me, now!" commanded Jeevana, her voice low but unmistakably hostile.

"Why?" Eshaan said, surprised. "We're on a date."

"No, we are not!" Jeevana sneered. She reached out and clawed Eshaan's hand from her leg as if it was a disgusting leech. "That wasn't the deal."

"Deal, baby? Oh yeah, it was," said Eshaan, all the while trying to reach her thigh again.

"Hush!" called a man seated behind them, "you two better take your business outside. Some of us are trying to watch a movie here!"

"Shut up!" Eshaan snapped at him.

Momentarily distracted, he lifted his hand to point a finger at the stranger.

Jeevana used the disruption to get up. The large popcorn that sat between them tumbled to the ground like a house of cards. Panic grabbed hold of her as she rushed out of the row, stepping on people's feet unaware. This earned her a few harsh responses, but she had to get out and get away from this creep. Moments later Eshaan was at her heels, calling after her.

Coming back from the concession stand, Janaki saw Jeevana bursting through of one of the other multiplex's halls. Jeevana seemed utterly upset, her face flushed, her eyes glazed. Janaki tried to wave at her, but Jeevana did not seem to notice. Moments later, Janaki saw the guy that she had presumed was Jeevana's secret boyfriend rushing after her. Oh, oh, she thought, just started dating and already their first lovers' quarrel. She smiled to herself. These two, unlike Abhaya and Chetan, did not have her, Janaki, as a director to manage their budding relationship.

Back in the theater where Abhaya and Chetan were left alone, Chetan was rehearsing the line that Janaki had suggested, finding the gumption to say it aloud. He was very nervous, maybe the most nervous he had ever been in his life. Sweat trickled down his spine. Chetan was glad the theater was dark enough that no one, including Abhaya, could notice. Abhaya, he would tell her, I hear you're interested in programming. I like it, too. What programming language do you use? The second part of the sentence was his, not Janaki's. Janaki just told him to talk technology and computers with Abhaya since it was a topic she would enjoy, but Chetan had come up with the question about the programming language all on his own. He felt rather proud of himself.

Before he had a chance to say anything, he heard a buzz from Abhaya's phone. A text message was coming in. He saw her reading it intensely, and then, visibly upset, she got up and rushed out.

Chetan remained seated, uncertain what to do next. The movie was about to start. Where is Janaki? he thought. Should he follow Abhaya or wait? Just then, as if hearing him calling her, Janaki appeared through the entrance opposite the one that Abhaya had exited. She made her way back to their seats, carrying a large popcorn and some candy.

"Where is Abhaya?" she asked when she finally reached Chetan. "Restroom?"

Chetan shrugged his shoulders and dropped them. "I don't know, but I don't think so," he replied. "She didn't say anything. She got a text, seemed very upset, got up and just ran out."

"And she didn't say anything?" asked, Janaki, more surprised than concerned.

"Nope," said Chetan, "not a single word. What should we do?"

"What do you mean?" Janaki looked at him. "We go looking for her. This is not typical for Abhaya. And I'm her friend." As the opening titles of Yaara Silly Silly rolled across the silver screen, Chetan and Janaki fled the theater with Janaki still holding onto the popcorn and candy.

CHAPTER 45

NEW DELHI

By the time Jeevana was out of the multiplex, she was running more than walking. Her mind was in a daze. This is not happening, she kept on telling herself, this is not happening. She could hear Eshaan following her a short distance behind, yelling for her to stop. That only made her move faster. She did not want to speak with him. She was done, even at the risk of losing of her job. It was simply not worth it.

Trying to stay within areas that had street lights, even if most were not functioning, Jeevana took a couple of unfamiliar turns. Somehow she ended up on a narrow street, her path mostly blocked by a group of young men. They appeared to be drunk. Not good. With Eshaan at her heels, she took the first available exit to her right. That landed her in an even narrower street, barely wider than an alley. It was poorly lit. Jeevana was breathing hard. Physically she was not in great shape. Hours spent sitting at work left her with no time to exercise.

Shortly after entering the alleyway, Eshaan, who was more fit than she, caught up to her. He grabbed Jeevana from behind, calling "Stop! Take it easy! Calm down!" But she did not, she could not. Instead Jeevana found herself struggling with Eshaan. The scuffle, somehow, seemed to only get him more excited. Eshaan is stronger than he seemed, she realized with horror. Within minutes, a small crowd made entirely of men circled them. During her struggle with Eshaan, her tightly woven shirt got ripped at the shoulder. Her bra strap showed against her smooth naked skin. The men surrounding them were staring at the scene, some with hungry eyes. Most were drinking her in. Only a few showed disgust, but apparently were afraid to interfere.

Jeevana's heart was pounding hard and her vision blurred. She felt trapped like the young gazelle she once saw on TV as a child. It was running slower than the rest of the herd, followed by a lion.

By then, Eshaan had her in his grip, her back pressed tightly against his chest. With one free arm, he tried to fondle her breasts. But Jeevana was not the one to easily surrender. She was kicking and trying to bite his arms.

"Anybody here want a piece of her?" she heard Eshaan calling aloud to the gawkers. "Come help me hold her and you can have a go." The crowd of men were hesitant, even the ones with lust in their eyes. Three started to edge in, grabbing Jeevana by the arms and legs. One aggressor was trying to remove her clothing. When Jeevana screamed her lungs out, Eshaan tried covering her mouth, but it seemed no one could hear her. She felt doomed. News images of a recent rape victim, a college student that was attacked brutaly in public, floated through her mind.

Just a street away, Abhaya was walking fast in no particular direction. Leaving the theater but minutes earlier, her mind felt shattered in a million pieces and heartbroken. She saw nothing and heard very little. How could he write that reply message to me? My own real-life prince, rescuing me from all of this? All her fantasies about him, all her dreams about the future, all her hopes were falling into a bottomless pit.

Through a mist of confusion, she heard shouts–or was it screams?–of a familiar voice. It bored a hole in her cocoon. Can it really be...Jeevana? Not possible. But the voice was exactly like her sister's. Abhaya changed direction and entered a semi-darkened alleyway. From a distance, she could see a circle of men, maybe ten maybe more, standing around a few people. A struggle was going on. She figured out that the screams that she had heard must have come from the center. She couldn't see clearly and the shouts were now somewhat muffled, but she was drawn to the source.

As Abhaya came closer, her eyes opened wide. She felt dizzy. It was indeed Jeevana, stripped half naked, and several men were trying to remove the rest. A fleeting thought, completely random, passed through her mind, Jeevana always preferred really tight jeans which were hard to put on, and even harder to take off. So far, this seemed to have worked in her favor.

"Get off her!" she found herself screaming while pushing through the circle, forcing her way in. "What are you doing! Have you all gone mad?" Before she knew it, Abhaya was in the center with everyone staring at her, especially her shocked sister. That awkward moment seemed to have lasted an eternity.

That is, until the young man holding her sister in a tight grip from behind, measured Abhaya up and down. A thin cruel smile on his lips, he said, "Well, well, well, what have we here?"

Half-dazed, Jeevana still recognized her sister, and yelled, "Abhaya, get away! Now!"

But Abhaya did not get away. She just stood there, taking in the situation, John all but forgotten. With a calm she had no clue she could muster, she said, "Let her go and you can have me instead."

One of the man in the inner circle broke away from Jeevana and came up behind Abhaya, grabbing her viciously. She was a mouse to his cat, sometimes bringing her near and sometimes nearly releasing her, as if still deciding her fate.

Eshaan burst out laughing, "Why let her go? Why have one when we can have two!"

"No!" shouted Jeevana, "Don't you dare touch my sister!"

Chetan and Janaki ran from street to street, looking feverishly for Abhaya.

"She left only moments ago," said Janaki to Chetan. "She couldn't have gone very far, could she?"

"I don't know," replied Chetan. "This neighborhood has a bunch of alleys and smaller streets," he said. "She could have taken any one of them."

They passed alley after alley. Most were empty, but in one, a small crowd had gathered. A commotion of some sort seemed to be breaking out, but the indistinct grunts and shouts made it impossible to figure out. Janaki and Chetan were just about to pass on to the next street when a loud "No! Don't you touch her!" rang out from the center of it all.

"Oh my God!" cried Janaki, turning pale, "that's Jeevana."

"Jeevana?" asked Chetan confused.

"Abhaya's older sister!"

"I'm calling the police." Janaki pulled out her phone and dialed the police.

Chetan rushed toward the circle of men. Janaki followed close behind, phone glued to her ear, hoping her signal would relay the location since neither of them knew exactly where they were. In the narrow spaces between the gawkers—those who wouldn't participate but would gladly be spectators at this dog fight—Chetan and Janaki saw two young women and saw that they were Jeevana and Abhaya.

Chetan felt his pulse quicken, his heart a large beating drum. Fear nearly gripped Chetan's feet, gluing him to the ground, yet a stronger irrational drive sprouting in his guts caused him to burst into the inner circle and assume a martial arts front stance.

The men stared at him, bewildered. Where did this fellow come from and what exactly was he trying to do? Once again time seemed to be standing still, but not for long. Chetan identified the person closest to him; the one that was holding Abhaya in a tight clutch. He directed a well-aimed round-house kick at the guy's kidneys. The offender yelled in pain, letting go of Abhaya and falling onto the ground. He stayed down, wailing, while his arms reaching to massage his bruised back.

Chetan did not stop. Using the confusion that his first kick created, he angled his next blow, a particularly high front kick, one that Arjuna always admired. His shoe connected with the chin of the one standing in front of Jeevana, trying to pull her pants off. The attacker yelped in pain and fell back. Only two remained of the inner circle. The guy who was holding Jeevana's legs let go and retreated to the outer circle, obviously terrified. The other guy still had Jeevana seized by her small waist.

Just moments earlier, the man holding Jeevana had an amused smirk on his face, but now that expression was gone. He pushed Jeevana violently enough to send her crashing to the ground, and out of nowhere, pulled a knife. Its blade, glinting in the dim light, was not very long, but it was sufficient to do serious damage.

Chetan's martial arts instructor's words echoed in his mind. "When attacked by a person carrying any type of knife, retreat if you can. It isn't worth the risk. It doesn't take much skill for a man with a blade to cause injury."

Yet Chetan could not run away. That was not an option. His heart thundered. Adrenaline pumping, he could only hope that his opponent was not highly skilled. Chetan's lips silently whispered a prayer to the great warrior, Lord Hanuman. He removed his light coat, winding it around his arm as an improvised shield. That was another lesson he learned from his instructor. Use any means available to you, including a piece of your clothing, to either extend your reach or protect your arm. It can make all the difference when fighting against someone with a knife. The two men circled each other once, twice, and then Eshaan savagely slashed right and left, waving the knife, before lunging at Chetan.

Chetan evaded the thrust with a sidestep, partially blocking the blade with his jacket-shielded arm. Eshaan, quick on his feet, turned to follow. Eshaan's next plunge of the knife managed to slice into Chetan's lightly protected forearm. The layer of clothing prevented the knife from going too deep, but it was just enough to tear the flesh. Chetan's nerves screamed in pain, but he refused to listen. He was a fighter, a warrior. He felt like Hanuman reincarnated. For those precious few moments, pain did not exist.

Out of the blue, a cloud of white fluff was flying at Eshaan. It was Janaki. Standing nearer than she had ever hoped to be, she flung the contents of her popcorn bucket at Eshaan. For a moment Eshaan halted his attack, disoriented. That one moment was all that Chetan needed. He closed the distance between them in half a step.

With a textbook scissor kick, the ball of his foot connected with Eshaan's ear. A soft cracking sound coincided with Eshaan flying sideways and collapsing on the ground. Eyes shut, blood streamed from his ear, Eshaan lay deathly still. A stray cat hissed nearby, and police sirens' soft wails grew louder and louder. The crowd murmured, as if awakening from deep hypnosis. Jolted, most turned and scampered away like frightened mice.

"Let's get out of here," said Jeevana, who meanwhile had gotten up and tugged her half-opened jeans back on. She struggled in vain to cover herself with remnants of her shirt.

"Here," said Abhaya, momentarily waking up from her own state of shock. She took off her sweatshirt with the large panda eyes, and handed it to Jeevana, her hands shaking. "Wear this."

Jeevana whispered "Thank you." Her voice shaky, she then turned her head to look at Chetan. As if noticing him for the first time, she said, "And thank you."

Abhaya echoed her sister. "Thank you, Chetan. We're so grateful."

Chetan, who kept his head down so as not to stare at Jeevana's partially exposed breast while she was dressing, nodded his head in acknowledgment.

"Shouldn't we stay and file a report with the police?" suggested Janaki, who felt left out. After all, a small voice at the back of her head whispered, if it wasn't for me throwing the popcorn, this could have ended up very differently.

"What for?" said Jeevana. "You know the police here. They'll lock us up as if we were the offenders. Especially since this creep is well-connected," she said, pointing at Eshaan. He lay still on the ground, eyes closed. Only his chest showed signs of life, heaving slowly. "Let's go."

Janaki nodded and pulled at a dazed Abhaya. Chetan remained standing nearby, as if nailed to the ground. Blood dripped slowly from his wounded arm, although the cut did not seem to him to be very deep.

"But where can we go?" asked Chetan. For a moment they stood still in the desolate alley.

"I don't know," said Jeevana, "But one thing is for sure, we have to get out of here." She picked a direction and started walking. The others followed, grateful for her lead.

Lagging a couple of steps behind, Janaki noticed a shining object on the ground. It was a phone. She picked it up without breaking a stride and slipped it mindlessly into her handbag. Catching up to Jeevana, Janaki asked, "Where are we heading?"

Receiving no reply, Janaki continued, "I would have invited you to my house as my parents are probably still out, but if they've come back early, we'll have a lot of explaining to do."

By then they were out of the alley and heading toward the livelier area of the city. Jeevana still did not answer. Her head was turning from side to side, searching like a lighthouse beacon. Abhaya and Chetan just followed behind silently, lost in a whirl of events. Abhaya's mind resembled a computer CPU facing an information overload.

Some minutes later, Jeevana said, "Let's head there," pointing at a building.

"Why?" asked Janaki, "what's there?"

"It looks familiar," responded Jeevana. "If this is what I think it is, then we're in luck. I think it's a pub where my friend works. She'll know what to do. She always does."

CHAPTER 46

NEW DELHI

"Thank God!" cried Jeevana as the small party arrived near The Colonel's Last Stand. "That's it! That's indeed where my friend works!"

The pub entrance was not very busy given it was still early in the evening. After a short exchange, everyone decided that Chetan, whose arm was now wrapped in a cloth torn from Jeevana's ragged shirt, would go in to look for Prema.

Moments later, he came back with Prema at his side. With a frown etched onto her forehead, Prema inspected Jeevana like an insurance claims adjustor would a property after a hailstorm. She then seemed to remember what her friend may have needed most and rushed forward to hug Jeevana as a mother would a lost child.

Jeevana, who until then held herself together, broke into a torrent of sobs on Prema's shoulder. Prema hugged her, stroking the back of Jeevana's head.

"Now, now," Prema whispered into her friend's ear, "it will all be alright. No need to worry."

Abhaya and Janaki stared at the two friends embracing before Janaki stepped toward Abhaya to hug her. Abhaya stiffened up, but moments later her back relaxed. She wanted to cry, to let it all out, but tears would not come. Her mind became a tightly shut clam with the events of the past hour playing in the far distance like her neighbors' noisy TV set.

Chetan was unsure what to do. Feeling out of place, he stared at his shoes. A couple of guys passed by and whistled at the hugging women. This made Chetan straighten up and turn sharply to face them.

One of them said, "Chill out, buddy. No one here is looking for a fight," and they moved on.

Chetan remained on guard.

"Let's go in," said Prema. "Follow me. We'll use the service door. We can figure out what to do once we're inside." The service door at the back led to a small storage room that smelled quite bad, a combination of spilled alcohol, mold and spices. Jeevana and Abhaya found places to sit, while the rest remained standing, forming a small circle. The single bare bulb, hanging from a wire, shed a harsh light.

Janaki was the first to break the awkward silence that ensued. "What's next?" she asked. Catching herself, as if by habit, she extended a hand to Prema. "By the way, I'm Janaki."

Taking her hand, she said, "Prema."

Then looking at the boy, Prema said, "And you said your name is Chetan, right?"

Chetan nodded his head yes but otherwise remained silent.

Eyeing the creeping red stain on his arm, Prema asked, "Are you hurt?"

Chetan barely nodded his head.

"Yes," volunteered Janaki. "He saved us. If it wasn't for him—"

"It was nothing," said Chetan, appearing embarrassed.

"No, it was not!" protested Janaki.

"At any rate," Prema broke in, "you're hurt. Let's take care of that first. Give me a moment." She left and went into the pub.

Moments later she came back, holding a first-aid kit. Removing the soaked piece of torn shirt, she inspected the cut on the arm. By then the bleeding had all but stopped. Prema took out a disinfecting solution. "This may sting," she warned while squirting the liquid over the wound.

Chetan squinted but said nothing.

Prema then applied a generous amount of ointment and wrapped the area with gauze. "There," she said sounding satisfied. "Just remember to redo this later and keep it clean. It shouldn't take too long to fully heal."

"Thank you," said Chetan. He moved toward the back of the room, found a crate, and seated himself on it.

"Now what?" asked Janaki, looking at her wristwatch, "I cannot stay out for much longer. My parents will be back home soon and there will be questions to answer if I'm late."

"Can you tell me what happened?" asked Prema. "All I know is that you were attacked."

Janaki was about to speak, but Jeevana went first. She relayed the evening's events to Prema in broad strokes.

"I see," said Prema when Jeevana was done. "One thing's for sure. We all must," she paused and looked around, surveying them all.

She then repeated, "we all must vow to keep this a secret. And not just for now, but forever. This can never, ever come out."

Janaki nodded yes.

Jeevana looked at Prema and said, "Yes, of course."

They looked at Abhaya who was gazing into space.

"Abhaya?" asked Jeevana.

"What?"

"You heard Prema?"

"Heard what?" Abhaya said, still sounding confused.

"About all that happened this evening," explained Jeevana, "remaining a secret?"

"Oh, of course," said Abhaya, becoming more alert.

"Yes," said Chetan, when all eyes turned on him. "Not a word to anyone, ever."

"Good," said Prema. "So we are all agreed. This is, obviously, very serious."

A knock came on the door connecting the storage room with the pub. Prema opened it narrowly and exchanged some words with a fellow employee. When she closed the door, she turned to the others and said, "I really have to get back to work. I've been out for too long. One more thing is left and that's to get you home safely. I'll go to the pub and call a taxi. You can share it and have the driver drop you off at your homes." Prema then turned to Jeevana and asked, "Do you have money to pay for the cab? I can lend you some."

"It's okay," volunteered Janaki. "I'll take care of it."

Jeevana ignored her and told Prema, "It's fine. I have cash."

After one last round of hugs, Prema disappeared into the noisy pub.

CHAPTER 47

NEW DELHI

Late the next morning, Jeevana and Abhaya were having coffee at Jeevana's favorite breakfast place. The peaceful setting was a far cry from just an hour earlier when Jeevana felt gripped in terror. She was drowning. Sharks surrounded her. Whenever she tried to ascend to the surface, their vicious teeth would snap, forcing her back to the depths of oblivion. Waking up within a start, she realized it was just a nightmare, something she had not had in years. Sharks had been a paranoia of hers ever since seeing a documentary about those sea beasts as a child. Lying in bed, she could feel beads of sweat running down her neck, all the way to the small of her back. Memories of last night flooded her mind. Jeevana's breath became fast and shallow as panic took hold of her.

With extensive mental effort, Jeevana calmed herself down, but her hands still clutched the sides of her bed. I'm okay, she told herself. I'm safe, safe at home. She looked across the room at her sister, turning in bed, and wondered if she, too, were having bad dreams. Quietly, she rose and took a quick shower. She wanted to freshen up, so she could appear calm and well put-together for her sister's sake.

Twenty minutes later, Jeevana shook Abhaya in bed, saying, "Wake up! You and I are going out. My treat."

"Who?... Why?... What?" mumbled Abhaya, still half asleep, "I didn't, I really didn't. I just wanted to help," she said, sounding confused. She rubbed her eyes and glanced at the alarm clock. "8 a.m. Really?" Then her eyes grew wide and her face went pale with horror.

Jeevana could only guess that she too was thinking of last night. Jeevana watched her all the while, holding Abhaya's hand until her breathing calmed down.

"It's okay," Jeevana was telling Abhaya, "we are home, safe. Nothing to worry about."

When the sisters had arrived home late the night before, it seemed that Lakshmi, the Goddess of Luck, was shining on them. Their parents were both out, possibly for a nightly walk. The sisters went to their room, showered and were in bed by the time their parents returned.

"You, me, breakfast, chat, plan," Jeevana said. "Now let's get a move on it, before Mom is back from the market and Father back from his morning rituals."

As she dressed, Abhaya's memories kept on drifting in and out, recalling last night in vignettes. It all looked like a movie, like someone else's story, but not her own. She had never imagined herself playing the role of a heroine, ready to sacrifice herself for her sister. Did any of this really happen? It all seemed so unreal. Her shocked mind shoved these images down in some corner of her brain, revealing only a frame at a time.

"Where do you want to go?" asked Jeevana.

"You pick," answered Abhaya. She was too tired and too confused to think. "But wait, why do we need to go out? If Mother and Father are away, can't we just stay home? I don't think I want to leave the house." Sudden fear reflected in her eyes.

"We can't talk here. There is no real privacy. Rest assured, Mother and Father will be back soon. And besides, I remember reading somewhere that it is important that we go out," she continued. "We are both still in shock," she said in a voice reminiscent of their father's lecturing. "We need to go out. It is psychologically important." She smiled at Abhaya, hiding her own doubts and concerns. "Besides, it is daytime. We'll go to a place we know on a road that's safe." "But," she glanced at her wristwatch, "we need to go out, like now."

"Okay," responded Abhaya unconvinced, and headed to the bathroom to get ready.

An hour later the sisters were munching on paranthas, a shallow fried wheat dough. Jeevana's parantha was filled with spiced potatoes while Abhaya's had cheese.

"The tea here is really good!" commented Abhaya, her mouth full, a fact that did not stop her taking a sip from the hot drink. This was her first visit to Bakul's Breakfast and Lunch.

"Mmm-hmm," agreed Jeevana, her mouth stuffed as well.

They both ate like ravenous beasts. Neither had eaten a thing the night before. In mere minutes, their bellies were full. With their teacups refilled, the sisters watched the distant glitter of the Yamuna river.

Sneaking a peek at Jeevana, Abhaya realized this was the first time the two of them had ever gone out together alone. She smiled and turned her gaze back to the river just as Jeevana sneaked a glance in her direction.

The silence between them lingered for a long while. There seemed to be no rush, nothing urgent to do, no important places to visit. They sat there for maybe five, ten minutes, but it could have easily been five hours.

Jeevana turned to Abhaya. "Well, little sister, it seems you're not that little anymore."

Abhaya, as if shaken from a daydream, shook her head and smiled at her sister.

Jeevana continued, "I just wanted to thank you. What you did yesterday evening was very selfless."

"Hmm?" responded Abhaya, not quite sure what Jeevana was referring to. "Oh!" she said. "That! That was completely useless, and probably quite stupid."

When Jeevana looked at her puzzled, Abhaya explained. "They were about to... well... hurt you, and there I was, throwing myself at their feet. And what for? They would have had me, too. As I said, completely useless and ultra-foolish." Abhaya smirked, trying to hide her embarrassment at this line of discussion.

"Not quite," responded Jeevana, her voice soft yet serious. "You did what you thought would help me. The result may not have been what you expected, but it takes nothing away from your intention, courage and self-sacrifice."

"I wish I was as sure as you," replied Abhaya. "The way I see it, if we compare this to science, it is all about results, and this 'experiment' had gone quite bad."

"You completely miss the point," said Jeevana. "You were ready to sacrifice yourself for me. No one has ever done this for me." She paused. "Furthermore, when I was your age, I can tell you for sure I did not have what it takes to do what you did. And I know that for a fact." Jeevana sighed but explained no further. Instead she said, "I've misjudged you. In a time of real need, you didn't turn your back and run away, taking care only of yourself. You forged forward and offered all that you had. You're something special, Abhaya. And you're true to your given name: 'fearless'."

But I was afraid! Abhaya wanted to protest, yet she knew what her sister meant. She could not deny that.

Jeevana continued to look at Abhaya who, instead, looked at her hands, unsure of what to say or do.

And then emotions flooded Abhaya. All that had happened last night came roaring back: the terror of it, the distress, the fear, but also the love. Abhaya's misty eyes turned from a drizzle into a downpour. She wept without uttering a sound but kept her eyes fixed on her sister.

Jeevana looked at her a moment longer before rising, coming around the table, and pulling her sister into her kneeling embrace. Abhaya quietly sobbed on her sister's shoulder. Time again stood still, or maybe moved at the speed of light. Whatever it did, it left the sisters untouched.

When they were ready, the two of them left the restaurant and headed down toward the river as if by unspoken agreement. They walked close to the water's edge, each keeping to her own thoughts. So many questions flowed into Abhaya's mind, questions she wanted to ask her sister but did not feel she could. "How did you end up in that situation? You're always so careful, so wise. How did you end up with that creep, Eshaan? You're a much better judge of people than that. What was the deal with Prema? I remember her somewhat from years ago. Weren't you best friends? Why did she disappear from your life? Was she the one you were alluding to when we spoke a while back about friendship? And what will happen next, now that you've lost your job?"

Jeevana's mind was spinning. *I saw the writing on the wall. It was there all along, loud and clear. Why did I agree to meet Eshaan? Did I really believe everything would go smoothly? Such wishful thinking. Am I that naïve? I should have just quit work. But the money.... What now? Well, that job is lost, anyhow. Meanwhile, I ended up not only risking myself but also Abhaya and her friends. This is all my fault. All my fault. Thank*

God for Abhaya's sacrifice, and also for her friend, Chetan, rescuing us. And thank God for Prema. What would I have done without her? I don't deserve such a friend.

"So what now?" Abhaya asked, shaking them both out of their tangle of thoughts. "I know I was pretty dazed, but if I recall, I heard you say yesterday evening that this guy–Eshaan?–was high-ranking at your work. Jee, what if he died? Or, what if he didn't die and he identifies us? And I presume you can't go back to work. Without your salary you said we cannot meet the rent. This means that we will be kicked out of the apartment."

Jeevana thought for a moment, looked around and pointed at a bench. "Let's sit down," she said, sounding tired. They sat half-facing each other. "Unfortunately, I cannot answer all your questions, but maybe we can discuss a few."

Abhaya nodded and paused.

"Tell me," Jeevana asked, "how much money have you made in your little secret online endeavor?"

"Oh, I don't know," Abhaya said without seeming to give it much thought. "I didn't check the last payment I received but maybe around eight, nine."

"Eight, nine what? Hundreds? And in what currency? Rupees or dollars?"

Completely nonchalant, Abhaya said, "No, no.... somewhere in the neighborhood of eight to nine thousand, and of course in US dollars. That's how they pay online." Distracted by a handsome young man walking by, Abhaya missed seeing her sister's jaw dropping, but she did turn her back when she heard Jeevana gasp.

"Abhaya," her sister said, staring at her with a mixture of perplexity, honor and embarrassment, "you realize that with only half that amount, Father could pay the rent on the apartment for one full year?"

Abhaya looked puzzled, as if Jeevana were speaking a foreign language. She heard the words but they failed to register in her mind. Then a lightbulb went off in her head. "Oh!" Abhaya cried out, her face brightening, "Wow! Yes! Of course! I see it now." A second was all it lasted before her face darkened again. Her thoughts turned to herself. *This is the money I need for my escape. I saved every penny. I need it.* A storm of emotions was swiveling inside her. *But my family... I cannot abandon them. I want to leave, but they are my only family.*

Another realization came to her. *I don't want to abandon them. As much as I can't stand Father and Jeevana, and even sometimes Mom, they are my family.*

Jeevana watched her sister's shifting expressions. "All right. You look as if you've just been to heaven, hell and back again. Since I can't yet read your mind, tell me, what's the matter?"

Abhaya did not respond.

As if treading on thin ice, Jeevana added, "I know you were planning to use the money to run away, but...."

"No!" exclaimed an upset Abhaya, "It's not that. Not that at all!"

Jeevana said nothing.

Abhaya sighed. "It is true that I did save that money for a goal. But in all honesty, I was sitting on this money all this time and just never made the connection that it could be a solution for our issues at home." Her shoulders collapsed inward and head dropped onto her chest with shame. "Never," she whispered, "not even once."

Jeevana said, "You quoted science to me earlier, remember?"

Abhaya nodded her head.

"It's the end result that matters, you claimed," continued Jeevana.

Somewhere down the street a mridanga drum was playing, underscoring the chanting of some reclusive holy men.

Jeevana said nothing more. She stared at Abhaya, her expression warm.

Abhaya knew that Jeevana wanted her to figure something out, to come to some conclusion on her own.

As the sacred music faded in the background, Abhaya's expression cleared up. She turned to her sister and said, "That's why I would like to give all of this money to Father."

"All the money?"

"All of my money," replied Abhaya.

"Maybe just keep some?" offered Jeevana. "After all, you worked hard to earn it. You should enjoy it, some of it."

"All the money," repeated Abhaya, without a hint of regret or reservation.

"And how about your plan to run away from home?" asked Jeevana cautiously.

Blushing a little as she looked at her sister, Abhaya said, "That can wait. No worries. I can make much more money. I'm quite good at what I do."

"I know you are," said Jeevana, smiling.

Abhaya laughed, which caused Jeevana's smile to lapse into laughter.

The sisters' laughter merged harmoniously with the fading drums.

After they had both calmed down, Abhaya said, "the issue is that Father cannot know where this money is coming from, and surely not from me."

"Right," said Jeevana. "I may have a way. Give me some time to think through some options, but right now, I have to go. I have some errands to run before meeting Prema for lunch."

"Oh, you have the life," teased Abhaya. "Busy as a bee from breakfast to lunch, not a worry in the world..."

"I wish," replied Jeevana as she got up from the bench, "but not quite yet."

"Oh no!" said Abhaya.

"What?" asked Jeevana, turning back to face her.

"I completely forgot! Mom grounded me and here I am, out with you."

"Mom? Grounded you?"

"Yes... long story, but the bottom line is that I was not supposed to leave home without her permission."

"So what were you doing out last night?" asked Jeevana.

"Well," replied Abhaya, "I did get permission for that. Well...not exactly for going out to the movies, but for going to study with Janaki. It's another long story. The question is, what should I do about being out this morning?"

Jeevana considered this for a moment and then said, "Don't sweat it. I'll call Mom on my way to Prema and tell her that I asked you out for a one-to-one sisters talk. I'll tell her you did warn me that you were grounded but that I talked you into this. I'll take responsibility. Mom would love the idea of the two of us going out," she smirked. "She hinted to me in so many words that it would give her great pleasure to see us connect. Trust me, it won't be an issue. Just head back home from here and you should have no trouble at all."

"Okay," said Abhaya. "I'll do that."

"See you later, Sis," Jeevana said as she walked away.

"See you," replied Abhaya, and she added in a much softer voice, as if tasting the word for the first time: "Sis."

Despite needing to head back home, Abhaya stayed at the bench a while longer, staring at the Yamuna river. She needed more time to reflect, and watching the water did her good. She reflected on its mystical wisdom, her roots, and her future, which seemed all wrapped in mist.

After a time, she rose and headed toward her neighborhood in anything but a straight line. She allowed her feet to carry her wherever they would go. Not knowing how, Abhaya found herself standing in front of a familiar sadhu, the same holy man sitting on a small carpet that she had passed once before with Janaki. Eyes shut, half-naked, and forehead carrying marks of white ashes, the sadhu was still seated in that same meditative pose. In the weeks that passed by, he may have never moved from his place for more than a few minutes here and there. That was not uncommon for holy men who were known for taking all sorts of unusual vows.

Abhaya stood there, watching him, recalling their last encounter, their staring battle, or at least that was how she remembered it. People passed by, not giving the two of them a second look, when suddenly the old man's face stretched into a wide smile. Abhaya found herself smiling back, not really knowing how or why, but smiling and feeling deeply contented.

She continued to observe the sadhu, no longer challenging him in her mind to open his eyes and duel. The holy man nodded his head in her direction through closed eyes. She took his nod as approval. Abhaya bowed gently and moved on. Happiness like a flower bloomed in her heart.

CHAPTER 48

NEW DELHI

Janaki was sitting in her room, staring at a cell phone. Looking for her own phone that she had dumped in her handbag right after calling the police, Janaki pulled out another one instead. It was the one that she'd picked up off the street after the fight. Until that morning, she had forgotten about it. Janaki recognized the phone as Abhaya's. She reasoned that Abhaya must have dropped it during the attack. The device was still charged and working, although a long ugly scratch decorated its otherwise smooth face.

Janaki knew there was no password. Despite her knowledge of the hazards related to internet security breaches, Abhaya never bothered to password protect her own phone. Janaki had nagged her about it, but Abhaya, being stubborn, said that unlike Janaki, she never lost valuable items such as cell phones. The arrogance, Janaki thought. Yet she thought it without animosity. Given yesterday's events, she felt protective of her friend, akin to a lioness toward her cub.

After some hesitation, Janaki made up her mind to check the messages. She needed to know what caused her friend to rush out of the theater the way she did. The texting app opened up onto Abhaya's thread with John. Janaki, a fast reader, scrolled quickly through the exchange, her eyes widening all the while. Was her friend out of her mind? It was quite obvious that John was just being flirtatious, nothing more, nothing less. What had she been thinking? Janaki wondered. No worries, she thought, I'll fix it. With John out of the picture, Janaki hoped to maneuver Chetan to take John's place in Abhaya's heart.

"Janaki dear," came her mother's voice from the dining area, "will you join us for breakfast?"

"Coming!" responded Janaki. She was indeed quite hungry.

Her father, a large balding man who preferred to wear dark business suits, even on weekends at home, was reading the morning papers while her mother poured him coffee. "Such violent acts are happening not just late at night, but in the evening, too," he muttered to no one in particular. "Something must be done! The police here are completely useless."

"What now?" asked Janaki, although the butterflies in her stomach hinted at what he was about to say.

Her dad read aloud, "Listen to this: 'In yet another merciless attack, a young professional male (name reserved by the editor for privacy) who is a manager at a large help desk firm, was beaten unconscious in the early hours of the evening. The victim received a strong blow to the head, possibly with a hard object, resulting in a severe concussion and loss of memory. He was left for dead until found by a police patrol that was alerted to the area by a Good Samaritan.'"

Hypnotized by the news piece, Janaki hardly noticed she was called a Good Samaritan.

Her father continued. "'Police suspect this act was done by a gang member, possibly as part of an initiation ceremony since the victim's wallet was not taken, thus ruling out a robbery. No eyewitnesses have come forward at this time and the Good Samaritan who reported the event remains unknown.

"The police are currently requesting the help of the public with any information about the attack. The victim's family is offering a reward of 50,000 rupees. The victim is expected to recover but doctors are skeptical as to whether he will regain his full memory or make a full mental recovery.

"This attack," says Jayesh Babu, a civil rights advocate, "illustrates again the need for better lighting in the streets as well as enhanced police patrols. It is inconceivable that our citizens would continue to live in fear in our own city." If you have any information...'"

Her father looked up from his paper. "This Jayesh," he muttered, again more to himself than to anyone else, "is always pushing his nose into others' business, making a self-promoting agenda of whatever will net him political gain."

"True, dear," agreed Janaki's mother, "but he does have a good point. This must stop. I just dread each time our Janaki goes out in the evening.

Imagine if something like this happened to her!" She turned a loving smile toward her daughter, a smile that morphed into concern. "What is the matter dear?" she asked Janaki. "You look so pale."

Janaki realized that her face was showing more than she wished and quickly improvised. "Oh," she said, "it's just that I still have... you know, my..." and pointing down toward her belly while sneaking a worried look at her father, concerned that he might overhear, "my period."

"Oh!" said her mom, nodding her head in understanding.

I've got to tell Abhaya about this, thought Janaki, but how can I reach her when her phone is in my hand? And what do I do with it now? She had no issue telling Abhaya that she'd picked it up for her yesterday evening. In fact, she was quite sure Abhaya would be very grateful, but she also felt that it might be best for Abhaya's sake to rid her of the phone. It might clear Abhaya's mind of her crush on John. Janaki knew it was silly, but in her mind's eye, "a new phone is a new beginning." Yes, she thought, I'll do away with that phone, maybe throw it into the Yamuna as a sacrifice, and say nothing to Abhaya, not about the phone and definitely not about what I think of her exchange with John. Let fantasies rest in the past, or for that matter, at the bottom of a river. She hurriedly finished breakfast and set out to see Abhaya. After all, she reminded herself, Abhaya is grounded, so it is probable that she'll be home. I can go visit her under the pretext of school work left over from last night. Again, she grinned to herself, praising her own craftiness.

Chetan woke with a start. He shook his head, trying to rid himself of the numbness surrounding his skull. It felt as if his head were under constant pressure, wearing a practice helmet that was too small. All night he had had nightmares, dreams of facing a hostile crowd while fighting a large animal. The creature appeared as a shape-shifting vicious dog, a wild satanic cat, a hissing poisonous snake and a raging bull. Chetan was trying to strike it without much success. The crowd around the ring booed him, throwing rotten tomatoes and white confetti, or was it popcorn?

Arjuna was there, too, as his trainer, encouraging him at times and mocking him at other times. Sometime during the night, Chetan realized his fighting was to save a maiden tied to a tall pole above the ring, as if in a computer game. The captured heroine's face was also shifting–one moment it was Abhaya, then Janaki, then another, older woman he did not fully recognize. And then, just as he was about to throw a winning kick at the head of the beast, the entire ring collapsed, and he was falling into utter darkness. That was when he woke up, drenched in sweat and hurting. "It's okay, I'm okay," he kept repeating to himself speaking softly, "It's just aftershock."

Chetan was grateful that he had once absorbed a lecture about the psychology of combat and its possible aftereffects that his martial arts instructor, a retired ex-commando, had given them. It included a description of ASD, Acute Stress Disorder, a condition experienced by untested fighters after facing high stress levels. "The body takes time to digest and get rid of it," his teacher explained. Chetan remembered the list of symptoms, including the headaches, numbness, vivid dreams. "In extreme cases, such a condition could turn into Post Traumatic Stress Disorder, but for the most part, it should clear in a few days to a few weeks. Meditation is a good tool for treating this condition."

That suggestion surprised the class. Chetan never imagined it would be his fearless instructor who would teach him mindfulness techniques.

"Meditation is also a good tool prior to competitions. We will dedicate fifteen to twenty minutes every class over the coming weeks to practicing mindfulness techniques. I expect each and every one of you–including you Arjuna–wipe that grin off your face or you will soon find yourself giving me a hundred pushups–to practice these at home every day."

Chetan, a dedicated student, had followed his instructor's command. By now, he had a good grasp on how to enter that state of mind quickly. He spent the next twenty minutes in deep meditation. That is, until his phone buzzed.

It was Arjuna. "Good morning, chicken feet! I'm waiting for you for breakfast and practice. Where in heaven's name are you?"

Before Chetan had a chance to respond, another message pinged.

Arjuna again. "I'll forgive your tardiness only if you tell me you spent yesterday evening with a nice girl ;-)"

Chetan thought about his promise. He replied, "Sorry. No such luck. I just overslept. Heading out in 10 min. Please order the usual for me. I'll be there in 20 min."

"Okay, boss. You the man, the cat slayer, the lady's knight on a shiny white donkey."

Chetan knew Arjuna was tempting him into his favorite text duel, expecting him to correct donkey with a horse. Not now, not today, he thought. He placed the phone down and slowly got out of bed. His arm throbbed with pain. "Ouch! And I forgot that I also need to replace the bandage!"

Chetan sighed in exasperation. This was worse than the fight itself. The phone buzzed again. What now? Arjuna can be such a pain in the butt at times.

Chetan debated sharing the events of last night with his best friend. On the one hand, he was eager to do so–Arjuna, being the giant of a person that he was, never had to put his martial arts skill to practice. People always made the smarter choice of avoiding a confrontation with him. In that respect, Chetan would have a tale to share that would make even Arjuna envious. But on the other hand, Chetan vowed–they had all vowed, Abhaya, Janaki, her sister and her sister's friend–to keep everything absolutely confidential. The sister's friend–Prema, he remembered–reiterated to them time and time again how bad this could turn if the story got out. They, and most certainly Chetan, would surely be arrested and thrown in jail. The justice system in this region was no different than anywhere else in this country. That is to say, it was anything but just. He may be a minor, and he may have come to the defense of women, but the way things were, the one with the most money wins.

According to Abhaya's sister, the guy he fought last night came from a wealthy family. No, Chetan would keep his lips sealed. Not a word to anyone, not even to Arjuna. His phone buzzed again. All right, all right already, muttered Chetan, as he picked it up. There were two messages, both from Janaki.

"Good morning, Chetan. Just checking how r u doing?"

That's nice of her, thought Chetan, very kind.

"I guess ur still sleeping or can't answer. OK. Buzz me when u can. ttyl."

Chetan typed a quick reply, confirming he was fine, and hurried to the bathroom. He was going to be late on top of already being late.

CHAPTER 49

NEW YORK CITY

Rache had just arrived for her Sunday afternoon shift at Jose's Place.

"Rache," called Dina, the host.

"Yes?" she replied, eager to punch in.

"Some guy dropped by a letter for you earlier," continued Dina. "He asked that I give it to you in person. He was actually quite persistent. Cute fellow, though, so I agreed."

She handed Rache a sealed letter that had "Rache/Jose's Place" written on front. "A secret admirer?" winked Dina, "or a new job offer?"

"Thanks," Rache said, snatching the envelope and shoving it into her back pocket. She was curious, but she was late enough and not about to reward Dina's nosiness with a dignified reply. She went to the employees' tiny lounge to punch in and finish her preparations, such as touching up her makeup and tying on an apron. By the time she was done, the envelope in her pocket was all but forgotten.

CHAPTER 50

NEW DELHI

"This may actually work," said Jeevana to Prema while the latter busied herself chopping salad for their lunch. She was seated by the small table in Prema's cozy apartment. The strong indirect sun flecked the kitchen floor with bright yellow dancing spots.

"Of course it will," Prema said. "All things end well in our fairytale." She brought the salad to table and they started to eat.

"So let me repeat this, just to make sure I have it right," said Jeevana in between bites. "Abhaya will transfer some of the money she made into my account. I'll bring the money home and say that I was solicited to take another position elsewhere, and that this is the recruiting bonus. I'll also add that the new job pays much better so my paycheck going forward will be double what it was before. That will suffice. I don't think my parents will question it. They are quite gullible when it comes to my world."

"Exactly," Prema said. "And as I mentioned, I have some good news for you on that other front."

"Okay," said Jeevana, "but before you go on, my sister will probably continue to insist that all the money she has should be used. She's a little, well... hard-headed."

"Ha!" Prema burst out, laughing. "Seems like it's a family trait." She winked at Jeevana, who was still too invested into her own line of thought to notice. "Okay. This is how to play it, if Abhaya acts that way."

"Oh, rest assured, she will," Jeevana said.

"Right. Explain to her that bringing in so much money all at once will look suspicious. What you will give your dad–about half Abhaya's savings– will be plenty to cover rent for a half a year and possibly much more. We'll worry about the rest later. Abhaya should hold the rest of the money in her account if and when it's needed."

"Abhaya will be disappointed."

Prema looked at her and smirked, "Well, if she's so eager to get rid of the money, I can always find good use for it."

"Like what?" asked Jeevana, "Give it to the poor?"

"Are you kidding me?" exclaimed Prema. "No, no. There's this handbag I've had been eyeing for a while."

Both friends giggled.

When their laughter subsided, Jeevana reminded her, "You mentioned some good news? I could use some now."

"Well...." started Prema.

Janaki paced the street in front of Abhaya's apartment. Looking up, she saw her turn the final corner. "Here you are!" Janaki called out, relieved. "I went up to your apartment, but your mom said you were out with your sister and didn't know when you'd be back."

"And here you are," replied Abhaya. "What's up?"

"I tried calling you on your phone," said Janaki, "but it went directly to voicemail."

"Yes," replied Abhaya. "I seem to have misplaced it. It sucks. I've never done that before."

"Hmmm," Janaki nodded while recalling her decision to dump Abhaya's phone into the river earlier that morning. Although she told herself at the time that she did it to protect her friend, there was a tinge of satisfaction in the act.

"All my contacts were in there," moaned Abhaya. "My photos–well, for these I do have a backup in the cloud, but not for all as I was running out of space. I also never bothered backing up my texts."

It looked as if the final words pained Abhaya.

Janaki kept her mouth shut.

Abhaya shrugged. "Oh well, I guess it's time for a new page."

Janaki nodded her head, full of understanding. She was half-smiling to herself. This was exactly what she hoped would happen. Boy, am I good at this! Janaki looked around as if checking for spies. "Let's go to your room," she whispered. "We shouldn't talk so freely here."

Abhaya agreed.

Once settled on Abhaya's bed with the door shut tight, Janaki pulled an article from the morning paper out of her purse. She placed it in Abhaya's hands, pointing to the story about the attack. Abhaya took her time reading it and then she re-read it. Raising her head with naked rage in her eyes, Abhaya stared at her friend.

This is the Abhaya I know, thought Janaki, fierce like the Goddess Durga. Deep in her heart she envied that in her friend. She was glad to see that the attack had not reduced her friend's ability to express her full emotions. When Abhaya hates someone, she thought, she really hates them. There is nothing tainting her feelings. Not like me. I have to hide my reactions like everyone expects me to.

"This is outrageous!" exclaimed Abhaya. "We should let them know who the real victim is, and who is the villain!"

"Are you crazy?" exclaimed Janaki. "This is good news! It means that the police haven't a clue and probably aren't able to crack it. This is great, so long as the four of us—no, the five of us, including your sister's friend—keep our mouths shut."

Abhaya, eyes narrowed, still steaming. Despite her wits, she did not seem to get it.

"Look," added Janaki, "this is India. Despite all the latest efforts to fight corruption, this country is still ranked high up there when it comes to bribery. This guy, the one your sister was dating, is wealthy, or, from what I understand, comes from a very wealthy and influential family. Who do you think the police and judges would believe? A bunch of teenagers, or those who will pay a hefty sum under the table to have a verdict levied in their favor?"

The words washed over Abhaya as if they were a bucket of ice-cold water.

"I'm sorry," murmured Janaki, her voice softening, "I really am. But look at it another way. Justice was served. And Chetan is the one who served it."

"You're right," said Abhaya.

In the silence that followed, echoes of the neighbor's TV news broadcast reverberated through the wall.

"Speaking of which," said Janaki, not wanting to miss the opportunity she crafted beforehand, "what do you think about Chetan?"

Abhaya gave her a confused look. Her eyes said, "What are you talking about?" When Janaki remained silent, Abhaya spoke. "Well, he's kind of cute and I'm very thankful to him. He didn't look the type that would do what he did last night, did he? But I guess, as my sis is fond of saying, 'Never judge a book by its cover.'"

Janaki smiled. "How about," she started asking when there was an unexpected knock at the door. Abhaya's mom peeked her head in.

"Lemonade, girls?" she asked, her melodic voice half-singing the words.

"Sure!" responded Janaki before Abhaya had a chance to refuse. That, she thought, would buy her more time.

Abhaya's mom smiled kindly at Janaki before closing the door.

"What if," continued Janaki, picking up where she left off, "I can arrange for another movie-night. And this time," she added, reading a flicker of suspicion crossing her friend's face, "we will invite Chetan to join."

Dummy, Janaki reproached herself, I almost tipped my hand that yesterday evening was a setup. She continued, "I mean, so that there are no chance encounters, I'll see if Chetan can bring a friend so it won't be so awkward. And maybe," she added, going on the offensive before Abhaya had a chance to squeeze in a word, "next time, you might not be so preoccupied with your phone. Maybe you could act more civilized!"

"Look who's talking!" protested Abhaya, taking the bait. "Ms. mobile phone herself!"

"Not true!" argued Janaki, "I may text a lot but...."

"You can say that again," she laughed.

"—but," continued Janaki, ignoring the interruption, "I don't do that while on a date with someone." She quickly bit her lower lip. I was doing so well, and now I'm screwing it up.

"I didn't know it was a date," said Abhaya. Not missing a beat, she added in a voice dripping with suspicion, "Janaki, was that whole chance encounter with Chetan yesterday orchestrated?"

"No, no!" Janaki vehemently denied. "What I meant to say is that it became a sort of a date, once Chetan joined us."

"I see." Abhaya remained unconvinced.

Just then, the door opened, and Abhaya's mom stepped in carrying a tray with two glasses filled with lemonade and a small dish of sweets. "Here you go," she smiled, placing the tray down before turning to leave the room.

Using the distraction to change the topic before Abhaya could continue her investigation, Janaki asked, "How did it go with your parents last night?"

"Luckily, they were still out when Jee and I got back. We must have been fast asleep by the time they returned. I didn't hear a thing, and neither did Jee."

"Good," said Janaki. "So how come you went out with your sister this morning?" she asked.

"My sister arranged it." She was getting tired of Janaki's questions.

"Anything interesting? I mean in the conversation between you and Jeevana?" poked Janaki.

"Not really."

Janaki could tell that Abhaya was still upset with her over Janaki's revelations at dinner the other day. She decided to press on, regardless. Janaki sipped her lemonade and reached out for another sweet. "So what do you say?" she asked, her mouth half full. "Can I arrange a date? I think we have to make it up to poor Chetan. There he was, landing an evening with two gorgeous girls, and he ends up having one of them run out on him while the other throws popcorn at him," she giggled.

Despite herself, Abhaya smiled, too. "Oh well, okay," she said. "Looks like it's not such a bad idea to go out with someone who can double as my own personal bodyguard."

"A bodyguard," squealed Janaki. "I like that!"

"But wait until you hear from me to set it up," said Abhaya. "Don't forget, I'm still grounded, and I have to work things out with my mom. And I don't want to pull what we did last night anytime soon."

"How long until you're off the hook?" asked Janaki, worried that this could potentially put a damper in her new plot.

"Not long," assured her Abhaya. "Judging by my mother's better mood this morning, I expect I'll be able to patch things up with her soon. I hope to be free again next weekend."

"Good," responded Janaki with a sigh of relief, reaching out for another sweet.

CHAPTER 51

NEW YORK CITY

Ending another long shift, Rache returned to the employee lounge. Taking off her apron, she heard something fall to the floor. It was a letter; the letter Dina handed her hours prior. "Crap," Rache muttered. She had completely forgotten about it. Punching out, she left the restaurant and entered the subway, heading home

Twenty minute later in a half empty subway car headed to Queens, she finally relaxed and opened the envelope.

"Dear Rache"

Hmm... She quickly shifted her gaze to the bottom of the page looking for a name, a signature. Sure enough, she found one: John.

Who the heck is John? She read on, "You may not remember me,"

No, I don't, thought Rache.

The mysterious sender seemed to have been guessing her thoughts as he wrote, "but I sure do remember you."

An admirer? wondered Rache. Was Dina right? I hate that host, always so full of herself. Or maybe it's from someone complaining about my service.

"I will forever be thankful."

Okay, not a complaint. This sounds more promising.

"I'm the guy who used to come to Jose's every weekend for brunch, always ordering the same huevos rancheros."

That rang a bell, but Rache had so many customers. Who was this guy?

"Anyhow, you probably still don't know who I am, and that's okay."

Very kind of you. Now get on with it!

"What you may remember is that I'm also the guy who just yesterday morning had his girlfriend [who, incidentally, is also named Rachel (and sometimes Rache)] walk out on him."

Now she remembered. That's the guy who stiffed me with the bill, she thought. She read on with increasing interest.

"At any rate, when that happened, I froze–please excuse the cliché–like a deer in the headlights. You kindly came over and encouraged me to follow the one I love, the only one I ever loved. If it wasn't for you, I might have lost her forever."

A little dramatic, maybe, but so very romantic! Rache allowed herself a smile.

"You see, my Rache, was very upset at me-"

You can say that again...

"and through no fault of my own,"

Why do guys always believe it's not their fault?

"she thought I was in love with another woman. It's really too complicated to explain in a brief letter, so I'll just summarize the rest."

Yes, please do.

"Rachel was upset at me, but also annoyed that she needed to work on a weekend, and a lot of other life-issues in general. She went to her office and was planning to resign as soon as her boss came in. Her plan was to pack a suitcase and just take off somewhere around the world. To travel on a whim. It's not something she would usually do, but that's where her head was after leaving the restaurant. If that had happened, I suspect I would have lost her, possibly forever. But because of you, I showed up at her office just before her boss arrived, and after a short quarrel, I was able to explain the misunderstanding. On the spot, I asked her to marry me and she said yes! We are engaged!"

"We further agreed it would be best for her to resign. She hates that job. She's been unhappy for a long while. She and I will be headed for a couple of weeks to the West Coast for an unplanned vacation, after which we may actually, if we like it, relocate. She can use a change of pace and some distance from her family, and I would love to be closer to Silicon Valley, given my new venture."

Wow! Too much information. This guy was dumping details on her, way beyond what she expected or could grasp.

"I'm sorry, I know it is way TMI and that you probably have no clue as to half of what I'm talking about it. But let me reiterate the bottom line: I'm eternally thankful."

"Separately, I also realized that I left in a hurry and did not pay my bill. Sorry about that. I didn't mean to stiff you. To set things right, I'm enclosing a check for a hundred dollars. It should cover the meal and the tip."

Holy–, that's a killer-nice tip! The bill had been about $25.

"Many thanks again. I'm not sure if I'll have a chance to see you again at Jose's before we leave New York City, but, at any rate, this story is not something I could have entertained you with while at work, so a letter seemed a better idea."

"My very best wishes, John"

Rache smiled and even wiped away a tear. She felt quite emotional.

"Briarwood / Main Street," came the announcement through the subway's speakers.

Rache cursed when she realized that she had just missed her stop. She would have to backtrack several blocks. Oh well, she further thought, it was worth it.

CHAPTER 52

NEW DELHI

Late in the evening, Abhaya was getting ready to call it a day. Sitting on her bed with no phone for texting friends, she felt restless. More than restless, she felt as if she were missing a limb. Well, she thought, maybe not a whole a limb. Maybe just a finger. Or at least a fingernail. Whatever. Tomorrow. Tomorrow after school, I'll go and buy myself a new phone. I know I committed all the money I have to the family, but paying for a cell phone will hardly make a dent in those funds. I deserve at least that.

Large yellow cat eyes stared down at her from the "Walk on the Wild Side" poster above her sister's empty bed. One day I should find this film. I wonder what Jeevana found in it?

Another thought occurred to her. Where is Jeevana? It is getting late. She shouldn't be out so late.

Argh, she caught herself, I'm becoming a mother hen. Stop it! But she could not. Her mind obsessively went back to the prior evening with all its horrors. And that was not funny. Not funny at all, she thought. She already dreaded the dreams this night would bring.

The door opened and Jeevana stepped in.

"Where have you been? It's so late!" exclaimed Abhaya. Her face was flushed with worry.

"I spent a lot of time with Prema," answered Jeevana unapologetically. She seemed oblivious to her sister's concern. After taking off her shoes and peeling off the nice shirt she was wearing, Jeevana plopped onto her bed. "By the way, I have a few updates," she said.

"What happened?" Abhaya's concern was about to grow into a full-size panic attack. "Is everything okay? Are you okay?"

"Yes, yes," replied Jeevana, "it's just been a long and...well...interesting day."

"Not like yesterday's interesting day I hope," said Abhaya.

"No, no," said Jeevana, "a different type of interesting. All in all, a much better one, and if you cut me a break for a moment and stop asking so many questions, I might actually be able to tell you something."

"All right. I'm sorry. It is just that you're making me nervous. Go on."

"To start with," said Jeevana, "turns out that our incident last night made it into the morning news. Have you heard about it?"

"Yes. Janaki showed me the paper. I'm not sure what to make of it. She thinks we are in the clear."

"So it seems," agreed Jeevana. "That is, as long as we all keep our mouths shut. I really don't want this to come out, for our sake as well as for the sake of your boyfriend–what was his name? Chetan?"

"Right," Abhaya nodded her head but added, "and for the record, he's not my boyfriend."

Jeevana did not seem to hear. "We were lucky and should consider ourselves such. I have given it a lot of thought–it was all so horrible!–but you and I have each other for support. We need to talk about it, share. Whenever you feel afraid, don't hold it in. Talk with me. I promise to do the same."

"Okay...." said Abhaya, a bit surprised.

Again, Jeevana was no longer treating her as a baby sister but rather more as an equal. She liked it, and she liked how much closer she already felt to her sister.

"The other reason I stayed late had to do with some favors Prema did for me. I didn't deserve this from her, but that's Prema. She is one of the kindest people you'll ever meet." Jeevana was getting emotional. She took a moment to collect herself and continued. "Anyhow, between yesterday and today, Prema already moved ahead on some opportunities for me. She realized I would not be able to go back to work at the call center. This was even before we heard that the creep Eshaan would probably not regain much of his memory. But even if I knew he wouldn't, I wouldn't want to go back to work at that place. Not ever. But I need a job."

"Turns out that two of her contacts came through. One is a customer of hers at the pub, a young executive who works at a different help desk center. Prema contacted him and he agreed to give me an off-the-record interview. That's where I was this evening. He hired me on the spot."

"That's wonderful!" interjected Abhaya.

"Yes, it is," agreed Jeevana. "It's pending approval, but he assured me I can consider it done. I'll hear the final word from him within the next twenty-four hours. It would be a part-time position, but it's a start. My salary will be half of what I was making, but our parents don't need to know that, and you and I have already discussed how to address the needed funds."

"Yes, and about that," interrupted Abhaya again, "I know I pledged all the money I made."

"Are you having second thoughts?" asked Jeevana.

"No, no, it's not that at all. It's just that I really need to get a new cell phone. It seems that during the attack, I lost mine. I can't live without one. I'll buy something simple, not expensive. Please?"

Jeevana smiled. "First of all, you don't need to ask for permission. It is your money. You earned it."

"I know, I know," said Abhaya, "but I promised."

"Second," Jeevana cut her off, "I spoke about this with Prema and she brought up a good point. We cannot bring in all that money, not all at once. It will look suspicious. So you will transfer only half of it to me and keep the rest. If more is needed some months from now, we will worry about it then."

"But I wanted to give it all!" protested Abhaya.

"And that's okay," said Jeevana. "Your intention is what matters here. And, as with science, it is the end result. No need to make a show of it. Besides," she winked at Abhaya and, stealing her friend's line, said, "if you really want to get rid of the money, there is this handbag both me and Prema were eyeing...."

Abhaya's frown turned into a smile. "Wait! Wait! There was this bag that I was eyeing. Perhaps it's the same one...Maybe the three of us can go shopping together one day–on me!" She chuckled.

"Now that's an idea," smiled Jeevana.

"You mentioned two contacts Prema had for you?" asked Abhaya.

"Oh yes," replied Jeevana. "The other one is a professor at the university I was attending before I had to drop out. He joined the faculty shortly before I left. I didn't really get a chance to meet him. Turns out he takes yoga classes with Prema and they sort of became friends. And no," she quickly added, seeing Abhaya's raised eyebrows, "not that sort of a friend. He could be her father! But it seems they both enjoy an occasional conversation over a cup of tea, and so she has his ear–as well as his private cell phone number. She called him this morning and had a long chat. Bottom line is that he's going to meet with me later this week, and if he likes what he sees, he might be able to arrange for me to have an assistant laboratory position at the university. You know I was on full scholarship but once I dropped out, I lost that privilege. Even if I get back to studying, the funding allocated to me has already been assigned to someone else. But if I come back as a lab assistant, I can study part-time. Not only will it be tuition-free, but I'll also make a little money. Granted, it will be very little money, but still...."

Abhaya's face glowed. "This is simply wonderful!" Abhaya exclaimed.

"Hold your horses," warned Jeevana. "Let's first see if he likes what he sees."

"And how can he not?" said Abhaya. "And if he can't, just tell him you're my sister. They'll let you in."

Jeevana laughed. "I can believe that."

They both were giggling once again.

A knock came at the door, and their mother stuck her head in. "What is going on?" she wondered, fully puzzled. "Are you girls all right? I don't think I've heard you laughing so much in a very long time."

"Yes, Mom," responded Abhaya. "All's good."

"All right," she said. She smiled and closed the door.

Waiting a few moments for their mother to be out of earshot, Jeevana whispered, "You see, everything happens for a reason and all in good time."

"I don't really believe that," responded Abhaya frowning. "You, almost getting... you know, violated, and me, almost, well, the same?"

"You don't have to believe it," replied Jeevana softly. "That's okay. But one day, you may, just may, come to realize it. I, too, am still learning to accept it."

"To each her own," said Abhaya. She knew she would never believe that something good could come from assault. It seemed to be a lame excuse that people used to forget a tragedy and move on. "By the way," she added,

"I meant to ask you, what do you think? Should we get Mom her dining room table back? I see her face each time she passes by where the table used to be. I swear it's like someone seeing a ghost."

"No," said Jeevana after a short pause. "Father would absolutely not appreciate it. But I wouldn't worry about it right now. I have little doubt that once some money comes in–that is, your money through me–Father will do the right thing and get it back himself. You know, it may not always seem that way, but I know for a fact that despite his hard shell, Father loves Mother very much."

"Oh, I know. Trust me, I know, too," Abhaya said quietly.

Jeevana gave her a probing look, but Abhaya didn't explained further.

CHAPTER 53

NEW DELHI

"You see," said Janaki to Chetan, "it all worked out, just as I planned." She cornered him at the schoolyard later that week during a break. The text that he sent the day after the attack simply said, "Thanks. I'm fine," and she wanted to make sure that he was indeed okay. She also wanted an acknowledgement for her important role during that dreadful evening. He may have been the star of the show, but in her mind, she was the director. While the star gets the fame, the director gets the credit.

"What?" exclaimed Chetan. "As you planned? With Abhaya getting attacked, and all of us almost getting killed, or, at least, seriously injured?"

"Keep your voice down!" Janaki shushed. "We don't need the whole world to learn of this. We all took a vow of secrecy, remember?"

She liked the idea of all of them sharing a secret. It made her feel special and important, as if she belonged to a secret society, an elite group of justice seekers, much like in the movies, at least in the ones with the superheroes. The fact that these films were based on comic books did not matter.

"Who came out the hero?" she challenged him, ignoring his points about the violent turn of events.

When Chetan kept quiet, she volunteered, "You did!" Smugly, she repeated though a bit more softly, "Just as I planned."

Chetan just rolled his eyes.

"Listen," she added as if inspired by an afterthought, "Would you and your friend–I forgot his name, the big fellow–like to go out with Abhaya and me to the movies this weekend? Maybe this time, it will be with a little less real-life drama."

The offer caught Chetan by surprise. His naturally open expression disclosed his naïve delight. "Sure!" he said. "I just need to check with Arjuna, but I don't think it'll be an issue. I think he actually... well... fancies you. So yeah, I'd love to!"

Ha! thought Janaki, ignoring Chetan's comment about Arjuna. Thus starts the sequel to my play. Boy, I'm so good at this, she smiled. Bollywood, be warned. Here I come!

Later that afternoon, Abhaya was sitting in front of her computer. She was checking the freelancing website. Two new messages awaited her in the inbox. The first one read:

"Dear Abby,

Thank you for submitting a bid."

Abhaya's eyes skimmed through the rest of the message, searching for keywords. "Unfortunately, we have...."

Abhaya started pursing her lips as the rejection began to form. It reminded her of a sunny midsummer day suddenly being taken over by a dark cloud, but she caught herself. Turning her grimace into a smile, she announced aloud to no one in specific, "Their loss!"

Her gaze captured the name of her pseudo character, Abby. Abhaya narrowed her eyes, lines of thoughts forming over her forehead like waves across a stormy ocean. And then, struck by inspiration, she clicked "edit." Moments later the screen name "Abby" became "Abhaya."

"Are you sure you want to make this change?" an automated message prompted.

"Yes," clicked Abhaya. Somehow this made her pleased, but it was insufficient. She looked at Abby's image of white skin and blond hair, smiling back at her from the screen. Abhaya hesitated, her index finger hovering over the mouse. She knew all too well the possible financial ramifications if she proceeded with these changes. People with foreign names and foreign faces cannot be expected to charge as much hourly as people with Western names and appearances. She had been there before and experienced the disappointments. Abhaya bit her lip, her finger tapping on the edit link. She looked again at her name and the photo of Abby.

"No!" she said aloud. "This simply will not do." If they won't have me for who I am, they won't have me at all. She edited Abby's photo, deleting it, and inserted one of her own, an image of the real Abhaya. At least my page profile still includes all the positive reviews from the half a dozen other jobs I've successfully completed. That should help me win new work.

Looking at her updated profile, Abhaya smiled. She liked what she saw. Abby, Abhaya thought to herself, is definitely not as interesting and mysterious as Abhaya. I like Abhaya much better. She then rushed to open the second message in her inbox. Not much time left, she realized. Her dad would be coming home in a few minutes. They had another Internet lesson to do together. Father asked her earlier this morning if "they could give it another shot."

With the little scheme she and Jeevana had pulled together, funneling money his way through Jeevana's new fictional job, tensions in the house calmed down and her dad became much more amiable. He actually smiled at her when she left for school this morning, a refreshing change.

The second message in her inbox was from a small Australian firm looking for a PHP developer; PHP being a programming language Abhaya was quite good at. That bid she won, and it made her smile. She copied the name of the company representative, the one that signed the acceptance message, into Facebook search. By chance or not, his name was... John. Is that a good or a bad omen? Abhaya wondered. In her mind, she had already nicknamed him Kangaroo John to distinguish him from the New York Long John. Since her father had not yet arrived, Abhaya copied the Facebook profile link onto her new phone and texted it to Janaki.

Abhaya texted, "Check this one out."

"Ok."

A moment later, Abhaya wrote, "A new client of mine. Did you notice his name?"

"No. Go on"

"John! I think I'm going to call him Kangaroo John. Kind of cute, isn't he?"

Janaki sent an emoji rolling its eyes. "Oh no, here we go again."

--- The End ---

ACKNOWLEDGEMENTS

To my dearest wife, Yael, and my cherished kids; a source of constant inspiration.

Special thanks to Tamara Fish, whose assistance during the process of writing, proved crucial to completing this work. My thanks are also extended to Star Galler, who corrected many of my short stories, as I started on my writing career path. Star is also the one who suggested that this tale be made into a novel.

My gratitude to my MJP editor Lara, for her excellent guidance, as well as to my dear friend Scott Korbin, who introduced me to David. Much thanks also to various helpers along the road, including but not limited to my family, Mary Payson, and Prarna Desai. Finally, big thanks to the entire Morgan James Publishing team, including David, Jim, Gayle, Megan, Christopher, and many others for making it all happen.

ABOUT THE AUTHOR

Ronen Divon resides in beautiful Cary, North Carolina, with his wife and four kids: a set of triplets and singleton. Israeli-born who spent twenty-five years in New York prior to relocating to NC, Ronen brings into his work as a writer, a unique blend of mixed cultures and philosophies. An award-winning filmmaker (BFA, School of Visual Arts, NYC,) with additional training in mixed media, Ronen is also a yoga and Tai Chi instructor, a healer, a spiritualist, and a business entrepreneur with rich life experience, and keen, honest observations about life. To date, Ronen published two children books, a host of short adult fiction, as well as many articles and blog posts. You are invited to connect and follow Ronen on social media as well as on his website www.est1964.com.

Morgan James Speakers Group

www.TheMorganJamesSpeakersGroup.com

We connect Morgan James published authors with live and online events and audiences who will benefit from their expertise.

 Morgan James makes all of our titles available through the Library for All Charity Organization.

www.LibraryForAll.org

CPSIA information can be obtained
at www.ICGtesting.com
Printed in the USA
BVHW041639041118
532125BV00002B/166/P